Lost and Found

Sheldon Greene

LOST
AND
FOUND

Random House   New York

Library of Congress Cataloging in
Publication Data
Greene, Sheldon.
Lost and found.
I. Title.
PZ4.G81316LO [PS3557.R3875] 813'.54 80–5274
ISBN 0–394–51250–2

Manufactured in the United States of
America
9 8 7 6 5 4 3 2
First Edition

To those who have helped,
especially Judy

Contents

Lost and Found

1.
Lost and Found

"I." "I" is the first word that comes to me. But it's not my intention to write about myself, except as a part of Bolton. Bolton is my home, though I haven't been here as long as many of the people I'll be describing. I only came here . . . how long ago was it? The years keep passing. It was 1947, July 14 to be exact. An important day, almost like a birthday for me. I had been living in a D.P. camp and came straight from there on an airplane from Frankfort to New York with a few stops.

I am looking at an old photograph of myself taken in 1947, a melancholy Mendel with recurring nightmares. I've learned to live with them, or maybe time has reduced their severity. In 1947 they were as strong as a seizure, only I didn't lose consciousness.

I was still quite thin in those days. The food was ample

in the D.P. camp, but it took time to gain weight. There is a young American soldier beside me in the photo, Mark Levinson. He was from Bolton, detailed to the camp because he spoke Yiddish. We had two common interests, chess and philosophy. We had both studied Kant, he before the army and I before Treblinka. He brought me to Bolton, as good a place as any other for me since I was believed to be the last of my family.

Of course, coming to a town is not becoming a part of it. So how did I, Mendel Traig from Zamosc, become a part of Bolton, Pennsylvania? The Israeli Post Office, a Polish customs official, Estelle Cantor and many others had a part in it. It wasn't only Mark's doing. I miss Mark Levinson. He was so healthy, or seemed so, and my health was so fragile then. It's not too good now, but age wears people down.

Once in a while I am tempted to take my chessboard out to the cemetery to play with Mark on his grave. Of course, I'd have to move for both of us, but otherwise it would be just as before. Mark never talked much during chess games and neither does his son, my current partner.

I spend a lot of time in the cemetery. Maintaining it is one of my jobs—arranging for funerals, the care of the graves, landscaping. It's a beautiful garden if I do say so. Of course, the cemetery is not my principal responsibility. Most of my time is spent with the Synagogue and Educational Center. I handle everything from ordering the library books to monitoring the janitorial service. There are a lot of details to attend to, but it really doesn't take that much time. Don't tell the board. They might reduce my salary and it's low enough as it is. If they didn't give me the apartment in the building, it wouldn't be enough to live on, at least not well. With the apartment I can buy as many books as I want.

It's a comfortable form of survival and lets me do what I really enjoy. For more years than I can remember I'd been at work on a history of the Jewish community of the town of Zamosc, a town in Poland near the Ukrainian border. I was spending all my spare time on that manuscript until Miriam Edelstein came home with the Torah.

Miriam was a widow whose late husband had been born in a Polish village. He had always wanted to return there for a visit, but had never managed the trip. With more money than she could use, given her limited interests, she decided to go herself. But to her chagrin, when she got to Poland nobody had ever heard of the village. She spent hours in the Jewish Community Center in Warsaw talking to the few old men and women who came there. Although she was able to converse in Yiddish, she could pick up no trace of her husband's town. Even the Ministry of Religious Affairs could offer her no clue.

She was ready to return to Paris when she was visited by an old woman, shrunken and stooped, dressed in a long shabby gray coat and carrying a shopping bag. The woman was ill at ease and kept glancing around apprehensively, even in the privacy of the hotel room. To Miriam's disappointment she knew nothing about her husband's hometown. No, she had come on her own business. She had seen Mrs. Edelstein at the community center and thought that she might be interested in Jewish relics. With some hesitation, her bony hands trembling, she produced from the shopping bag a Torah scroll wrapped in a newspaper.

She was poor and sick, she explained. Her family, the few that had remained, had left Poland during the anti-Semitic purges of the sixties and she had stayed behind, as her husband had been too ill to leave. Now she was alone, with a small pension, and she needed money, not very much, a hundred dollars, even fifty dollars would help. As for the origin of the Torah: her father, a distinguished rabbi, had received it from another rabbi prior to his deportation by the Germans. It was nearly the last of her father's possessions. She had sold everything else but his silver pointer, which she would retain as a remembrance until she died.

The old woman watched Miriam anxiously, her head bent upward against the weight of her stooped back, her almost colorless eyes watering. Without hesitation Miriam Edelstein gave her ten ten-dollar bills and asked for her address, but the old woman refused to give it, afraid to get mail from America. She took Miriam's hand in hers and Miriam felt the spasmodic loosening and tightening of her grip. Then she bent down, kissed the Torah and left the room without another word.

Miriam left Poland the next day but almost without the Torah. A customs official refused to let her remove it from the country since it was part of the cultural heritage of Poland. Thirty dollars silently pressed into his hand convinced him that, relic though it was, it fell within an exception of the rule, being a commonplace Torah of nondescript lineage.

Word of the Torah preceded her and Miriam Edelstein returned to an unusual welcome, a visit by Rabbi Bing and several members of the board.

"Is the Torah in good condition?" asked Nudelman, the president of the congregation.

"Oh yes," replied Rabbi Bing, "considering it's probably one hundred and fifty years old. Let's introduce it to the congregation on *Shabbat*."

More than the usual number of worshipers showed up for the *Shabbas* service, curious to see the new Torah and hear the rabbi read from it. Not that it would sound any different from any other Torah, but word had passed that the rabbi would do the special consecration ceremony, something like on *Simchath Torah*. This he did. The Torah was removed from the ark. It was homely, with plain dark wood rollers and an unadorned yellowed cover, not even a fringe.

The rabbi held the Torah up over his head, gave it to Feinberg, the treasurer, who marched up and down the aisles letting people touch or kiss it as they wished. Meanwhile, the rabbi and the congregation sang a joyous song; at least those of the congregation who knew the words sang. As the Torah was returned to the *bima*, the rabbi said a few kind words about the generosity of Miriam Edelstein before commencing the reading of the week. This portion, as it happened, was about the Egyptian bondage of the Jews.

The rabbi unwrapped the bindings and opened the scroll, but he couldn't begin the reading. The words were blurred, as if damaged by water. The parchment was streaked in places and many words had nearly washed away. The rabbi frowned as he studied the scroll, looked up somberly and said, "The Torah is a bit damaged. We'll have to use another."

After the service the congregation could talk of nothing else but the damaged Torah. Some people blamed the rabbi for not examining it before he used it. Others poked fun at Miriam for having spent good American dollars for a worthless souvenir. Nudelman, the president, was philosophical. "What do you expect?" he remarked. "After all that Torah has been through, don't you think it has a right to be a little tired?"

After dinner I returned to the sanctuary, as I always do after a day of services, for a look around. Mrs. Moss, for example, is forgetful. She often leaves her reading glasses behind. In the winter there's usually a scarf or a pair of gloves under a seat. In truth, I like to go there when the lights are dim and the eternal light over the ark where the scrolls are kept seems brightest. The sanctuary is still warm from the congregation, there's often a hint of perfume in the air. It's almost as if the room is filled with bodiless worshipers. Sometimes I think that it is, for after all, shouldn't the dead have the right to a *Shabbat* service of their own? They paid dues all their lives, so why should they stop using the sanctuary? Occasionally I think I can even hear them chanting or feel a slight movement in the air as one of them goes up to the *bima* for an *aliya*. Whatever. I like it then, more than when the place is filled with people.

That night as I walked around putting up the seats, a vague restlessness overcame me, then a sudden tearfulness, and I felt myself drawn to the *bima*. As I stood before the blue velvet curtain of the ark, I was caught by an impulse to look inside. I drew the curtain, opened the sliding doors and faced the Torah. I found myself picking it up in my arms, and as I walked up the aisle, returning to my apartment, I had the feeling that I was carrying a young child.

I placed it on my desk and stared down at it. It seemed familiar, but Torahs all look pretty much alike. How many times had I read from one in my father's small synagogue in Zamosc? I thought of my *Bar Mitzva*, the first time I had actually read from the Torah in public. I unwrapped the Torah and turned to the portion I had read then, dealing with the sacrifice of Isaac, which I had thoroughly memorized during my long preparation for the reading. Now the words sprung out at me in greeting. As I came to the fourth line, something nudged my memory— a letter, the letter *resh*. Different scribes have different styles and like to embellish certain letters; sometimes a *resh* is adorned with a crown. This *resh* had not one crown but five!

My heart pounded with the thought that this Torah was the very same one that I had read in the synagogue as a child, the same one that my father, brothers, uncles and grandfathers had studied. I started to tremble. Images of the old synagogue enveloped me like a prayer shawl: I saw before me my whole family, my lost family, all of the people whom I had loved, who had loved and nurtured me. The tears began to fall from my eyes and they fell on the Torah, making it seem as though the Torah too were weeping. Damp spots were appearing on the words, forming into droplets and running down the parchment, blurring the words in their path.

With eyes burning I looked at the blurred text and heard a voice in my head. Not one that I recognized; it was an old voice speaking to me in classical Hebrew, the Hebrew of the Bible:

What had I been doing with myself all these years?

Writing a book about Zamosc, I thought proudly.

What about the place I lived now? Did I write about it? The people? What did they do for a living? The rabbi?

I tried to answer but I knew I thought more about Zamosc than I did about Bolton, where I had spent almost half my life. I was still living in Zamosc, and I had to confess that the past had more meaning to me, more reality, than the present.

You don't care much about this place, do you?

And I thought, There are no miracles here.

Have you looked around you?

I had to answer, No.

Then what do you know of miracles?

I know about miracles in Zamosc.

Remember Zamosc. Don't forget Zamosc. But live where you are.

Such was the lesson I learned from the battered old Torah. At first, it seemed commonplace wisdom, a cliché. The more I thought about it, the more sense it made. For a long time I had thought of myself as a kind of ending—the end, at least, of my family. There were no more thoughts of ending that night, and I felt instead a quiet joy, the glow of sandstone in the late afternoon.

Early in the morning I put the Torah back in the ark and returned to my room exhausted. When I awoke I put away my unfinished Zamosc manuscript and haven't touched it since. But it wasn't until I got the letter that I started to write about Bolton, the American *shtetl*.

Next day, the rabbi took out the Torah to see if the faded writing could be restored by a scribe. He went through it column by column and found that all the lettering was legible, a little faded with age; the ink was brown, but readable.

2.
The Luftmensh

Doubtless no one would have ever heard of the *luftmensh* if I hadn't innocently asked Sidney Cantor something like "Have you ever heard from that fellow Rivkin?" I asked only to make small talk the night of the UJA dinner. It was not like him, but Sidney didn't respond at first. He just looked at me with suspicion in his eye, and after sizing me up, as if he wanted to know exactly why I asked the question, he said, "I'll tell you about it sometime." And within the week he did.

But before I get into it, let me share a brief description, more a view, of Bolton from the Pittsburgh Road. It's the way strangers and returning residents first see Bolton, lying in a cradle of round rolling hills, just where the Monoganessen River escapes from a narrow valley, takes a wide bend and stretches before slipping between the hills again. What it looked like a hundred years ago I don't know. But now it is a tight town where gray houses crowd together, the close weave of railroad track comes undone against long black buildings and tall smokestacks belch dense gray clouds. The air smells of sulfur and soot turns everything gray. The clatter of steel wheels, the pulse of diesel engines, the clash of metal, the quake of drop hammer, overlay the bird's song and the river's murmur. But on the coldest night a returning traveler like Sidney Cantor sees warm yellow fires through the dirty windows of the mill, and the hills of ash glow yellow at the top and smolder like little volcanoes.

BOLTON CITY LIMITS said the sign, lit for an instant by the headlights of Sidney Cantor's pearl-gray Oldsmobile. It was the last turning of the highway and the lights of the town appeared all at once.

One by one, Sidney, now impatient, traversed the familiar landmarks: the junkyard, the all-night diner, the mill, the bridge with its gray girder frame, Main Street, the stolid brick City Hall, the bank with its Roman ornamentation, the storefronts, the neon marquees of the Ritz Theater and finally a narrow residential street with well-tended lawns and spacious two-story houses.

Sidney Cantor always felt a sense of welcome relief when he returned home, and despite his apprehension this particular night was no exception. He stopped in front of his house, turned off the lights and the engine, slid out from under the steering wheel—thinking he was gaining too much weight—and looked up at the bright lights of his house.

Estelle was probably reading in bed waiting for him. His son, Noah, was, no doubt, downstairs watching television when he should be studying.

The familiar creak of the wide oak floorboards in the

front hall greeted him. He walked through the living room, turning out the lights as he went through the French doors into the flickering phosphorescent glow of the family room. Noah, tall and angular, was slouched on the sofa, a glass of milk in his hand. "Why didn't you turn off the lights?" Sidney asked.

Noah looked guiltily at him for a moment, then his gaze returned to the television. "Mom left them on for you," he replied, his adolescent voice squeaking.

"All of them?" Sidney asked, and traversing the family room, he entered the kitchen, surveyed its colonial maple décor with satisfaction and put the kettle on for some tea. The evening paper lay folded on the table where Noah had left it, the sports pages up. Sidney sat down heavily and instantly began reading.

"The water's boiling." He looked up and saw Estelle, her face shiny with cleansing cream, wearing a long quilted bathrobe that made her look lumpy. She came to him, leaned over and gave him a kiss on the forehead. He responded by squeezing her thigh without looking up from the paper.

"I see the Beavers won today," he said softly. "They're in fourth place now."

"Oh!" She put the tea down in front of him on the aqua place mat and sat down across from him. Without looking up, he reached for the sugar bowl, took out two cubes and, missing the cup, dropped them on the table. "You don't have to look at me, but you might at least look where you're putting the sugar," she said.

"You're right."

"So what did they serve?"

"The same as last year: dry roast chicken, Neapolitan ice cream for dessert, fruit cocktail before."

"And the speaker? What did he say?"

"The same as last year too. Things are terrible, the needs are greater."

"And what did you pledge?"

For the first time he looked at her, his brow creased, then without replying, he stirred the tea and took a sip.

The wrinkles in her forehead deepened and her voice, usually sharp, grew more shrill. "You pledged what we decided before the dinner, didn't you?"

"Of course."

"And no more?"

He sighed audibly. "Estelle, you know I'm the local chairman."

"So you gave more again. I knew you would. You were there with all those rich men from Pittsburgh, the ones that can buy and sell you, and when they all stood up and announced how much they were increasing, you had to do the same. Even though we will need an extra five thousand dollars to send Noah away to college next year."

He sighed again and looked up at her from the paper.

"Will you please stop reading the paper!"

He nodded and brushed the newspaper aside. "I *am* the chairman. I've got to set an example. I won't be chairman again next year and we can decrease the pledge."

"But we'll have to borrow some of the money."

"So? We've never borrowed before?" His voice, usually smoky, raised in pitch and took on a different cadence. "We'll pay it back. Be thankful I'm healthy and business is good. So we'll pay it back."

"Dad, can I have the car tomorrow night? There's a basketball game in Elwood City." Tall and ungainly, Noah stood in the doorway, leaning against the doorframe, watching him expectantly. Sidney looked at the tight-fitting stovepipe jeans, faded on the knee, the baggy blue sweatshirt, his son's long neck and finally his face, gaunt like the rest of him. He smiled and thought, He's grown so tall, taller than both of us. It must have been all the milk.

"Who are you going with?"

"Um, just Bill and Stoney."

"And Susan Anderson?"

"I guess so," Noah mumbled.

Sidney sucked his lips into his mouth but said nothing.

"What about it, Dad?"

"If you promise to be home by eleven."

Noah smiled and said, "Thanks, Dad." He took another glass of milk, gulped it down and left the kitchen, saying, over his shoulder, "Night, Mom. Night, Dad."

Sidney finished his tea and went to bed, but sleep avoided him. He could hear Estelle's regular breathing as he lay still on his back, wanting to turn this way and that, afraid that his motion would disturb her. Heavy, throat-catching thoughts entered his head. He hadn't told Estelle the truth about their finances. He never did. He didn't want to worry her, she was so easily disturbed. Three times he had made short-term loans at the bank and two were in default. Not that business had been bad, but he was out twenty-five thousand dollars because of the bankruptcy of that big hotel account and he just couldn't recover from it. None of the jobs he had gotten in the past year could begin to make it up. He had used up all of their savings, all but the two-thousand-dollar emergency fund. He had even sold the little stock they had accumulated, of course at a loss. The problem wasn't only that he had to borrow the three thousand dollars he had pledged and that he would have to pay it all within three months, the night of the annual UJA dinner, but that he didn't know where he could even borrow it. He thought back on the evening, the build-up of tension as one by one the wealthy had gotten up and announced their pledges. What increases—not just fifteen percent, but twenty-five percent, even forty percent. He didn't know how they could do it every year. At least twenty of them had pledged more than thirty-five thousand dollars each. Together they had given over half a million dollars. Then his name was called. It was too hot in there and he was sweating. He took a sip of water, cleared his throat and prepared to say "Two thousand dollars," but he couldn't say it. He stood there, and they all seemed to be looking at him. He tried again, but it wouldn't come out. He rubbed his fingers on the skirt of his jacket, took a deep breath and said, almost inaudibly, "Three thousand dollars." It was a thousand more than last year. The chairman nodded his approval and called the next name, he couldn't remember whose. He was feeling a little weak and flushed.

The illuminated dial of the clock on his bedside table said one-thirty, and still no sleep. Estelle would think that they had pressured him into the increase, and perhaps they had. But he could never compete with the big *machers* in Pittsburgh, whatever he gave. Maybe Estelle was right; but maybe she wasn't, he thought. He wanted to think that he had done it because there were people who needed it more than he did. But I haven't even got it not to need it, he mused.

The next weeks passed heavily for Sidney Cantor. He always had several irons in the fire, but none of the major jobs turned out. It seemed that he was always underbid by one of the bigger plumbing suppliers out of Pittsburgh. He didn't understand how they did it; he was shaving his margins so thin as it was. Passover was coming, that was good. The income taxes were coming due, that was bad. The local fund-raising dinner wasn't far behind and still he didn't know where the money was coming from. Of course, he could write a check and take it back the next day, but it would be all over town within twenty-four hours and he would be humiliated. Why did the chairman have to write the first check? Why couldn't he just announce his pledge like they did everywhere else? Maybe he could just break with tradition this year, but then, of course, nobody would stand up and make their pledges. A sickening image came to him: he was standing there on the stage waiting for someone to follow his pledge. The crowd would be sitting there waiting for him to write his check. What would he say then?

The first night of Passover came and things hadn't changed, but Sidney Cantor didn't care. Passover was his favorite holiday. It always had been since he was a little boy and had first read the four questions, drunk the four glasses of sweet dark wine, dipped the eggs in salt and felt the sharp sting of raw horseradish in his nostrils. Sidney's Passover was always as he remembered it: a houseful of people, including some of the people in town with whom no one else wanted to have Passover—the people without family, the poor, the eccentric, the unpopular. Tonight it would be the Fiedelsons, war refugees from Poland who ran a threadbare used-rug store. They had no family here and their only son had moved to Nebraska—or was it Kansas?—and he seldom wrote, let alone visited. Then there would be Zalman Katz; no one wanted him because his stomach growled and he ate enough for four. He had no family either. Joe Schwartz was a dishwasher in the Burger Hut. He was a little retarded and he had two different color eyes; no one wanted him. Eppi Kalb was a retired shoe salesman and a widower; he couldn't stop talking. And, of course, there was always his aunt and uncle and the cousins, not only from town, but from the nearby towns, for Estelle's gefüllte fish was celebrated in five counties, not to mention her honey cake.

It was only half an hour before the guests would begin to arrive. I had been there since midafternoon. My excuse for coming early was to bring over some extra folding chairs from the synagogue. Actually, it was to serve as a willing taster of the food. Noah and I were busy setting up card tables and the chairs, and Sidney had just finished pouring the Carmel wine from Israel into an ornate crystal decanter that had belonged to his mother, of blessed memory. He was standing in the living room selecting a hiding place for the *afikomen* when the phone rang.

"Sidney, this is Harry. Harry Lesher."

"Harry, you don't have to give me your last name. In the twenty-five years that you've been calling, I should recognize your voice."

"I know, it's a habit I can't break from the office. Listen, Sidney, I've got a favor to ask you. Can you make room for one more tonight? There's a stranger in town, an investment counselor from Beverly Hills, California, who doesn't have a place to have *Seder.* I would have him here, but you know how Libbie is: when she's got it in her mind how many people she's going to have, there's no changing the plan. I know Estelle is different. So what do you say?"

Sidney paused, waiting for another sentence, and asked, "Is he Jewish?"

"Of course he's Jewish, would I send you a *goy* on Passover? So it's done then, I'll bring him over. You'll love him, he's charming."

"Wait, what's his name?" But it was too late, Harry had already hung up.

The call elated Sidney. It was good to have a stranger for dinner on Passover. The table was always set for one more and the door left ajar for the prophet Elijah, who was supposed to visit every Jewish house. "Estelle," he called through the kitchen door, "we've got an Elijah for dinner tonight, a stranger in town from California."

It seemed as though he had hardly hung up the phone when he heard a brisk, insistent knock at the door. Opening it with the expectation of seeing one of the local guests, his eyes widened with surprise as he saw a heavy man of medium height dressed in a fashionable but baggy brown suit. The coat was opened, revealing a tight belt, above and below which the fat protruded much like a bundle that had been tied too tightly. Sidney just stood in the doorway. The stranger met Sidney's surprise with a relaxed, good-natured expression. A large smile opened his full lips, showing irregular yellowed teeth, and his eyes, deep-set in his fleshy face, glowed with good feeling and even a spark of amusement at Sidney's unconcealed surprise.

Advancing a step, his hand out ready to grasp Sidney's, the man said with a pleasant modulated voice, "How good of you to have me tonight, Mr. Cantor. Elijah is truly welcome at your house, or at least a poor imitation of him. My name is Simon Rivkin."

"Well, let's not stand in the doorway, Mr. Rivkin."

"Simon. Don't stand on formalities."

"Simon, call me Sidney. Come in," Sidney said, ushering him into the living room. "Sit down, there in that armchair, uh, Simon." Sidney introduced him to me, repeating the name tentatively as if he was getting used to it, watching Simon fall heavily back into the chair as though he had been dropped from above. "Can I get you something to drink, a little Seven and Seven maybe?"

"No, thank you. I'll just wait for the Passover wine."

"I'll do the same then," Sidney said, nodding his head as

he sat down on the sofa. "I'm afraid my wife is still in the kitchen, in the middle of preparations. You'll meet her later."

Simon said nothing but continued to smile and regard Sidney with his warm green eyes.

"I understand you're in the investment business. What brings you to Bolton?"

"I'm sure you know the Lewisons, Phil Lewison? We were concluding a transaction, the sale of a parcel of land near Phoenix."

"A retirement place?"

"No."

"How much land, if I might ask?"

"Well, I'm not sure I should say, but . . . you look like a discreet man," Simon answered. Looking at Sidney intently and leaning forward, he said in a lowered voice, "Fifteen thousand acres; irrigated cotton land. Of course, he's not the only partner in the venture, but don't misunderstand me, he's not the smallest investor, by no means the smallest."

"You mean to say Phil Lewison's going into the cotton-farming business? I don't believe it. Did you know that, Mendel?"

I shrugged, as investments didn't interest me at the time.

"No, it's just an investment. We expect to sell the parcel within six months at a respectable profit."

"Well, if it's not intruding too much, what kind of a return would you expect in such a short period of time?"

"Understand, Sidney, this is a highly leveraged deal. He should . . . quadruple his money," Simon replied, looking matter-of-fact.

"That's a fantastic return."

"Not really. We do it often enough, but I admit this one's particularly good."

"Are you looking for other investors, small investors?" Sidney asked.

Simon frowned and shook his head. "I'm afraid it's too late for that one. It's closed. But there are others. In fact, there's one that I'm putting a little money into myself that I'm sure will double my money in no more than thirty days."

The thought of such a short-term profit made his pulse quicken. Sidney wasn't a self-destructive gambler, but he did enjoy the regular once-a-month poker game with a few of the boys from the synagogue men's group. And he loved to win. It always made him feel like he'd gotten something for nothing. He liked to play a hot tip at the track or invest in a flyer on the stock market if a friend had some inside information. But the stock market hadn't been so kind to him lately. In fact, his losses during the last recession were the start of his current financial predicament. Still, he hadn't lost faith, despite his bad luck, for he knew that it was just a matter of having the right information at the right time. He was intrigued, even excited, by what he had heard, but before he could pursue it the doorbell rang and the other guests began to arrive.

The *Seder* glowed with the warm light of one hundred candles. Sidney looked around at the tightly packed group after the last song and thought that for the first time it was just as it had been when his grandfather had presided. A sense of kinship filled the room, and for a moment he thought he saw crowded among the guests his grandparents, uncles and aunts and behind them, like shadows, an endless line of celebrants, each smaller and less definable than the last, fading back even to the beginning of time itself. Then, abruptly, the daydream passed and he found himself looking squarely into the warm green eyes of Simon Rivkin.

We sat for a long time at the table, drinking tea, devouring Estelle's honey cake and fresh fruit, talking among ourselves about the mundane misfortunes and windfalls that break the routine of small-town life. Reluctantly, we broke up shortly before midnight, and when all but Simon had left, Sidney offered to take him back to his hotel.

As Simon was about to get out of the car in front of the Roosevelt Hotel, he turned almost as an afterthought and said, "You remember that investment I mentioned earlier in the evening?"

"Yes, of course," Sidney replied, feeling the same quickening as he had earlier at the thought of such a profit. "You're a lucky man. Those kind never come my way. They all *sound* good, but mostly they fizzle in the end."

Simon nodded and said, "This one is a sure thing or I wouldn't be doing it. It's an opportunity to purchase some warrants on stock which is going public in three weeks at" —he paused—"exactly *three times* the price of the warrants."

Sidney thought of the emergency fund, the two thousand dollars in the savings account. If he could invest the money, he would have six thousand dollars in just three weeks, more than enough for the UJA contribution. Then doubt punched through and he thought, What if it's like all the rest, something unexpected happens and you're lucky if you get half of your money out? And the man's a stranger. Besides, he hasn't asked me to participate. It won't do any harm to ask, he concluded.

"Simon, close the car door a minute unless you're in a hurry. I want to ask you something. Do you think . . . I could get into this investment? I have a couple of thousand lying around . . ."

Simon shook his head. "I'm sorry, Sidney, but it's all

committed. Tomorrow is the last day to act and I've reserved the last five-thousand-dollar block for myself. In fact, I've got to wire the money to Phoenix tomorrow morning. You won't believe this, but I have the five thousand in cash with me."

"I always miss the boat on the good ones."

Simon studied him for a time, then said, "You know, Sidney, you're a good person. You extended hospitality to a total stranger on such short notice. You had all the people in town to your *Seder* that nobody else wanted, didn't you? You did, didn't you?"

"Well, I—after all, it is Passover."

"Sidney, you know money comes to money. I don't really need the profit on this deal. I get lots of opportunities like this. I'll tell you what, I'll let you participate for say . . . two thousand dollars."

Sidney's spirits leaped, but immediately he thought, It must be too good to be true. If he's willing to cut me in, there must be something wrong with it, and he said, "That's damn good of you, Simon, but I'm just not lucky. It wouldn't work out and we'd both lose in the end."

"You're afraid. Afraid you'll lose your money, aren't you? Or are you afraid to give it to a total stranger?"

"No, it's not that," Sidney protested. He knew, however, that he was afraid to trust a stranger, even one for whom he had such a good feeling.

"You're right to doubt, of course; there are so many dishonest people," Simon said as he drew a leather wallet out of his inside coat pocket, removed three crisp notes and offered them to Sidney. "Take this, put two thousand dollars with it and send it to an address I'll give you with this message: 'Exercising Bollingworth option to purchase warrants, five-thousand-dollar block, Simon Rivkin and Sidney Cantor. Send warrants this address.' Use those words exactly," he added, writing the address and message on a piece of notepaper.

Sidney looked at the money in his hand and recognized three thousand-dollar bills. "I've never seen a thousand-dollar bill before."

"I always carry a few of them. They take up less room in your wallet and you never know when you'll need the money. Of course, I carry a special insurance policy with Lloyd's, just in case." Simon paused and looked at Sidney. "Now do you think you can trust me, Sidney? I'm putting the whole matter in your hands, even the possession of the warrants. We'll settle up later. Besides, they'll be in our joint names. You see, Sidney, I know that I can trust you with my money. At least some of it," Simon added.

The decision was already made for Sidney. He put the money, the address and message in his pocket, barely able to contain his excitement, and thanked him profusely as Simon moved his heavy frame through the car door. As he was about to close the door, Simon bent down and looked at him, a look that was redolent with good feeling, and he said, "Goodbye and God bless you, Sidney Cantor. And don't forget the wire, first thing in the morning. I'll be in contact with you when I get home."

With that he closed the car door and Sidney drove off, catching a last glimpse of Simon in the rear-view mirror.

Driving home, Sidney was so preoccupied that he missed the turn into Flower Street. As he went up to the door, he resolved not to speak of the investment to Estelle, as she would worry. If for some reason it did not work out, he would simply say that he had needed it for the business.

The next day, as soon as the bank opened, he withdrew two thousand dollars from his savings account and hurried to the telegraph office to wire the money to Phoenix. Then he carefully folded the receipt and put it in a compartment of his wallet, feeling like a hen with a newly laid egg.

But Sidney's euphoria was short-lived. It shattered like a broken mirror a few days later when he casually met Harry standing in line at the bank. When Sidney thanked him for sending the guest for Passover, Harry looked embarrassed and said, "I'm sorry about that, Sidney. We had him to dinner after all. Eddie called to tell you he wasn't coming, didn't he?"

"No."

"I'll kill that kid," Harry spit out through tight lips. "I hope you didn't wait too long for him. He was such a nice man and he had such good ideas on investments—"

Sidney interrupted: "Who are you talking about? He came to *my* house."

"You mean he came to your house the second night of Passover? I thought he was leaving town."

"No, he came the first night."

"Who?" Harry asked, his voice growing shrill.

"Simon Rivkin."

"Oh! But Krasny ate with us."

"Who's Krasny?" Sidney exclaimed.

"Krasny's the man I called you about who came to our house after all."

"Then who was Rivkin?" asked Sidney, the blood draining out of his hands.

"I've never heard of him. I—I thought you were kidding me when you mentioned a guest. But I've never heard of Rivkin. There was a Max Rivkin, a doctor in Beaver Falls, and he had a brother named Jack, but he moved to . . ."

Sidney did not stay to hear the rest of the sentence. He went directly back to his shop and called Phil Lewison, but the line was busy. He tried two more times in rapid succession, all the while nervously cracking his knuckles until, on the fourth try, the phone rang, but Phil took so long to answer. His heart nearly stopped as he heard Phil Lewison's voice. He was sure that Lewison would confirm the business deal, and in his excitement he began the conversation in the middle. "Lewison, this is Sidney. It's about Rivkin."

"Napkins?" came the response, as Lewison was a little hard of hearing.

"Rivkin," Sidney repeated more distinctly.

"Oh, Rivkin." Sidney relaxed, but after a moment, "Who's Rivkin?"

"The investment broker from Beverly Hills."

"I've never been to Beverly Hills in my life, Sidney. How would I know him?"

"But, Phil, you did business in town with him last week."

"Oh, him. But his name wasn't Rivkin. It was, ah—I'm terrible with names—it was Krasny."

After a long pause, Sidney said weakly, "Are you sure?"

"Of course I'm sure. Where did you get the name Rivkin? Unless you're talking about that Jewish family over in Beaver Falls, but they're not in investments, unless you call a junked car an investment. So how are the plans for the UJA dinner? How many, Sidney, are coming?"

Sidney hardly heard him. "What? Oh yes, everybody," he muttered.

"What?"

"Everybody. Well, sorry I bothered you."

"No bother. I'll see you at the dinner, if not before."

Sidney hung up, called Beverly Hills information and was elated to learn that there were two Simon Rivkins listed. He called both and spoke directly with one, a retired pathologist who had never heard of Sidney. The wife of the second Simon Rivkin explained that her husband was a furrier and had not left California in twenty years. Next he checked with Phoenix information for a listing of the Bollingworth Company, but there was no such listing.

He called the Roosevelt Hotel. Their records would show a forwarding address, but he was shocked to find that not only was there no address, there was no Simon Rivkin listed in the guest register. In a panic he called the other hotels and motels, but no one had any record of Rivkin. Sidney slumped in his chair, struck his forehead with his fist and shook his head. An assumed name. He had been conned. Giving him the three thousand dollars was just a ruse to overcome a sucker's suspicions. By now Rivkin, or whoever, had picked up the money, his and Sidney's.

It could have been worse—he could have given Rivkin three thousand dollars. As an afterthought, he called Western Union to see if the money order had been picked up. The manager assured him it had or the Phoenix office would have sent him a status report within five days of transmission. Despite all the evidence that he had been tricked out of his money, Sidney still wanted to believe that it would come out all right. Perhaps he had the spelling wrong. Maybe it was Rifkin, or maybe the desk clerk had overlooked the entry. Simon was so nice. But aren't con men always the most believable people? If they weren't, nobody would trust them. Sidney opened both hands in a gesture of resignation. Rivkin or no, his big problem still remained the three-thousand-dollar check he had to write to start the pledges. Days passed and he went on as usual. The arrival of the mail, the sound of the telephone gave him palpitations, a sense of unease afflicted him especially before he went to sleep, but no one, not even Estelle, would have guessed that he was troubled.

Then two days before the UJA dinner, as Sidney was seated at the cluttered desk in his cramped office, costing out a prospective order on the calculator, the phone rang. It was Western Union, letting him know that his money had been returned unclaimed by the Phoenix office. The money order had been put in the wrong file or it would have been returned sooner. He could come in and pick it up at any time.

Sidney felt both relief and disappointment as he abandoned the shop and, without even locking the door or putting up a sign, walked the two blocks to the telegraph office to claim the money. Only when the check was secure in his coat pocket did he begin to think about what he could do.

He could see clearly what had happened. Western Union had made an error and the money had never been delivered. Rivkin's contact or even Rivkin tried to pick it up in Phoenix. What must Rivkin think of him—that he had kept the money? Wouldn't Rivkin have contacted him, unless he was really a con man? If he was he might just have thought it was too dangerous and turned his back on it. On the other hand, maybe he wasn't a con man and was simply too busy. After all, what was three thousand dollars to a man of Rivkin's means? Sidney rationalized.

It could be worse, but he still was one thousand dollars short of making the pledge unless he used Rivkin's money. That would be stealing, and stealing from a rich man is still stealing. No, he couldn't bring himself to use money that did not belong to him, whatever the circumstances. He would have to feign sickness and let the vice-chairman handle it. He had done the best he could. A poor man had no business being chairman of a fund-raising drive in the first place. Charity is just like business: if you haven't got the cash flow, you can't pay the bills, Sidney concluded.

So it was final: he would give up the honor to a rich man, for the vice-chairman was more comfortable than he. To be sure, he felt regret at the finality of it, regret that he couldn't get up and say to the whole congregation what he felt about charity, things he had wanted to say, regret that he didn't have enough money to give ten thousand dollars, even twenty thousand dollars; it would feel so good. Perhaps someday.

At dinner Estelle started to question him about tomorrow's fund raising: who couldn't come, whether he had prepared a speech. But to all of her questions he was noncommittal. He wanted so much to relieve himself of the burden and tell her about their finances, about what he must do tomorrow night, but he said to himself, Why make *two* people unhappy? So he contained himself, answered the questions and changed the subject. After dinner, he busied himself around the house with minor repairs, made some last-minute phone calls about the food and the tables and chairs and, exhausted, went to bed earlier than usual, without even watching the eleven o'clock news.

That night, or rather early the next morning, he had a dream; a dream so vivid it might have been real; a dream that makes reality seem almost dreamlike by comparison. He was at his grandfather's *Seder* and all of his relatives were around him, all the familiar uncles and aunts, now long dead. All of the details were so sharp, the smell of the chicken soup, the blue Chinese garden pattern on the Passover dishes. But the striking aspect of the dream was the moment when the door was opened for the prophet Elijah. At first there was only a warm spring wind, gentle and fragrant, and then Elijah really appeared, only it wasn't Elijah at all, it was Simon Rivkin. The alarm clock's electric buzz brought him out of the dream, yet not quite out of it, for he could still feel the sense of it as he got up, put on his robe quietly so as not to wake Estelle and went into the bathroom. Even as he looked into the mirror, he still saw, over his right shoulder, the whimsical glance of Simon Rivkin. Startled, he turned his head to look over his shoulder, only to see a blue towel on the rack behind him.

He shaved and the dream atomized, at least until, as he was spooning a measure of instant coffee into his cup, he again thought he saw Simon Rivkin's face, this time at the bottom of the spoon like a shattered reflection in water. He sat down at the dinette table, hardly aware that he was eating rye toast and butter, when a wave of feeling enveloped him; it passed but left him calm and sure.

That night, after the usual chicken dinner, Sidney didn't feign sickness. Instead, he got up and spoke. He spoke of the tradition of generosity, of charity, of the needs of those less fortunate, of his feeling of oneness with them. It was brief and it was over within a few minutes. Then without hesitation, without even so much as a tremor, he wrote a check and handed it to Abe Nathanson, the treasurer, whose eyes widened as he declaimed in a loud voice to the very heavens, "Five thousand dollars."

Sidney sat down beside Estelle, feeling weightless joy, for he saw all around him not only his familiar neighbors but others, and among them were his grandfather, his uncles, his aunts, his father and his mother, those whose faces he knew only from faded pictures in the family album, people whom he had never seen, gaunt people dressed in plain gray tunics and some wearing broad black-and-white stripes, so many that to describe all of them was beyond his powers. And among them, far back in the crowd, one face stood out, the only one, in fact, who seemed to be looking right at him—the amused, approving, indulgent face of Simon Rivkin.

3.
A Letter

The week of the UJA dinner the mailman brought me the letter. Just looking at it there on my desk with its Israeli stamp made me feel, well, a little light-headed. With no family and no friends other than here in Bolton, all I get in the mail outside of New Year's cards are bills and advertisements, not to mention solicitations for charities, but this was none of those. No, this was a personal letter addressed in a vertical European script that somehow looked familiar, although all of them do, as if there was only one teacher of writing in all the Polish first schools. Yes, Polish, the script looked Polish. Just a letter, but seeing it made me tremble like birch leaves in the wind, for I had—how many years ago—given up receiving it. Yet in my fantasies, even in my dreams, it would come to me, that letter, from some distant, even forgotten, even disliked, member of my family. Denial set in, and tearing the envelope open, I reasoned, It's probably just a personal solicitation for a contribution to a *yeshiva*.

It began with a hopeful "Dear Mendel." I skipped over the cramped text right to "Your beloved cousin (I hope), Ephraim." I laughed out loud. It was Ephraim, my closest childhood friend, more like a brother. The writing was a mature version of his script, I recognized it. And it was his sense of humor; he hadn't lost it despite all that had passed. I pulled open the envelope, hoping for a photograph, but there was none, and with the same movement opened the thin paper, rattling in my trembling hands, and deciphered his Polish.

"Can it really be you?" the letter began.

It is beyond all hope after these many years of believing you a victim of the Nazis. If it is you, I know that you must have thought the same, since I'm sure you heard no more of me after I disappeared that day. You must have thought that the Germans took me and that I didn't survive, or we might have found each other after the war. Don't imagine that I didn't try to find someone from our family, but it seemed that every road led to a crematorium. I still doubt that you are my Mendel Traig, and you will probably respond to me, if you respond— you will respond with a New York accent or some such regional dialect, if it can be communicated in writing. Or you will write in English "Return to sender" or "I don't understand Polish," something which tells me that you are not you. I am resigned to that, although I cannot accept it, for I have believed through everything that there was someone else left of our blood, and even now as I write this letter I believe it, and I believe it is you, living for all I know in the wilderness of western Pennsylvania among the Indians, who, having been subjugated long ago (unlike some of our neighbors, some think), are no longer hostile. If you write, perhaps you will tell me, Where exactly is Pennsylvania? Is it near Chicago? And when you have told me about your life and I have done the same, you will tell me what it is like to live there in America. I suppose it's very different from our Zamosc.

If you are not my cousin Mendel, perhaps you will still write and tell me something about yourself. It is good to receive letters from faraway places.

If you are my cousin Mendel, I have some important news for you that concerns reparations paid by the German government in your name, which have been in an Israeli account, unclaimed, for twenty-five years and which, if not claimed in the next year, will be forfeited.

Before I tell you the details, please give me some proof of your identity, such as your mother's maiden name, your father's middle name, your address in Zamosc, the name of the teacher at the school and whatever comes to mind. How good it will be to see these names written by someone else. Until then.

I put the letter down, and as with the Torah, my tears fell on it, diluting the ink but not the words. For the second time my old life had returned to me with a rush of pain and joy. First the Torah had called up memories with its old and timeless words, and I had touched it knowing that here in this same place was invisibly etched my own father's touch. The release of sadness, the evocation of memory had in some way prepared me for this writing, not timeless but familiar. I reread the letter and I laughed, laughed like a crazy man alone on an island for five years who, walking around a large rock, suddenly sees not a stranger, not a cannibal, but his best friend. Yes, I laughed and wept and laughed and wept at the same time, so much so that Rabbi Bing, passing my door on the way home, knocked politely, then came in, a look of concern on his face, and said, "Are you all right, Mendel?"

I told him through the laughter, "I'm fine. You see, I've

just won the Israeli sweepstakes and I've just heard the news."

Rabbi Bing, with a look of subtle incredulity, more like gas, said, "Really. I wasn't aware they had one. But in any event, what did you win? A trip to Israel?"

"Nothing like that," I said, calming down, "just a cousin."

"A cousin?" he repeated; then a look of understanding appeared in those small pale-blue eyes, visible one fathom down through his glasses, and as reserved as he is, he came over to my chair, squeezed my shoulder and said very quietly, "I'm very happy for you, Mendel." He touched my shoulder a second time, then he just stood there. I waited, expecting him to leave. Then just to say something, I said, "Leaving early?"

"I've got to go to the hospital." It wasn't the usual day or time for him to go, but I didn't think of that. He didn't want to cast a shadow on my happiness by telling me who had fallen ill, and without another word he left the room. In retrospect, I'm glad that he didn't tell me. I found out soon enough.

I hardly noticed the door close; I was already groping in the drawer for a pen that wrote and a clean piece of stationery. And I wrote, "Dear cousin Ephraim, you want proof, my mother's name, your aunt's middle name, why, I'll give you the names of every aunt, uncle, cousin, housemaid, teacher, fellow student . . ."

I listed a dozen or so in mock biblical fashion, and as I wrote the names, they came alive in my mind for a moment. Then I told him some embarrassing stories, like the time he came to stay the night at our house and wet the bed. Silly of me to remember that, let alone repeat it. I thought to cross it out but left it in; why stand on formality with so dear a friend? Besides, I knew he would have done the same, and why not get the jump on him? He was so irreverent, Ephie; that's what we called him. Nothing special about it, but much that was special about him.

I finished the letter and mailed it immediately, even driving in Tevya, my Chevy, downtown to the post office to make sure that it had the right postage. Mr. Soder inspected it, calculated the postage and said, noticing the family name on the address, "I didn't know you had some family over there, Mr. Traig."

And the words tasted like cinnamon on cake as I replied, "Just a cousin, Mr. Soder, but a *special* cousin."

He nodded as the stamp thudded down on the envelope BOLTON, PENNA., JULY 20, 1978, and it took its first step out of Bolton, halfway around the world.

4.
The Golem

The High Holy Days were approaching, barely two weeks away, the seats for the services still had not been assigned and there was no one to do it. Sarah Millstein was sick, unconscious, even near death, and she was the only one who knew where people sat. For fifty years now Sarah had served as the secretary of the congregation and carried in her head the history and social hierarchy of the community. Only she knew the order of their coming to Bolton, the key to the seating. No one but Sarah really knew if the Nudelmans came before the Fishbeins, the Rosenzweigs before the Kozinskys, the Epsteins before the Pomerantzs, the Gordons before the Tuckers or the Krantzs before the Cohens. Nobody but Sarah knew that, for if you asked the Krantzs they would tell you that they came first, and so would the Cohens and the Nudelmans and all the rest. Why? Because everybody wanted to be among the first families to settle in Bolton, the first to complete a *minyan* in the Pomerantzs' living room, the first to choose a rabbi, the first to make an *aliya* at the first service. Yes, only Sarah remembered that. But there was Sarah, laid out like a corpse on a tilting bed in a private room at Mercy Hospital. Ciel, her oldest daughter, composed but with a blotchy case of the hives, was sitting next to her bed as Nudelman, the president, and I paid a visit. The creases on Nudelman's forehead were bottomless as he studied Sarah's thin, wrinkled profile.

"Did you see her lips move?" he whispered to me. "She must be trying to tell us where people—" But he broke off in the middle of the sentence. Nudelman reached down and touched her forehead ever so gently. When he looked up his sad hound eyes were glistening. "Look at her eyes, she recognizes us," he said, the words sliding down a sigh.

An emergency meeting of the board was called for no other reasons than to deal with the problem of the tickets. Present were Finkelstein, Nudelman and Roe, the newest member, who had come to town only within the last five years, having been relocated when the National Casualty Insurance Company built its regional data-processing center on a two-acre site north of the Bolton city limits. Of course I sat in too. It was a good thing Roe was there. He was an administrator with a reputation for solving problems in a practical way. So despite his junior status in the community, all eyes turned expectantly to him as we discussed the crisis.

"The biggest problem," said Nudelman, "is that if we ask everybody where they've been sitting, they'll all say the row in front of the real one and we'll never know for sure who just doesn't remember and who wants to move up."

"How were the seats assigned in the first place?" asked **Roe.**

"The usual way," said Finkelstein.

"You'll excuse me, but what way is that?"

Finkelstein looked confused. "It had something to do with when you joined the congregation and something to do with how much you've contributed," he said, clearing his throat. He had a nervous habit of clearing his throat whether or not he was nervous; he did it all the time.

"That sounds manageable," said Roe, squinting over our heads. "We'll forget making any survey of the congregation to avoid the confusion at this late date. You and Nudelman will simply reconstruct it from memory."

"It's not that simple," said Nudelman, looking like calamity was stalking him. "In addition, there are the health **problems.**"

"Such as?"

"Some people are a little hard of hearing. They must sit close. Then there are others who have poor eyesight. They too must sit close. There are those who sit on the aisle because they often get up during the service. There are people who sit in the back because they have bad feet and don't like to walk to the front."

"That sounds manageable," said Roe. "Simply make a list of the health problems, and we'll assign them seats first and work around them."

"But we still have the social problems," said Finkelstein.

"H'm," said Roe, looking thoughtful and taking out his pipe.

"Please don't smoke," said Nudelman. "My asthma."

Roe drew his lips together. "I forgot. What are the *social* problems?"

Nudelman continued, looking relieved as the pipe returned to the pocket: "Without mentioning names"—he tossed his head to the side—"mentioning names: the Fish-beins aren't speaking to the Hammers, so they can't sit next to each other. The same with the Phillips and Howard Baer; Sophie Baer is all right, but she must sit next to Howard. There are a few more like that."

"I see," said Roe, softly biting a fingernail. Finkelstein cleared his throat and Roe shot him an irritated glance. "Is that all?" Roe asked.

"There are some other social problems as well. You know that there are some people who . . . who people don't care for generally. You know what I mean. *Why* did Sarah have to get sick?" Nudelman bayed sorrowfully.

"Don't worry. It'll be difficult, but it's manageable," said Roe. He paused and looked at each of us. "I'm going to do it all on the company computer."

"The computer!" Finkelstein gasped. "You want to put all the congregation's dirty linen in the computer?"

Nudelman tossed his head to the side and snorted. "The computer. Not such a bad idea, if you could."

"It's simple, but you have to help me with the program."

"The program? We never have a program on *Rosh Hashanah*. The prayer book is the program," said Finkelstein with scorn on his face.

"No. We've got to feed the information into the computer so that it will issue the tickets." And with that introduction Roe proceeded to give us a simple course in computer programming, and we reconstructed, as best we could recall, the seniorities and eccentricities of the congregation. All of this Roe took down in cryptic notes in the margins of the congregation roster. Well, we didn't finish with the last name until one-thirty, there was so much disagreement. Roe smiled with assurance. "Don't worry. By tomorrow night, the next night at the latest, you'll have your tickets."

No sooner had he left than he took out and lit his pipe. No sooner had he left than Nudelman looked at Finkelstein and me, raised his eyebrows and said, "I'll believe it when I see it."

Finkelstein just cleared his throat and looked like he had overeaten.

The next night Roe called Nudelman and told him apologetically that he couldn't get any computer time to do the job. The following night he called again with the same explanation, and all the while the High Holy Days drew nearer.

"They'll impeach the board!" Nudelman muttered to himself as he hung up.

Finally, two days later Roe appeared unexpectedly at Nudelman's door, triumphantly brandishing a thick envelope. "Here they are," he exclaimed. "You'll see they even have the names on them. Just put them in the window envelopes and mail them. They'll get them a couple of days before the service."

Nudelman examined one of the tickets. All the information was there, neatly typed out in the quavery letters of the computer. "It looks a little like Hebrew, doesn't it?" he asked, looking appreciatively at Roe. Nudelman patted Roe on the back and added, "Roe, it's good to have you on the board."

That same night, Nudelman and I stuffed the tickets into the window envelopes and mailed them. It was so simple. With the last ticket, Nudelman shook his head and said, "Sarah will be disappointed when she recovers and learns that she has been replaced by a machine."

The first night of *Rosh Hashanah* arrived and a triumphant Nudelman was at the synagogue door personally greeting the congregants, looking at each of them with an eager expression, soliciting comments on the new tickets, but to his dismay not everyone was happy.

Some were sullen, others were cold, while a few of the people who he wasn't even close to greeted him like a returning son. He was perplexed, that is, at least until he entered the sanctuary and took his place on the *bima* to the left of the ark. Then as he looked around, he understood. People with bad eyes were sitting in the back. Fat people were sitting on the aisles blocking the rows. Enemies were next to enemies. The poor had the places of honor while the rich were behind posts or crowded in the corners. Nudelman was so embarrassed that if he could, he would have crawled into his *yarmulke*. The antagonism from the rear was giving him chest pains. He scanned the crowd and found Roe sitting near the middle of the room. Nudelman caught Roe's eye. He raised his eyebrows and widened his eyes, but Roe just smiled uncomprehendingly. Roe doesn't understand. He doesn't know that there is anything wrong. That's what comes of trusting an important job to a newcomer, Nudelman said to himself. What went wrong? It was the computer. It did the whole thing backwards, he mused, his face flushing with indignation. A machine and a newcomer! Some combination. Neither of them knows what they are doing. Then his eye fell on the people in the front rows: Shapiro, the used-furniture dealer; what's his name, the one who washes dishes in the café; the widow Maltz, who does child care; the others; and touched by their happiness, he grew calm. The rabbi walked solemnly to the *bima* in his white silk robe and began the service.

Sarah recovered from her stroke, somewhat impaired in her faculties, though able to reconstruct the traditional seating plan, but Nudelman would have none of it. "Why should you bother, Sarah? The new seating worked a miracle. The deaf could hear, the blind could see, the lame could walk, enemies talked and the poor, the poor seemed the richest of all of us. It was as if God's hand had reached down and touched us all," Nudelman said. Sarah only smiled, but it was clear she understood.

5.
Morning Coffee

Morning coffee with Estelle Cantor had become a ritual every Tuesday. It wasn't so much the meeting of the executive committee of the Sisterhood—she was vice-president and program chairman and I was there to help with logistics. Nor was it the coffee cakes that she often baked—not the best in town but creditable, especially the one with almond paste. Neither of those. I enjoyed talking with Estelle, being with Estelle. As with Nudelman, there was always something to talk about and the conversation was nourishing, sometimes even filling.

Most of the people in town don't talk much about national, even international, happenings, but Estelle a few years back had participated in a study group at the library on American foreign policy and since then had taken an interest in what we, I mean the big WE, were up to around the world. Don't misunderstand, she was no Hans Lowenthal, I think that's his name, which tells you the depths of my knowledge. But she did read *Time* magazine regularly, she watched the network news as well and unlike most people she enjoyed talking about it. Since Sidney, her husband, didn't know Nigeria from Siberia (perhaps that's too harsh), Estelle would usually save her observations for either me, Linda Joyce or Harriet Rosenzweig, who had taken the course with her.

This particular day, however, the conversation was international but personal, for the day before I had received in the mail after a delay of six weeks (due, I later found out, to a postal workers' strike in Israel) a reply from my cousin Ephie. By the time I was sitting at the table in her kitchen, I had reread the letter so many times that I probably could have recited it like an oration. With the first cup of coffee cooling in front of me, the aroma of the cake teasing my nose and Estelle sitting across from me, an open, attentive expression on her face, I read, or rather paraphrased, the entire letter for her. (The letter this time was in Yiddish rather than Polish. Let's hope the next one isn't in Hebrew, or I'll have to take it to Pittsburgh to have some Israeli student translate it.)

"Don't dawdle, Mendel, tell me what it says," she chided as I studied it, choosing the words; it's not easy to keep the flavor of Yiddish in English, like trying to make Chinese food in an English tearoom.

The letter began, "My dear Mendel. So it's really you. Batya, my wife" (*so he has a wife; first question answered, but still no photographs*) "Batya is to be congratulated for finding you. She works for the *Sochnoot*—that's the Jewish Agency, which spends the money that the UJA collects in America. She thought that there was a remote chance that you were somewhere in America and could be traced through their donor lists; they are computerized. The records of the reparations entitlements had your name misspelled 'Triag,' although we didn't know about it until this year. Just what you'd expect from government clerks. I should talk, I am little more than that myself. Shame on me, but I'll get into all of that later, there's so much to say. Sure enough, her inquiry was answered and you were on it, complete with address. Generosity is sometimes rewarded."

"Isn't it the truth," interjected Estelle just as the timer bell rang. She held up her hand and said, "Wait till I get the coffee cake out of the oven." Potholder in hand, she opened the oven door and said, "So the computers have been busy this month. When they weren't scrambling the congregation, they were busy exhuming you. What next, I wonder?"

"If God wanted to exercise some influence over the world, he couldn't pick a better place to start." She returned to the table and I went back to the letter.

"Pardon me if I ramble; it's late at night and I'm weary from a long day—yes, sometimes even government workers exceed the regular day. Since by now you're probably curious about just what I do, I'll tell you. I have the Nigerian desk in the foreign ministry. Yes, even though they broke off relations with us years ago, we still have a desk, if for no other reason than to provide employment for self-styled African specialists like me. Actually, I'm overworked, but I like what I'm doing and don't mind it, most of the time."

Her coffee cake out of the oven and cooling on a rack, filling the room with the smell of cinnamon-butter and almonds, Estelle said, "What's this about reparations?"

"Wait, I'll get to that."

"Your cousin is worse than you are; he rambles all over the place."

"There's probably a traffic jam in his head, with everything he wants to tell me," I said, turning back to the letter.

"So now you know that I'm married and what both of us do. Batya and I met on a *kibbutz*. I came here after the war in the Aliya Bet, which the Haganah set up to by-pass the British immigration restrictions.

"She is a *sabra;* I'm sure you know what that is." (*What does he think, that I haven't even read* Exodus?) "She is a daughter of the *kibbutz* where they took me after I waded ashore in the middle of the night along with 134 other children who crossed the Mediterranean in a rusty old Turkish coastal steamer that must have done service in the Crimean War. That's another story. It's so late and I've got an early meeting, so I'll get to the pressing matter, the matter of the reparations account. As I said before, it's yours but will be forfeited to the government in less than a year if you don't claim it. I think it's about seventy-five thousand American dollars. The interest over the years since 1955, when it was first paid by Germany for the destruction of your family home in 1944, has increased it to that amount. But you'd better hurry because it's in Israeli pounds, and our inflation rate is so high right now, and getting higher, that at least in relation to the dollar, which isn't doing so good itself, it's likely to be considerably less by the end of the year. It's just too bad that the Trustee for Unclaimed Reparations didn't invest it in dollar-linked bonds or even bought a nice flat, but he didn't, so that's that."

"Mendel, you didn't even tell me about the money."

"It's just that finding my cousin was so momentous, I think I just neglected to mention it. Besides, I feel funny about taking it. It's like they think that they can close the account with some money, but, of course, no amount of money . . ." I broke off the thought and just looked at her, and understanding in her eyes, she nodded.

"Cake's cool enough to cut. How about a piece and some hot coffee? It's small enough compensation for sitting through this meeting," she said. "I think somebody's knocking. Just help yourself; you know where the knives are."

I debated waiting for the rest of them against having it when it was hot. Hedonism prevailed, so I found the cake knife where it always was and, listening to the high voice of Harriet Rosenzweig, cut a discreet wedge of coffee cake just as she preceded Estelle into the kitchen, saying, "Congratulations, Mendel." She had a lyric quality to her voice; she must have wanted to be a singer. "Congratulations," she repeated tunefully. "Estelle has already told me about the other half of the good news. You never mentioned the reparations money, apparently—at least no one told *me* about it." Her already small lips tightened into a line, while Estelle, standing just behind her, rolled her eyes.

I turned my hands up, opening them, and a piece of the cake broke off and fell on the floor. As I picked it up I said, "It just didn't seem that important at the time, compared to the other news. Besides, who knows if I'll get it? My cousin says the time has almost run out."

"Maybe Henry can help. After all, since there's not much time, a lawyer might expedite things." Probably just the opposite, I thought. "Call him. I'm sure he'll be glad to talk to you about it." I said nothing, my mouth was full of cake. "Better yet, knowing you, you won't do it. I'll have him call you, although he'll probably say it's unethical."

"We won't snitch on him," said Estelle on her way to the door in response to an insistent knock.

"Maybe," I said, thinking that I'd rather not get anyone else involved.

"When are you going to get Sidney to fix the doorbell?" said Linda Joyce, the emphatic tone of her voice resounding down the corridor.

"He won't do it. I've asked him. He says it discourages door-to-door salesmen," answered Estelle.

"So did your cousin tell you how much money is involved?" Harriet asked with a hollow look of expectation.

I had been waiting for that question. Estelle could be trusted not to spread it around, but Harriet would, if she knew, tell Heda Finkelstein, and the whole town would know by sunset. It's not that I'm such a private person; I have nothing really to keep from anyone. It's more that I couldn't get used to the notion that I might come into such a sum of money. Why, even in shrinking dollars it seemed like a lot. So all I answered was "He's not sure."

Her eyes narrowed in appraisal. "He must have given you *some* idea?"

"Oh, four hundred thousand or five hundred thousand, maybe."

A perceptible gasp. "Dollars?" she said with a mixture of incredulity and awe.

"No, lira," I answered, stifling a giggle.

"What?"

"You know, Israeli pounds."

"Yes, of course."

Estelle rescued me at that point. She understood perfectly. "How about some coffee, Harriet?" And without waiting for a response, she continued: "What would you think of having that rabbi from Altoona for a program, that one who does the delightful readings from Sholem Aleichem?"

"Hardly anybody came the last time," said Linda Joyce contemptuously.

"Yes, but there was four feet of snow on the ground, as I recall," said Harriet.

"No more than a foot," Linda Joyce retorted, and the meeting started itself. Fortunately for me, I had to leave in the middle of the meeting, missing the long discussion which ultimately molded into the Jewish cookbook project.

6.

The Authentic
Jewish Cookbook

Sophie Feld's term as president of the Sisterhood was remembered for years, not for the considerable good that
she accomplished, but for the single crisis that developed
under her leadership. In Bolton, the Sisterhood's function
was to raise money for such charities as child-care centers
and old people's homes by sponsoring potluck dinners,
mah-jongg tournaments, theater parties and, of course,
the annual appearance of the faded mezzo-soprano from
New Castle who sang Yiddish folk songs a quarter octave
off key. Not content to leave well enough alone, during
Sophie Feld's term the Program Committee thought up a
new fund-raising device, one that would raise hundreds,
perhaps thousands, of dollars and would, moreover, with a
little promotion, put the Jewish community of Bolton on

the map, or so they thought. The idea? Compile a real Jewish cookbook.

Now, there were many cooks in the community who would have been honored to assemble an authentic traditional Jewish cookbook, but the inevitable Selection Committee gave the job to Sophie Feld herself. "I'll do the best I can," she said, surprised, out of modesty, at being chosen. "At least nobody is starving to death in my house."

That was an understatement: Phil, her husband, always had the heavy-lidded, self-satisfied look that goes with a piece of honey cake, a nice cup of tea and maybe even a good cigar. Cynthia, her daughter, looked a little like a goose being fattened for the holidays, all white, fluffy and round. Sophie was a larger version of Cynthia, with arms like loaves of rye bread and hips that swelled out as though under sixteen skirts. Let's just say that Sophie was as imposing coming as she was going. But for all her expanse she had a sweet, small face and a mouth so delicate you wondered how all the food got into her.

Sophie's stove had six burners and two ovens, going all day. She would use three or four pots to do what an ordinary cook would do in one, always mixing a little of this and that, sautéeing three or four items separately, then combining them in a new, fourth pot so the other three pots wouldn't get their feelings hurt. Who washed these pots? Not Sophie; she hated to wash dishes, but she could make a pile of dishes that resembled heaps of scrap metal at the junkyard. Her maid, Harriet, skinny as a tomato stake and mumbling to herself, would wash one pile even as Sophie would build another.

Almost everyone thought that Sophie was the queen of the kitchen. *Almost* everyone, for a few envious contenders gave the credit to Harriet. In any case, everything went well—at least until Sophie tried to reduce her recipes to writing. Weeks went by and she couldn't produce a line. She would sit at her kitchen table for hours, paper in front of her, pen in hand, but nothing would come out. She had never measured anything, never looked at a recipe; had learned it all just by watching her mother throw in a cup of this, a handful of that and a pinch of the other. She would set the oven by the feel of the dial and could tell when it was done by the smell, the look and the taste—no timers for her.

Finally she invited Estelle Cantor to follow her around and write down everything she did. That was no good, either. The presence of an observer in the kitchen made Sophie so nervous that she burned things, threw in the wrong ingredients and ruined everything.

Sophie gave up. After floundering around for a bit, the committee decided simply to invite anyone who desired to submit recipes. Imagine the response! However, every solution leads to two problems, because it quickly became clear as the committee culled the recipes that no one could agree on what constituted authentic traditional Jewish cookery.

What is a true Jewish recipe? Who can say, really? Jews have traveled around so much and lived so many places that—well, need any more be said? Was it the way Russian Jews prepared, for example, brisket, or the way the Litvaks stuffed intestines with groats? If there had been a Yemenite Jew in the town, she or he would have insisted that only her or his spicy stews were authentic—luckily, the dispute was limited to exponents of Hungarian, Latvian, Russian and Ukrainian, not to mention Polish, derivations.

Take the controversy over *blintzes*. A *blintz* is a thin pancake filled with cheese and usually eaten with sour cream, although some eat it with jam, others with cinnamon and sugar; but what to put on it was the least of the problems. First, was the *blintz* Jewish, was it Russian, was it Greek borrowed by the Russians or was it brought to Russia by the Jews? Was it generally Mesopotamian or unique to Israel? How to resolve these questions? Queries were sent to the Library of Congress, and one distraught woman petitioned the Prime Minister of Israel for guidance in the matter. The dialogue took a bizarre turn when one committee member who traveled to Mexico each year for a month insisted that the *blintz* had been borrowed from the pre-Columbian Indians and was, in fact, a refined form of the *tortilla*. The majority was quick to rebut it was the other way round: the presence of the *blintz* in Mexico was proof that Solomon's sailors, after circumnavigating Africa, had visited the New World, maybe even opened a restaurant in Tenochtitlán. It even confirmed that Columbus was a Jew. And so it went.

Then there was the question of what ingredients were allowed in a traditional Jewish recipe. In Bolton there was more than one cook who took shortcuts to the preparation of food, especially the use of canned cream-of-mushroom soup in sauces. Others resorted to ketchup, though surreptitiously. Ketchup was really going too far. But—was a pot roast really a pot roast if powdered French onion soup had been added as a flavor-enhancer?

"My mother never had powdered onion soup."

"But she had onions" was the reply.

"Onions are not powdered."

"In the winter she used dried apricots; why not dried onions?"

"Just because."

"Not just because," added a third voice.

"If they used dried apricots, it's traditional. If they didn't, then it's not."

"And what about before?"

"Before what?"

"Before dried apricots."

"That was a different tradition," answered the exponent of tradition, a triumphant light in her eyes.

Finally, selection of key recipes boiled down to a great cooking competition, the menu of which consisted of chicken soup, gefüllte fish, roast chicken with potatoes, peas, noodle pudding with raisins and cheese, and fruit compote. The judges were to walk down a long table, tasting a series of platters identified only by number. Imagine these judges, ten of the best eaters in the county, a total of 1,978 pounds, and all of them as carefully selected as the cooks. There they were, looking as earnest as gluttons on the morning of a wedding feast, earnest no doubt because of their weighty responsibilities.

Meanwhile, the cooks were all busy at the other end of the room, arranging a little parsley for a garnish, giving a little squeeze of lemon to the chicken soup, trying to look nonchalant. The tasting began.

Alas, some practical joker had laced the chicken soups with cayenne pepper, so that the judges all grew red-faced and had to leave off for twenty minutes while their tongues cooled down. Other than that, the competition proceeded smoothly. The tasting finished, the judges sequestered themselves in the library with tea and, rumor has it, Bromo Seltzer. Outside in the hall, the contestants milled about expectantly, talking nervously, doing busywork.

Finally at nine-forty-five the door to the library opened, and ten solemn and dyspeptic men filed out and waited, eyes averted, while Ben Davis read the verdict.

Who would have imagined that the winner in all categories was Rena Feitelson? The news broke like the shattering of a plate-glass window. Rena was a good cook, but not *that* good, certainly not good enough to take all categories.

Rena was a plain woman, she didn't talk much, the kind of person who spent most of her time doing things around the house and taking care of her children. Her husband sold ladies' ready-to-wear on the road, he was home only on weekends and they didn't entertain much. When the news broke, she didn't even look up from her knitting, although her face did flush and a little self-satisfied smile crossed her lips.

The judges looked around the room uncomfortably, feeling that they had made a few enemies, and cleared out. Swallowing their disappointment, eight or so women gathered around Rena. Where did she get her recipes? Was it her mother, her grandmother? To all these questions she replied with a slight tilt of the head to the side, a narrowing of the eyes and a "Mmm," until finally she said, "I have to tell you, ladies. None of these recipes were in my family. My mother, in fact, was a terrible cook."

"So? So?"

"So five years ago I went to a mah-jongg party in Pittsburgh sponsored by the Sisterhood of the Temple Israel."

"And there you met this fabulous cook. I'll bet I know who. Stately woman, Phyllis Schwartz?"

"No, it had to be Helen Kackner," said another.

"So tell us," came a chorus.

"It was neither of those. To tell you the truth," she said, dragging out her words, "they had this cookbook for sale . . ."

To this day, no one has ever again suggested that the Sisterhood publish a Jewish cookbook. Someone a few days later, it was probably Finkelstein, asked Nudelman what he thought about the whole business. He thought for a moment and said, "My wife's a good cook. But she just can't make gefüllte fish like my mother used to make it." Then he looked up, laughter in his eyes, and said, "And you know what? If I heard my father say the same thing once, he said it a hundred times."

7.
A Simple Form

If I had any reservations about consulting Rosenzweig, they evaporated when, several days after the meeting at Estelle Cantor's, I received a form in the mail; sixteen pages and in Hebrew; yes, Hebrew, the language of the Bible, now Hebrew, the language of bureaucracy as well—the fulfillment of a dream. I turned the pages one by one, and except for the first line, which called for my name, I couldn't understand a word of it. In ancient times the government and priests sometimes used an older formal language to communicate, I read somewhere, just as the Catholic Church continued to use Latin for fifteen hundred years after people stopped using it to buy groceries and tell off-color jokes. For all I know, that's precisely why they continued to use it, because it wasn't corrupted by pedestrian usage. I'll ask Father Shanahan about that the next time I see him. Again I looked at the form and thought that it would have been nice if the State of Israel had used ancient Akkadian and cuneiform script for its forms and regulations. It would have been all the same to me at least, and I wouldn't have developed these negative feelings about the language which were beginning to sprout. Reading the Torah in Hebrew, after all, hasn't frustrated me since I was a child and that was because I couldn't read very well in any language. Though I had to admire the typeface on the form, clean and modern, lacking the embellishments which carried over from the scribe, that is, if I could understand the words.

After only ten minutes that endless inscrutable form brought me to call Rosenzweig, if for no other reason than to see the expression on *his* face when he opened the envelope and saw what I saw.

It was worth the trip to his office. He turned the pages soberly, pulling on the pouch of one of his prematurely sagging cheeks, then he looked up and said, "Mendel, I can't read this."

"Why not?" I asked.

"We haven't got a *minyan*." We both had a good laugh.

"So call Nudelman and the rabbi and we'll get seven men together and have a bureaucratic service," I said as our laughter subsided.

He nodded, mirth in his eyes, and said, "Listen, that's no joke. Let's at least take it to the rabbi. He went to a seminary, after all, and he's fluent in Hebrew. He can surely translate it." I could see by the look on his face that he wanted to do to the rabbi what I had done to him, and before I could respond he was already looking up the number in his Rolodex and dialing. To be more precise he called his secretary and asked her to dial. He must have had a sore finger or something and couldn't do it himself. He didn't have anything else to do, because while he waited he just sat there drumming on the polished walnut surface of his desk, on the only place where the surface was visible, since the rest of it was covered with paper, yellow manila files, paperback books without eye-catching covers, which I took to be the latest fiction from the courts. The buzzer rang, and the humor still in his eye, but the resonant professional tone in his voice, he arranged to go right over to the rabbi's house with me and the document; he called it a document. Poor Rabbi Bing must have thought that Rosenzweig was bringing him something from a rabbinical court, a divorce certificate or something like that.

To his credit, the rabbi waded right in, but it was soon clear that he was over his head and drowning in bureaucratese. Considering the trouble he was having, Rabbi Bing was marvelous. Only by the twitching of his little finger and the little nicks he was making on his pencil with his fingernail could we tell that he was straining his mental lexicon to the limit with the translation, at least for the first five minutes, until humility finally got the better of him and he collapsed back in his chair and said, with a tired smile, "I hate to say it, but I'm not doing a very good job of this. Of course, if you want to leave it with me . . ." But he couldn't bring himself to finish the sentence.

So Rosenzweig and I had the second good laugh of the day on the way back to his office, and to my complete surprise he offered to help me, assuming I could get an Israeli student at Pitt to translate the form for him. He offered to help me without even discussing the fee, and even more surprising, he forgot to ask me just how much money was involved. Later I found that he hadn't forgotten. Harriet had told him that it was four hundred thousand

Israeli pounds, and he just hadn't yet gotten around to asking the bank what the rate of exchange was between dollars and lira.

On the way out of the bank building, I ran into Steve White, who looked at me as though he had been searching for me all over town, a strange reaction for one whose only contact with the synagogue or me that I recall was the funeral of his father, Aaron Weisblatt.

Yet there he was, greeting me like I was his long-awaited benefactor and eager to tell me something about his recent trip to Europe. Taking me by the elbow, he looked at me confidentially and said quietly, "You're a survivor of"—his eyes rolled in his head as he searched for the right word—"World War Two, aren't you, Mendel?"

"Yes," I replied, eying him with a mixture of suspicion and apprehension.

"Mendel, do you have time for a coffee at the Coffee Cup? I would like—would like to do something about my father's grave. You're the one to take care of that, aren't you?" This abrupt change of direction, albeit on the same general subject, aroused my curiosity. There was an urgency, a pleading in his eyes much different from the casual tone of his voice, which made me want to respond to him, and I willingly followed him, although I confess that he had me in tow.

8.
The Pewter Mug

All I know about old Aaron Weisblatt, Steve White's father, is the epitaph engraved on his tombstone. HE NEVER LOOKED BACK is what it said. He came from someplace in Eastern Europe, Lithuania perhaps, and it's rumored that his father was a distinguished rabbi. Unlike his father, old Aaron made a career in retailing and never cared much for religion. And neither does his son, Steve White, for that matter. Aaron is better left buried beside his wife, Emma, in a quiet corner of the cemetery. The Torah, after all, told me to honor the living, or have I already got it mixed up? In any event it was not Aaron's migration *from* Europe but his son's and grandson's trip in the other direction which interested me when Steve, in his matter-of-fact way, told me about it that day at the Coffee Cup.

Old Aaron died a year after Steve and Amy's son was

born, so they could not name the child after him, but they had no intention of doing so, although "Alan" might have passed. They called the boy William because Amy liked the melodic sound of William White. William, or Billy, as everyone called him, grew tall in the nurturing environment of Steve's two-story brick Georgian house in the wooded, hilly outskirts of Bolton. He was the only child Steve and Amy had and they concentrated all of their love on him. Unlike his father, he was not lured into the family business after school—there would be time for that. For Billy was a natural athlete, tall for his age, a good competitor and a team player. He practiced sports every night after class and came home exhausted to a huge meal and early bed. It seemed that he was always in training for something. Like his father, he was a mediocre student, but who cared?, he did so well at sports, winning varsity letters in football, basketball and track.

Graduation arrived and his parents both cried when they saw him win the Most Valuable Athlete of the Year Award, a presentation made personally at the graduation ceremony by the president of the Elks Club, the sponsoring organization. With the eighteen-inch simulated–gold-plated trophy on its walnut veneer base in hand, Steve and Amy cared little that Billy barely edged into the top half of the class. His athletic scholarship at Pitt was already secure, and they knew that he was basically a smart boy who would make a worthy successor to the family business. He had a lot of common sense, after all, and that was all that mattered.

Even before the excitement of graduation had receded, Steve, Amy and Billy, with six suitcases, including a new Tourister set bought for the occasion and a deluxe Kodak Instamatic, enplaned to Europe for a full month, the first time any of them had been there. Steve's curiosity for

Europe was nil, but several of their friends had gone and Amy was feeling excluded from all of the talk about the values in bone china in London, not to mention the leathers and tweeds, the perfumes and clothing in Paris, the elegance of the hotels in Nice and the quaintness of the little towns in the countryside.

Amy was sitting next to the window thinking about all of the things she wanted to buy. Steve was on the aisle checking his pockets for the whereabouts of the traveler's checks, passports and plane tickets, simultaneously making a mental budget and deliberating over the hazards of leaving their valuables in the hotel safe. As for Billy, he was looking forward to stealing a pewter beer stein from the Hofbräuhaus in Munich for his room at college. Steve studied the itinerary and thought of the only disagreement they had experienced in planning the trip. Steve still had doubts about going to Germany after all that had happened to the Jews. Amy did not feel very comfortable about going to Germany either, but it was Billy's graduation trip and he refused to go without seeing the beer halls in Munich. Not that he was overly fond of beer; he would not admit it, but he found it bitter and it filled him up too fast. Coke in a can tasted better. It was that beer stein. Steve had even offered to send away for one that he had seen advertised in a copy of *Playboy* that he had found in Billy's room, but that would not do. So, reluctantly, after London and environs (including a day trip to Stratford-on-Avon), Amsterdam (with a trip to the cheese market), Paris (including Versailles), they would rent a car, one of those small ones that were so unsafe, and drive to Heidelberg with a view of the Rhine en route, then to some picturesque old medieval walled towns that Russ Sage, the travel agent, had talked them into visiting. Really, it seemed a silly detour when they could go directly to

Munich, by-passing the cities on a kind of German turn-
pike which had neither tolls nor a speed limit. Steve
reached into his jacket pocket at the thought of the car
and was reassured to find the international driver's license,
thinking that it was so complicated to be in Europe as
compared with the United States.

They moved through their itinerary in a daze, the many
impressions blurring together like the shifting images of a
kaleidoscope. They could not study the details. There was
so much to do in any given day that there was not time.
And besides, Steve faithfully recorded every stop, photo-
graphing Amy in front of the Tower of London; Billy
eyeball-to-eyeball with a guard at Buckingham Palace;
Amy poking a red cheese somewhere in Holland; Steve
and Amy looking down at Heidelberg from the ruins of
a castle, and so on. Not given to hobbies except for the
biweekly synagogue men's club bowling league, Steve was
beginning to like taking pictures. The car, a Renault 12,
was more comfortable and roomy than they had imagined,
and but for the difficulty with the road signs and being
perpetually lost except on the open highway between
towns, the driving was almost pleasant.

Still regretting that they were not taking the Autobahn,
they filled the tank in Heidelberg on an overcast morning,
watching despondently as the meter raced through the
marks and pfennigs, and were on their way toward what
Russ Sage had labeled the "romantic way." They traveled
slower than usual that day. The neat green farmland inter-
spersed with small clustered towns, the fields that looked
as though someone had just cut the grass and pulled the
weeds, the geraniums festooning the stucco-and-beam fa-
çades of the tilting houses, had the appearance of illustra-
tions from children's books. Except for the stench of the
truck exhausts, there was nothing to mar the simple beauty

of the countryside, neither signboard nor junkyard. What did they do with their old cars anyway? Steve wondered. Despite himself he was taking a liking to Germany. The people, at least hereabouts, were nice and courteous, certainly in comparison to the rude, cold Parisians. But he found himself looking at every middle-aged man and dressing him in an SS uniform.

The afternoon brought them to a chain of old walled towns with narrow streets, peaked roofs and leaning walls. "Very quaint," they agreed. But the clouds opened, drenching them in the late afternoon, and darkness found them hungry and wet, inching along a narrow road behind a truck. The windshield wipers hardly kept up with the heavy rain, and the continual condensation on the inside of the windows almost totally obscured their whereabouts. Road signs were nonexistent or invisible, and only the blurred yellow light of an occasional roadside inn and Billy's confidence with the road map kept them on what they thought was the road to Munich. Uncomfortable as they were, the thought of a hot bath at the hotel which had confirmed their reservation for the night kept them going. Kept them going, at least, until the car nearly foundered in a dip in the road that had filled with water, and within a few hundred yards the engine was reduced to one cylinder, which bravely carried on until it, too, gave up. The car drifted to the side of the road, where it remained, pounded by the dense rain and spray from passing trucks. Billy volunteered to try to dry the electrical system, but he only succeeded in getting himself and the engine compartment soaked. Frustrated and helpless, Steve sat behind the wheel repeatedly turning over the engine until finally the battery, too, expired, and the three of them, irritated and helpless, sat shivering in the small car.

It was Amy who, after half an hour, calmly passed

around some crackers and cheese and suggested that a distant light might be a roadside inn. Armed with his pocket Berlitz, soaked by the hostile wind-driven rain, Steve pushed down the dark road toward the yellow light, finally bursting into a warm if austere dining room. The owner, an angular middle-aged man with thin reddish-blond hair who fortunately spoke English, studied him with watery pale-blue eyes as Steve explained their predicament. Nodding and wiping his hands on his apron, he turned and disappeared into the kitchen, leaving Steve standing in an ever-widening pool of rain water. A few moments later he returned with a boy Billy's age, whom he dispatched with a car to bring Amy and Billy to the inn. Steve he directed to the fireplace.

There was only one room available, cramped under the eaves and with two small mullioned windows, the double bed and chaise lounge taking all the floor space. They ate a late dinner in the corner nook of the warmly lit half-paneled dining room in the company of a few locals, who, after making an appraisal of the newcomers, went back to their liters of beer and rumbling conversation.

The meal came on a foot-long platter piled high with cooked red cabbage, hot German potato salad and roast veal. Billy bravely ordered half a liter of beer, which was, he concluded, not as bitter as American beer and even came in one of those pewter mugs that he coveted.

When they had finished dinner, the owner, Herr Reiter, suggested that they try the apple torte, and although Steve and Amy, at least, were quite full, they agreed out of politeness. Herr Reiter returned juggling three plates. Billy opened a road map on the table and said, "Could you tell us where we are on the map? I guess we got a little lost in the rain."

"Where do you want to go, Munich?"

"Yes."

Herr Reiter took his glasses out of his pocket and put them on. "Do you mind if I sit down?" he asked, and drawing the map toward him, he placed a stubby finger on a point and said, "You are here."

"Where are we?" Billy asked.

"Why, Dachau," Herr Reiter replied in a tone which reflected surprise. "You've come to Dachau."

The room was warm but Steve felt his spine contract. Amy grew pale. Billy, head down, continued to study the map. He looked up momentarily, a look of concentration on his face, and asked, "How far is that from Munich?"

Steve looked at the innkeeper and thought he saw a faint flush come to the cheeks of the German. Then hoarse laughter from across the room distracted him.

"The beer makes them happy. It is German bread," said the innkeeper, then turned to Billy and added, "Not more than thirty kilometers."

"Is this another one of those walled cities, like Dinkels . . . Dinkelsbühl?" Billy asked.

"It's a very old town with some historical buildings, but it's no rival to Dinkelsbühl," replied Herr Reiter, his almost colorless eyes fixed on Amy and Steve.

"If Munich is so close, Steve, maybe we should try to make our hotel tonight," said Amy, speaking very slowly. "After all, we do have reservations."

"Is the room too crowded for you, Mrs. White? I am sorry, but it was all we could give you. But you would be foolish to leave in this rain. Besides, it's out of the question. The service station won't be able to charge the battery of your car until tomorrow morning. I've already told Hans, the boy who brought you here, to take care of it."

Steve looked at Amy tentatively and said, "He's right, Amy, we'll get off to a good start in the morning, having had a good night's sleep, and we'll be fresh for a full day of sightseeing in Munich."

"And you'll have a good breakfast to start you off the right way, I promise you that," Herr Reiter added. Amy smiled unwillingly, but she smiled. Seeing it, Herr Reiter nodded and said, "I saw in the register you come from Pennsylvania. Do you live near Pittsburgh? I have a brother in Pittsburgh. He went there after the . . . in 1947. When you return, maybe you will telephone to him and tell him you saw me?"

"Of course, we'll be glad to do that," said Steve, feeling more at ease and urging Amy with his eyes to relax. "Would you like some more tea, Amy?" he said. As soon as he heard "tea," Herr Reiter got up and went to the bar. When the innkeeper's back was turned, her expression changed, revealing to Steve a mixture of horror and discomfort. She said only "Dachau," in a stage whisper. Steve reached across the table to touch her hand and nodded, feeling a lump in his throat as he watched the innkeeper return to the table, a steaming teapot held in his right hand and a half liter of beer in the left.

"Here's some more tea," and he again sat down.

"Maybe you shouldn't," Amy said to Billy, who said nothing but chastised her with his eyes.

"It's good for him, Mrs. White," he said.

Herr Reiter reached into his pocket and took out an old leather wallet, opened it and slid it across the table toward Steve. "Here is a picture of my brother and his wife and son," he continued, with a reassuring wink at Billy. "Of course, it's an old one. Gerhardt, their son, is about your age. He's serving in the American army now and my eldest son is at the same time in the German army."

At the mention of the army, Steve began trying uniforms on Herr Reiter. "I suppose you were in the army,

Herr Reiter?" Steve asked, doing his best to feign noncha-
lance, holding the teacup between table and lip.

Herr Reiter sighed. "*Ja*—and who wasn't in those times?
Little children, old men, everyone who could walk, before
it was over." His jovial expression gave way to a more
reflective mood. He fell silent, then a faint sad smile returned and he said, "Those were bad times for all of us
here. And on your side too."

No one responded. Steve shifted in his chair, suddenly
aware of a pain in his lower back. Amy looked across the
room at nothing in particular and fussed with her hair.

"Were you here during the war?" Steve asked, ignoring
Amy's urgent signals to change the subject.

"No. First I was in Africa, then Russia. I was in the re-
treat from Stalingrad; I lost three toes from—what do you
call it?—frostbite. I can still feel the cold sometimes. But
at least I made it back; many are still lying there."

"When did you come home finally?"

"After the war. I was taken prisoner by your forces just
before the end. I'm only glad it wasn't the Russians."

"Did you see the camp when you came home?" asked
Steve hesitantly.

"*Ja*, I saw it," replied Herr Reiter, his tone subdued.
His expression flattened and his pale eyes were vacant for
an instant. Then the light returned and he said, "The camp
was mostly gone when I came back. They had already destroyed much of it. Only a few buildings remained."

"Is it nearby?" said Amy.

"It is very close. Just across the road, in fact," he said.

The tips of Steve's fingers felt suddenly like they'd been
in ice water. "Do many people visit it?" he asked.

"*Ja*. People come all the time from all over the world."

"There was a concentration camp here, wasn't there?"
said Billy. "We learned about it in world history," he added,

looking at each of his parents in turn, but Steve's head was in his teacup and Amy was again focused on the far wall.

Herr Reiter stacked three beer coasters and said quietly, "*Ja, ja.*"

World history resounded in Steve's head, and it came to him that they, he and Billy, had never talked about what had happened. They had talked a lot about sports, about cars, even about school, but never about the Holocaust. He had, he supposed, assumed that somewhere in his education Billy would pick it up. The thought struck him that the Holocaust meant no more to Billy than the Battle of Bull Run. It was just an event in the past. Surely now wasn't the time to talk about it. Besides, what would he say? What indeed did he, Steve White, really know about it?

Billy took a sip of beer, grimaced as he swallowed and asked, "Herr Reiter, where can I get a beer mug like this?"

The question released the suspended tension. The innkeeper's smile returned, and Amy came back from wherever she had been and finished her tea.

Herr Reiter leaned toward Billy confidentially, the kindly great-uncle look in his eye. "So you like our beer steins? All the Americans do, it seems. Now they are hard to come by. They use glass or even plastic now."

Billy's face fell at the thought of not being able to get one. "You wouldn't sell me this one, would you?" he asked.

"No, I wouldn't sell it to you"—Herr Reiter paused—"but I might give it to you." Billy's eyes widened.

"No, we couldn't let you do that," Steve protested. "Not if they don't make them anymore. But we'll be glad to pay you for it if you think you can part with it."

"I still have two hundred or so in the cellar. I bought a large supply when I heard they were becoming scarce. He shall have it as a remembrance." His expression sobered

for a moment. "Now if you'll excuse me, I must get back
to some chores. I will see you in the morning. And your
car will be parked outside as soon as the battery is ready."

With a little bow, he turned toward the kitchen. Steve
looked at Billy, whose eyes were on the pewter beer stein.
"Bed?" he said and Amy, fatigue showing, nodded.

The rain stopped before they went to sleep, and Steve
went to one of the small windows in the eaves to look out,
but a thick fog shrouded the landscape.

Steve and Amy read for a while in the dim light of the
bedlamps before they burrowed under the feather bed and
turned off the light. Tired though they were, they both
had a hard time getting to sleep, perhaps because of the
tea, and their feet would not warm up. At last Steve turned
toward Amy and said, "Can't sleep?"

"No. My feet are too cold."

"Put them on my legs and warm them up," he said.

The early-morning light suffused the clearing mist with a
purity, a total absence of color. Steve awoke and was
drawn again to the window. There, across the road, beyond a hedge of trees, still spectral in the undulating morning mist, were several long white barnlike buildings on one
side of a vast empty field—empty except for outlines of
foundations and a gravel road dividing it. On the far side
of the field, the top of a chimney protruded from a grove
of trees, and nearby were several shapes that looked like
monumental sculptures. As Steve watched, a milky film
enveloped everything, and there was nothing to see but a
void, chaos as it must have been before life came to the
universe, a compost of souls covering a barren world. But
Steve saw only a heavy mist closing off a monument so
abstracted that it conveyed no feeling to him. He turned

from the window and began putting on his clothes, trying not to wake Amy and Billy.

As promised, the car was parked in front of the inn. Herr Reiter saw them off personally, solicitous as before, reminding them to contact his brother on their return. They pulled onto the road as the sun groped through the mist, awakening the color of fields gleaming with condensed dew. As the car lurched forward, Steve said to Amy, "Should we stop here and see the memorial before we go to Munich?"

"Wouldn't it be depressing for a vacation, Steve? Billy, do you want to stop at the memorial?" she asked over her shoulder.

Billy looked up and turned his head toward the entrance. A large tour bus was unloading a group of nuns and priests. Nothing could be seen except for tall hedges, white fences and the backs of nondescript buildings. He turned away and said, "It looks like there's nothing much left now." Steve hesitated and his foot eased off the accelerator. The car had nearly stopped when Billy said, "It's okay with me, Pop, if you want to stop. It might be interesting. But shouldn't we get on to Munich?"

Steve turned toward Amy and his foot pressed down on the throttle. "Well, it is Billy's graduation trip."

"Do you want to stop, Steve?" The car had already passed the entrance to the parking lot.

"I guess not," Steve said. "We've already passed it and there's no point in going back. There's so much to do today. Besides, I saw it this morning out of the window, before the fog closed in."

Steve shifted into third gear, the car accelerated and he wondered whether the hotel in Munich would insist that they pay for the previous night.

9.
Money, Money

Someone, possibly a fund raiser for charities, once said, "If you want to make an enemy of a rich man, ask for his money." Certainly an overstatement and one that had no application to my life, since I neither asked others for money nor had much to give. Nevertheless, what there was left over from my pay I willingly shared with others, so much so that when the letter first arrived I had not more than $3,756 in the Bolton Mutual Savings Association. That's not much insulation against adversity, but I had learned in my life that when adversity really strikes, no amount of money or possessions will help, except possibly to delay the inevitable, but of course everyone knows that.

Why am I thinking about money? Since the news of the reparations and the receipt of the form, which was eventually completed and returned to the government office in

Israel (the particular name escapes me), I've had to think of it more than I did in the past, which was precisely almost never. Now that a sizable portion of money was in reach, I had to figure out what to do with it, and as I soon found out after word leaked to the general community, there are all sorts of experts in money management and disposition in Bolton. It seems in fact to be a greater diversion than stamp collecting, bowling and rose cultivation, all of which have their fanatic adherents who get together regularly. Up to now I had not known about the Money Club, which had its own magazine, called, of course, *Money*, and which met once a week in the board room of the bank. In fact, the bank president, D. P. Petersilge himself, and the local vice-president of the stock brokerage firm of Wallen, Fern and Sedgwick were frequent participants. There was nothing of the secretive rites which I understand to be associated with the Brotherhood of Owls, and none of the adolescent tomfoolery which is incorporated into the luncheon camaraderie of the Society of Optimists, none at all. The Money Club is just a lot of nice people—some of whom also belong to the Optimists, the Owls and the Model Railway Engineers—who want to learn how to keep, multiply or just live with their money. That's no joke, for, as I was learning, living with money isn't easy. I realize in retrospect that had I simply said publicly, possibly by an ad in the personal column of the newspaper, that I was receiving seventy-five thousand dollars in reparations, it would have been easier. But because I had been taciturn, if not evasive, the rumor took on its own reality, inflating like a hot-air balloon until by the time it had spent itself, my fortune was estimated to be alternatively five hundred thousand Israeli pounds, three million Polish zlotys and five hundred thousand American dollars, including a small house in Poland and a cooperative apartment in Jerusalem.

The first indication of the extent to which the rumor had in fact circulated was an invitation that I received in the mail, nothing fancy, just a postcard, to come to the next meeting of the Money Club, to hear a speaker from Pittsburgh talk about the "Pros and Cons of the Money Market Certificate." Before this I hadn't even known that there was a money market. I've always thought that you bought things *with* money, like food and clothing. So the first question that came to me was, What, just what, do you use to buy money with at the money market? I must confess that I was almost curious enough to go to the meeting; at least I put the card in a pile of other event announcements for the month.

Something else came to my attention. Curiously, people began treating me a little differently; at least so I imagined. Oh, not everyone, not my good friends. But Finkelstein, for example, looked at me the way the wolf looked at Little Red Riding Hood. He's not to be blamed, it wasn't for selfish reasons, it's just the affliction of the long-term treasurer of an institution that never has enough money, something like a chronic condition of low blood sugar. There was nothing obtuse about it. He never came out and said something like "Mendel, the synagogue has been good to you, so how about returning the favor?" All he did, besides the look, was to discuss confidentially the needs, those plums that the budget never provides for, like a new sound projector and screen, a new sound system, expansion of the record collection and, of course, the library, for he knew that was my weakness. I agreed with him totally, and although I didn't say it to him, I put them all on a little *Chanukah* list I was making, for about the only pleasure that

I was getting from the notion that I would have some money coming was the thought of what I could do with part of it. The money itself was still too much like the purchase price for an urn containing all of the family's ashes.

The second change that I noticed was a new tone and look of respect, the kind of look reserved for someone who has just won the Tchaikovsky Competition or the Nobel Peace Prize; a look that was totally undeserved, since I had personally done nothing more than open a letter. The money would make me no better a person, and very likely would make me a little worse, although I hoped not.

10.
Mimi

My mother used to say, "Children are like sponges: they absorb everything, keep it for a while and give it all back." What does that have to do with money? Nothing, but it has everything to do with children, and Mimi Finkelstein is a child, a child who I am very fond of, a child who likes me. Eleven years old, with not even the suggestion of maidenhood, but with the promise of beauty in her large brown eyes. She has the eyes of a fawn and long brown hair that reaches to her thin waist, hair that glows golden when the sun meets it.

Her mother, Heda Finkelstein, monitors all that passes in our town. Heda is a thin woman, though not unattractively so. I often think that she lives not on food but on personal events; she is sustained by gossip. Not malicious gossip; that is the province of Mrs. Wasserman, of which something will be said later. Any old event is good enough for Heda as long as it has human interest. She would have made the quintessential journalist. And that, I assume, is how it was that one day as I was opening the door of one of the schoolrooms in advance of the meeting of the youth group, the Young Israelites, I was approached by a smiling Mimi, who said, with her usual directness, "What are you going to do with all that money, Mendel?" Even the children call me Mendel; no formality for me, I am little more than a child with wrinkles myself.

I stopped, the key only halfway to its destination, and answered with the first thought that came to me: "Why, give it to you, Mimi. That is, if you can tell me what you would do with it and I approve."

Her eyes widened, if that was possible, they were already so wide, and she said, "In that case, Mendel, tell me what you would approve of so I'm sure to get it right the first time."

"That's an even better question than the first one," I replied.

"One question deserves another. That's what my dad always says."

"He does?"

"Don't you think so?" she said.

"You win."

"What do I win?" she asked, not content to let the game drop.

Remembering the key in the lock, I opened the door and withdrew it.

"You sure do have a lot of keys, Mendel."

"You still haven't told me what you would do with the money, Mimi, if I give it to you."

"Oh," she said, shifting from foot to foot. "First, I guess I would get my mother a new washing machine."

"And then?"

"And then I would get myself a new dress, but just one. And then I would get you all the books you ever wanted in your whole life, because you gave the money to me."

"And if there is some left, what will you do. with it?"

"Maybe—maybe I would use it to feed hungry children. Yes, that's what I think I would do. Do you approve of that, Mendel?"

Three or four children were coming down the hall, laughing and chattering. I looked up for a moment, then down at her. Her head was turned up as she waited for my answer. I put my hand on her shoulder, touching her soft hair, and said, "Yes, Mimi, I approve of that."

"Good. I'll tell my father. And, oh, I almost forgot. Can we add a new sound projector for the synagogue?"

"Tell your dad it's on the list, Mimi. And, Mimi"—she paused at the door as the others caught up to her—"turn out the light when the meeting is over. Your father would like that, too." That she didn't hear, as she was already inside, laughing about something with her friends. Children. I returned to my apartment in anticipation of a visit by Nudelman, thinking that there would still be time to go out and buy some cookies for Isaac.

11.
Giving Birth

Nudelman and his wife, Sarah, had been married twenty-four years and had reached middle age without children, and not by choice. At a time when most married people were looking forward to their grandchildren, they were planning a vacation to New Mexico. The *why* of not having children is usually shared only with close friends and relations, so it came as a surprise that a man such as Nudelman, a private man, by no means an exhibitionist, should be willing to disclose so much of these personal events with the understanding that one day, a few people, strangers to him and Sarah, strangers even to Bolton, might learn of his problem. It happened this way:

I had told Nudelman that I was writing this memoir about Bolton and, frankly, about America, since Bolton is a little piece of America, the one that I'm familiar with. Nudelman is a sensitive man, the type of person, in this country at least, who is not given to long philosophical discussion, but who has great insight. So from time to time I would let him read something of what I had scribbled, just to get his reaction, and he would comment, always with some sagacity. On one such occasion late one night after a meeting, I made some tea for him in my apartment and showed him something that I had written.

He said, with a smile, "Mendel, what you have written is interesting, but there is one thing lacking, one thing that Americans can't get enough of, like ketchup."

"What's that, Nudelman?" I said, feeling a little defensive.

"Sex," he said. "Sex."

"Sex?"

"Sex."

"Well, I—I don't know anything about that side of the community. What, just what exactly, are you talking about? Adultery? That kind of thing?"

"Whatever."

"I suppose there's no reason why I shouldn't have a little of *that* in it. After all, there's no life without it," I said. And I began to think about all the fornication and lust in the Bible that everyone always cites. "Nudelman, you may be right. I was reading a book awhile back about how important sex used to be—"

"It still is."

"I mean in the religious sense. Why, there's one theory that the Holy Ark was guarded in the temple in Jerusalem by two winged cherubim, one male and the other female, engaged in—well, you know what I mean."

"Mendel! Where did you get such a filthy idea?"

"It's true, Nudelman. I read it."

"Not everything you read is true. Maybe it was anti-Semitic propaganda."

So I let the subject pass. I drank my tea and he drank his and we each kept to our own private thoughts. Finally I said, "Nudelman, the whole thing doesn't have to be about sex. But it could be about having children."

"It's the same thing, isn't it?"

And then it came to me. "You had a child very late in life, you and Sarah."

"Wait a minute, Mendel, I didn't raise the . . ."

There you have the beginning. It's not like me, but I pried a little and eventually he told me what follows.

Nobody tried as hard as Nudelman and Sarah to have children. It was not for lack of feeling for each other or, for that matter, intimacy, but nothing ever happened, whatever they did and whatever they tried. And they tried everything from gynecology to folk medicine. First, of course, they tried the doctors one after another. Americans I've seen have about the same faith in their doctors as Irish women do in their priests. They consulted, taking turns, all manner of fertility specialists, only to find that the equipment was in good working order. That made them feel both better and worse: better because they couldn't blame themselves, and worse because if everything was working, why didn't something happen?

At first they thought that good timing would help, but despite the most elaborate record-keeping, the moment eluded them. Then it was the cold showers, the headstands, the vitamins, the special diets, even new loose-fitting underwear for Nudelman, putting aside the new jockey shorts just bought on sale. Next they tried, in turn, a little brandy before bed, the full moon and herbal tea . . . Time passed, years passed, the remedies were forgotten, pushed to the back of the medicine cabinet, and gradually they just stopped talking about it. They adapted their lives in different ways. For one, they took more vacations than the average couple of their age. A lot of people envied their freedom and they made good use of it. For years they drove into Pittsburgh twice a month for a play or a movie and dinner, something people with families did only occasionally and with a lot of advance planning. Sarah taught in the Sunday School; she loved the children and they loved her. They had a niece with whom they spent a lot of time. She would stay with them for a week or two every year, they sent her presents for all of the holidays and never missed seeing her on her birthday, so they were what a psychologist would call compensated, or something like that. It doesn't quite sound like the correct description of making the best of it. That's what they did. They made the best of it, and no one knew the ache that they sometimes felt when they came home to their empty, orderly and so quiet house.

In this way they went on filling the void in their lives, like the two sound people that they were. Then one night, long after they had given up any hope, after they had even rationalized that they were better off without children and too old to put up with them, Nudelman had a dream. Nudelman was not much of a dreamer; he worked hard and slept soundly, and when most of us are moving from profound sleep into a state of higher mental activity, Nudelman was already getting up and puttering about the house, preparing for another long day in his hardware store. So a vivid dream, not just a selected short subject, was something for him to think about, provided he could remember it on waking. In this dream his father came to him and in a mournful tone told him that he was disappointed because Nudelman had not produced any grandchildren. A straightforward dream, it was not the kind that prophets spin history out of, but to Nudelman a coffeepot is a coffeepot and a pocketknife is a pocketknife. In the dream Nudelman told his father that it was not for lack of desire that they had no children. His father answered that perhaps they had desired too much. To this Nudelman replied respectfully that they, too, had thought about that. So Nudelman's father looked at his watch and whispered a tip in his ear: "March 24 at two o'clock is the time." Then he went through a door which suddenly appeared in front of him, and closed it without so much as a goodbye. Nudelman woke up with the echo of the date resounding in his ears. The day of the dream was, by the way, only March 9.

He pushed the whole thing under the rug—after all, it was just a dream—but that night after supper, having nothing better to talk about, he told Sarah about it. After asking how his father looked, she shrugged and said, "I once had a cleaning woman who had a dream book. She would turn her dreams into numbers with the book and then play the numbers in Pittsburgh."

"How did she do?" asked Nudelman as he moved on another piece of bread.

"Sometimes she won and sometimes she lost. But when she lost, she always said it was only because she had misread the interpretations in the book."

"You didn't believe her, did you?"

"Truthfully, I never even considered it. As far as I could tell, it was as good a method of choosing a number to bet on as any other."

"That's true. So what if there is something to this number?"

"What if?"

"What if we did it and it finally happened?"

"A scary thought, after all these years of hope and disappointment." Her voice dropped and she looked over his head.

"The point is, do you still want a child, Sarah?"

"I had given up. We're too old now. You've got to be young and modern. We're a little out of date already, aren't we?"

"Mature, Sarah. Just mature and experienced. But what a good parent has to give a child is never out of date, Sarah, and it doesn't change from generation to generation."

What he had said kindled a light in her eyes, and he saw it across the table. "Could we really put up with all of that now, the diapers, the crying, the junk that you haul around; could we give up going out to the movies whenever we felt like it?"

"There's nothing to see anymore. They don't make them like they used to. Not for years."

"You see what I mean? We're out of date."

"Still, what if it really worked this time? Would you be willing to try? Just one more time?"

"And if it didn't? We'd have the disappointment and the wounds all over again."

"That's true."

"But I suppose I still would be willing to try."

"Then let's try."

"In the middle of the day?"

"It could have been the early morning. He didn't say which. Just like my father. He was never one for details. Tell you what. We'll try it both times."

"Are we up to it?"

"Sarah!"

"I'll make a light lunch and we'll even have a little wine, but not too much."

"What, in the middle of the night?"

"In the middle of the night I'll get up and make some tea."

So, telling nobody about this—they felt a little silly—they went quietly into training. Not in the precise sense; they simply got out an old book which related diet to fertility and potency, adding a little wheat germ here and a little yogurt there. Sarah just smiled and said nothing. She didn't want to disappoint Nudelman, but she knew what she knew, that it wasn't the best time of the month for conception. But why pour cold water on Nudelman, he was having a good time, and besides, hadn't her mother always said that thinking about something is often better than doing it?

On the day before the night, they were both feeling like kids who were going to the circus the next day and who liked clowns but were afraid of lions, tigers and bears. They went to bed with ceremony: Sarah put on her best nightgown and Nudelman a new pair of crimson pajamas. At this point Nudelman, a sound sleeper, put his faith in Big Ben, the faithful alarm clock. He knew that if Sarah had to get up at two in the morning, she would probably lie awake thinking about it, but what if at about one forty-five she drifted off into sleep? What then? It's always better to have spare light bulbs around the house, not to mention fuses, just in case. Even candles.

Nudelman was right, half-right. He fell asleep almost immediately. Sarah lay awake thinking that given the time of the month, the whole thing was highly improbable, and at one forty-five she looked at Nudelman, serenely asleep, and she decisively turned off the alarm and closed her eyes. Closing her eyes was one thing, closing her thoughts another. What would he say when he learned that without even consulting him, she had taken it on herself to give up what was to be their only ephemeral chance to have a child? They had always made decisions together. So at three minutes to two she shook him awake. At this time of the night, getting Nudelman up was no easy task, and without going into details, they missed the time by a full seven minutes. Nudelman's only comment before he went back to sleep was, "My father, he should rest in peace, was never a very exact man, so who knows? Besides, we've got another chance."

The next morning the telephone went off before Big Ben. It was Roth, Nudelman's principal supplier of bathroom fixtures, which were at that time in short supply, owing to a long strike in Indiana. Roth was in Pittsburgh for only one day with a catalog and some samples of a new Japanese line priced very competitively. Nudelman had to go, but it would be no problem, as he could easily return by noon. The car was almost new and he would leave plenty of time for delays. He dressed quickly, grabbed a piece of toast and "hit the road." His meeting with Roth lasted only twenty-five minutes. He placed an order conditioned on twenty days delivery, ordered a grilled-cheese sandwich to go with a slice of tomato in the hotel coffee shop and was soon back on the road. Stop-and-go city traffic irritated him, but he finally escaped from the city, only to get a blowout on the left rear tire. There was some confusion with the new jack, but he quickly changed the tire, throwing the spare into the trunk without bolting it down, and with grimy hands, feeling sweaty, he was on the road again, still with lots of time, at least a half-hour margin. Nudelman normally observed the speed limit, but today, with an eye on the rear-view mirror, he pushed it a little.

It goes without saying that our fathers didn't make up all of those old proverbs for nothing, and as he found out, haste does indeed make waste. Ten miles from Bolton he was clocked at sixty-three miles per hour by young Carl Petersen, Olaf Petersen's son, traveling in an unmarked state police car. Carl tried to hide his embarrassment when he saw that the offender was his up-the-street neighbor whose apples he had more than once stolen before reaching the age of conscience.

Nudelman was glad to see him, and he said, "Carl, thank heavens it's you. I'm on my way home and it's an emergency."

"Nobody's sick, I hope, Mr. Nudelman," said Carl, leaning on the window.

"No. To tell you the truth, Carl, it's a matter of a baby."

"You don't mean Mrs. Nudelman?" Carl was newly married, his wife was pregnant and he was thinking about such things.

"Yes. Well, no, not exactly."

"Well, I'm sorry, but I'm gonna have to give you a ticket," Carl said, his pencil finger beginning to twitch.

"Carl, listen, she *is* going to have a baby, maybe. Just write it out and drop it off at the house and I'll sign it. Send me the bill."

"If you're on your way to the hospital, I'll escort you. I can do that." Carl was feeling guilty. They had told him at patrol school that there would be moments like this.

"Don't worry, Carl, not now; maybe call me in nine months. But if I don't get home soon . . ."

A foxy smile crossed Carl's face.

"Carl, can I go now? If you must write a ticket, just put it on my account or something."

"Okay, Mr. Nudelman. I'm not supposed to do this, but . . ." Before he could finish the sentence, Nudelman had started the car. He spun his rear wheels in the gravel, accelerated down the road, leaving Carl, eyes smarting from the exhaust, and got home in time, even for a quick shower.

Nudelman and Sarah did their best to put the day behind them. He never once asked her, verbally at least, as the month passed, but secretly at the office he was marking off the days on his desk calendar. Even when the proper time had finally elapsed, he was restrained in his outward curiosity, assuming that if something was happening he would be the second person in the world to hear about it. Sarah, practical as she was, never took the dream seriously. She had gone along to indulge Nudelman, more as an adventure for its own sake than out of hope that anything tangible would result from it. When it was over she dismissed it as something to laugh about in the future; the "Weren't we silly even in middle age" kind of anecdote. By the time a month had come and gone, the experience had been moved into the attic of her consciousness, that is, until what was supposed to happen didn't happen. Even this she dismissed, for physiology, like the airlines, occasionally departs from its schedule. About this time she noticed an expression of curiosity, even suspense, in Nudelman's glance. Nudelman was waiting for a pronouncement, a health bulletin. Each day she asked herself, Should I say something to him, should I get his hopes up? and she answered, Not yet, he's had too many disappointments in the past.

At last the day came for the definitive test with the

rabbit. Not being a gynecologist, and not being a mother either, don't ask me to explain just how a rabbit becomes entangled in the fertility rites of American couples. Those who don't understand must accept it as a matter of faith. Those who do understand require no explanation. For me, they simply consulted a rabbit. He, or she, I don't know which, thought about it for a while and came back with the conclusion that Sarah Nudelman was in fact going to be a mother, God willing.

Then she finally said to him, "You're going to be a father," the stored-up suspense combined with the emotion of the moment was just too much for him, and he said, "Who's going to be the mother?" He was angry that she hadn't talked to him about it sooner, but then, he might have asked her. He saw at once that his quip had trivialized the moment, but it was too late to take it back. Somebody once said that humor is a way of concealing strong feelings. Well, what if it is? For me, humor is just about the only thing that distinguishes humanity from the other forms of life. One of the things I like best about Nudelman is that when a meeting is tense or dull, he often breaks the mood with a joke. Sarah forgave him, and as she thought about it, she realized that she had in fact excluded him from the process. Our strengths are sometimes also our weaknesses.

Sarah and Nudelman alternated, in the next few days, between joy and apprehension. The joy needs no explanation: any person can imagine what it is like when something hoped for and dreamed about finally is going to happen. Now, the actual happening is very often a disappointment, but at that moment of perfect anticipation, nothing can spoil it because it isn't tainted by an often imperfect reality. I, for myself, would rather eat an imperfect meatball than think about a perfect meatball. What caused the apprehension? Of course the fear that they were too old to raise a child, or even worse, that they were too old to bear a normal child. "What if it comes out already an old man, with flat feet, a hernia, even diabetes?" Nudelman said.

Sarah answered, "The odds are against it."

"But from what you've told me the odds were against its happening at all."

They passed their time in such speculation like medieval monks, although "fixation" might be a better term than "speculation." Nudelman thought of, spoke of nothing else, once they had gone public with the news. To say that it turned the community upside down is an understatement. If the telephone company had had the foresight to charge by the minute for local calls, they could have paid off all of their debts on the first day.

It took them about a month to get used to the idea. After that they began a minute articulation of the symptoms, ranging from the time and frequency of nausea to changes in Sarah's shape. Nudelman actually brought home an exact tape measure and made daily measurements, recording them on a chart, a highly scientific, if unorthodox, way of expressing his paternal interest. After all, what else could he do besides look solicitous, open car doors for her and give her a pillow for her back? As it began to happen, as her girth expanded and she slipped into more capacious clothes, she began to glow like a ripe peach on a sunny day. About that time came the little stirrings inside; the little creature was apparently teaching itself to swim.

Months passed and they heard about, and took, a course. There was all of this controlled breathing to take the woman's mind off of the pain, to help her to relax and to get the man involved in the process as early as possible. For him it was better than standing around and worrying, and for her it was better than the old-fashioned scream. The husband's function under this system of dual child-birth, according to Nudelman, was to simultaneously time the contractions, roll a tennis ball around on his wife's back, feed her ice chips, wipe her brow and gently massage her tummy. To hear him describe it, he did all the work and all she had to do was lie there.

About this time Nudelman and Sarah began to think about names and sex. Somebody gave them a name book, and there were so many deliveries of paper bags and boxes full of baby clothes and paraphernalia that their house took on the appearance of a Salvation Army collection center. Ultimately they had enough baby clothes for a battalion of babies.

Then came the child's room. The spare room was transformed, with bright new colors on the walls, blankets, a crib, a cradle, actually an antique cradle with a rocking mechanism, something the Pennsylvania Dutch had dreamed up, a changing table and all sorts of odd gadgets acquired at a baby shower, a kind of prenatal birthday party. "It looks more like we're going to assemble the baby from a kit than give birth to it," Nudelman commented when he saw all of the equipment.

Finally the countdown began with irregular contractions. By this time, according to Nudelman, Sarah looked as if she had swallowed a plastic beachball. Of course, Nudelman's jokes were only one side of the experience. The countdown continued, with the contractions coming and going. The little suitcase stood by the door like a dog waiting to go out. The house had never been so clean; Nudelman said Sarah was like a bird who couldn't stop building nests. He wanted to bring her down to the store to do inventory, but she would have none of it—the store was his domain and she had no interest in it at the moment.

Nudelman and Sarah made a trial run to the hospital, just to see what it was like, feeling self-conscious and evoking condescension from the maternity staff. It wasn't really a trial run; they had thought it was the real thing. After all, a little caution doesn't hurt. Outwardly they reflected calmness; just a couple of veterans. They joked about this. They were going to tell the hospital staff that it was their fifth child, a menopause baby.

The time to go to the hospital really came. The staff was helpful. Nudelman actually managed to do everything he was supposed to do. Sarah breathed like an athlete, endured the pain, and four hours later, Nudelman, wearing a white gown, was in the delivery room in soft light, holding Sarah's hand, watching the birth through a mirror. To his great surprise he was calm, and wondering, wondering. But even before he had time to speculate, the doctor was holding a small person; pink, with already open eyes, moving, breathing, complete and a boy. As the doctor was wrapping their child in a white cloth, Nudelman thought he saw his father looking over the doctor's shoulder, nodding approval. Then in a moment he was gone and the doctor was approaching him, handing him the bundle with only the head visible. He took a step back, then he reached out gingerly, took the child and showed him to Sarah, and between them was a special look of completeness.

Nudelman ended there, and where he ended, life itself continues, for here at the door of my apartment is little Isaac Nudelman, now three years old, holding his father's hand but preceding him.

12.

Going Broke

As Sidney Cantor finally found out, going broke was a little like dying and going to his own funeral. After all, what most of us do in life is work and accumulate things. Of course, we have a family, we see children grow and in time fly the coop, as my grandmother used to say, but aside from the family, we are known for the car we drive and the suits we wear. Not me, of course: I have no family—except for my cousin—and only two suits and neither is stylish. Or maybe they are again, I don't really pay attention to such things. More important than clothes are the house and the furniture, an antique or two, even a hand-signed original print obtained at the annual synagogue sale. Then comes the business, the new trucks parked in the lot next to the store, the recent modernization of the storefront, the new memory typewriter and so on. It's not that we aren't also made up of our deeds, our generosity, honesty, reliability, kindness, but these are like smoke, while the possessions are always to be seen, at least until you go broke, and then even they become like smoke. Which is why . . . But I'm repeating myself.

It was the last recession that put him under. It had nothing to do with Sidney's business sense or his skills. He was, everyone acknowledged, a good businessman, even too good, some people said. Understand that it's not for me to judge, I have no standards. Finkelstein handles the books of the synagogue; I, for myself, have a system which I learned about in Poland and which, I am told, is foolproof, not burglar-proof, but foolproof, a cigar box in which I put all that I receive and take out all that I need. Some people prefer a cookie jar, those of more modest means a sugar pot; for me a cigar box has always been sufficient. My father, a rabbi, never trusted the banks, a lesson Sidney should have learned. He, my father, not Sidney, used to say, "A banker, like the flooding River Zarb, gives to those who don't need it and takes from those who do," a maxim which I never personally tested.

As I said, it was the last recession. Sidney thought that he would work his way out of the hole in his finances caused by the twenty-five-thousand-dollar loss when the hotel went under. He had rights with the other contractors because he was the plumbing contractor, and finally, when the hotel was sold to new owners from Iran, he received forty percent of what was owed to him, enough to pay off two of the three notes at the bank but not enough to set his business right. This and all that came after he told me one night over tea in my small apartment after a meeting of the synagogue Finance Committee. He and I were there to keep the chairs from floating. He must have told me just to have told someone. Everyone needs to tell someone, and Sidney was not the type to spill his troubles to a crowd like coffee on a white linen tablecloth. So he told me because, I suppose, he understood that I wouldn't think any less of him because of it.

There he was, with only one forty-thousand-dollar note, or whatever the bankers called it, and two very good jobs which should have been profitable, when the recession came through like a wind blowing the smoke from the mill back across the better side of town. A bad metaphor because the one good thing about the recession was that the air in Bolton was decidedly better since one of the blast furnaces shut down for adjustments, leaving the workers to television, the repair of torn screens, broken storm windows and leaky toilets, not to mention the bars.

As for Sidney's plumbing contracts, they stopped too, but only after all of the materials which he had ordered for them had been delivered to his warehouse—that was what he called the shed and yard behind his store.

Sidney accepted this turnabout with outer calm. He threw himself into a poker game with the usual group from the Men's Club. It lasted until three in the morning and cost him no more than sixty-five dollars. "What's sixty dollars?" he said to Estelle the next morning as she poured his coffee. He raised it to his lips with the usual morning tremor. She, turning her back to return the pot to the stove, said calmly, but not without feeling, "Sixty dollars is sixty dollars."

And Sidney replied, not without irritation, "You don't have to tell me that. I know that already." Again he raised his cup and the tremor persisted, so he set it down again on the saucer, splashing a little on the place mat.

Watchful, Estelle mopped it up with a sponge and said, "Staying out so late isn't good for you, Sidney. You don't look very well. You should see Dr. Zucker. Let me make you an appointment . . ."

"No, Estelle, I'm fine. Just tired from last night. Everybody needs a little escape, a little recreation." He sighed, turned the newspaper over, looked at the front page without seeing it, sighed again, looked at the sports page, again without seeing it, ate a forkful of scrambled eggs and got up heavily as Estelle, having sat down to her own breakfast, watched in disbelief.

"Where are you going?" she said to his receding broad back. "You've hardly touched your breakfast. You haven't said a word to me. If losing the money last night affected you that way, you'd better give up poker."

Sidney turned and came back to her. His eyes for the first time that morning touched hers. He stroked her back, kissed her on the cheek and said, "I'm sorry, Estelle, it's not the poker. I've got an early appointment at the bank, a business deal. Very important."

Estelle, both hurt and a little mollified, looked up at him and said, "You should have said so. You *can* talk to me, you know."

"I know, I know, but why should I bother you with the business? You've got your job and I've got mine. You don't bother me with the cost of tomatoes and coffee, so why should I tell you about the unavailability of five-eighths-inch copper pipe?"

"Sidney, I know about such things as scarcity."

"I'm sure you do—from the supermarket."

She studied him, listening to his breathing, and said, "Sidney, you're breathing hard. Your face is red. Are you angry? I'm going to make an appointment for you with Dr. Zucker. I'll call you at the office and you'd better not miss it. You missed the last one and . . ." Before she could finish, Sidney raised his forefinger and swished it in her face. There was warmth in his eyes as he said, "Estelle, I'll be late, please don't go on. If it makes you happy, I'll see Dr. Zucker."

He kissed her again, tenderly, but with the thought in his mind that Dr. Zucker couldn't cure what was bothering him. Not today. The bank had extended the note three times and he hadn't even kept the interest current. And each time they had extended, they had taken more security; first the inventory and equipment, then the accounts receivable and finally a second mortgage on his house. And in a half an hour friendly, understanding Joe Kruger, the bank manager, would probably tell him what he had said on the phone—that there was no extending the note again.

And that was just what friendly Joe said, sympathetically, sincerely, but emphatically, and finally. He didn't want to do it, "but you're not the only one in town, if that gives you any satisfaction." It didn't. "The recession even affects the banks, you know. We, too, have our investors who depend on us for their income, the widows." Who will take care of my widow? The thoughts rumbled through his head like in a spin-drier as he walked the two blocks from the bank to his store.

"Good morning, Sidney." Amy White startled him out of his thoughts.

"Amy. I was thinking about something and didn't see you. Going shopping?"

"Yes, I'm off to Haneys; it's the semiannual sale. I never miss it."

She hurried on and he watched her go, watched her quick, lifting stride and thought, Always the sale, which is why you have it and I don't. Then immediately he disagreed and thought, I wonder if Steve White could help? I've never asked anyone before. It wouldn't be a matter of

money. Just a guarantee of the note. In the meantime
there are enough small jobs to keep the business going and
pay the small bills. I've got to do something. He's given me
five days, five days to do something. Now is the time to
have a brother, a well-off brother. You can sometimes im-
pose on your relatives, at least the close relatives, which I
haven't got. And as for Estelle's brother, he's a part of the
problem. A real hanger-on, first on her, then on both of
us. He owes us four thousand dollars from that Florida
real estate limited partnership that went bust. Even Estelle
thought it was a bad deal. He can't seem to hold on to
money either.

His store was locked; he had let the office manager go
last week. The lock wouldn't turn and he had the frantic
thought that the sheriff had already padlocked the place;
wasn't that, after all, what they do when the bank takes
over, or the IRS? Yes, they don't waste any time, the Feds.
They just come and close the place up and sell things off to
pay the taxes. They'll be here even before the bank. He
could feel a headache coming on, dull and pressing at his
skull. His face felt hot. It must be my blood pressure.
Estelle is right. I should have an examination, or maybe I
shouldn't. I would be better off with a fatal heart attack,
the kind that takes you quickly. The cash values of the
whole life policies are borrowed, but there's still the mortgage insurance and at least another forty thousand dollars in
term life. Estelle would be comfortable and Noah could get
a scholarship and some student loans. They must favor children without fathers. Oh God, why am I thinking like this?

He was inside the store now, feeling its burden like a
heavy winter coat on a warm day. Maybe we could move,
start somewhere else. I could get a job with another company and make more than I do here. Why didn't I incorporate this place? Why didn't I take Rosenzweig's advice

years ago? What difference would it have made? The bank would have had the house anyhow. Why didn't I sell the damned business five years ago and move to Arizona with the building boom? I'd be well-off by now.

He was in his office now, balefully surveying a pile of unopened mail; if you don't open it, you don't have to pay it, he was saying to himself, when he heard the door open and saw Sam Yanow step in and look around him as though he had lost something. What could he want? Sidney thought. He's always used Pitman Brothers in Pittsburgh. Probably just looking for a washer.

Sam looked up, saw Sidney, and with a look of apology he said, "Sidney, I'm sorry to bother you for such a trifle, but I've just been to the hardware store and they are out of a certain size washer and I'm trying to fix a leaky kitchen faucet." He held out his hand, showing Sidney a worn washer clasped between his thumb and forefinger.

"We might be able to help you, Sam." Searching through a few small drawers, Sidney soon located a washer that matched the worn one.

Sam, looking satisfied, pocketed the washer. "What do I owe you, Sidney?"

"Nothing. Just do the same for me sometime."

"Don't hesitate to ask if I can ever help you." Sam turned toward the door, then he said, "All by yourself today? Is the office manager out sick?"

"Yes. No. Actually she's not here anymore."

"Having a hard time replacing her, I guess."

Sidney said nothing, but he wanted to, wanted to tell this man who was no more than an acquaintance everything that he couldn't bring himself to tell his wife or his friends: that he had lost control, that he didn't know how to help himself, that he was afraid, so afraid of losing his home, of having to leave town, of having to make a fresh start at fifty-two. He said nothing, but the look on his face, a look of anguish, communicated to Sam and it was not lost on Sam, for he said, "You, uh, you seem to be troubled about something, Sidney."

"Well . . ." Sidney hesitated. Could he just ask his advice without going into details? After all, he was a successful businessman. "Do you—do you have a minute?" Sam nodded. "I, uh—this recession has affected my business."

"We're all feeling the pinch, big and little. Housing starts are down forty-two percent, according to *The Wall Street Journal*. And the tight money isn't helping. It's the Federal Reserve. This tight-money policy. I was just talking to Joe Kruger about it at the bank the other day. It's like a line of dominoes; it starts at the Federal Reserve Board and it ends with an unfunded project in Bolton."

"Yes. I was just talking to him too."

"I suppose he told you the same, didn't he?"

"In a manner of speaking."

Sam looked at his watch. "Well, I've got an appointment with Dr. Zucker, so I'd better be on my way. Thanks for your help with the washer. And if you're having difficulty with local bank financing, I'll be glad to introduce you to someone in Pittsburgh. They've got very liberal policies, even in these times."

"I just might take you up on that, Sam. Thanks."

The deadline came and Sidney had done almost nothing about it. He did try to collect delinquent accounts, without much success, although he managed to raise eight hundred dollars from one account, which reduced some of the delinquent interest and brought him another extension on the promise to Joe of another large payment. He had lied to Joe Kruger about this. He had no expectation of a large payment, and he sensed the chill in Joe's voice and knew that he had reached the end of his patience. Sidney thought of Simon Rivkin. That sort of thing happened once in a lifetime, like a long shot at the racetrack.

A week later it came in the mail, the first notice of fore-closure. The bank was going to sell his house, and the next day the Internal Revenue Service, as if by coordination, put a padlock on the store. They had seized his business assets, such as they were, to pay back taxes.

He drove up that morning only to see the notice on the door and the padlock. Sidney, feeling worthless, mortified, as if he had lost control of his bowels, started the car and drove away. He drove blindly, his eyes filled with tears, out of the town, away from the town, past the anonymous farms tended by people who didn't know him. Too anxious and frustrated to even think, he drove on until finally the motor began to stall and he saw that he was out of gas on a narrow country road.

He leaned back in front of his instrument panel, his hands on the steering wheel, fondling the soft, shiny black surface. Even the smooth, quiet power of the Oldsmobile was based on money. This was no time for philosophy, he thought, this was a time to find a telephone, call the auto club and get back to town. He got out of the car, closed the door, thought about locking it, then, concluding that there was nothing in it to steal, he shrugged his shoulders and began plodding down the side of the road. The road inclined slightly and he felt himself already getting short of breath. I'm not used to walking, especially out in the country. Doctors always recommend exercise. He looked about him at the quiet rolling landscape: clouds as light as down sailing on a blue sky, a meadow with a few black-and-white cows, heads low, tails switching. On the ridge was the peaked roof of a farmhouse, behind it the cylindrical silhouette of a silo. He only partially saw these things, for he had always been one to drive through the countryside, his eyes on the road and his mind on the destination. But now that he was walking, despite his agitated state, he was even aware of the cut-grass sweetness of the air and the shy warmth of the morning sun on this dry Indian-summer day. He found the farmer in his barn. He willingly filled an empty five-gallon can with gasoline from the storage tank and drove Sidney back to the car in his pickup truck.

On the way home he bought some sweet corn and beefsteak tomatoes from a farmer's stand and resolved to finally tell Estelle about the imminent loss of both the business and the house. He got home about twelve, but she wasn't there. There were meetings that she went to on Tuesdays and Thursdays. One or the other club, he never was sure which. He walked around the house looking for something to do. Descending into the basement, he approached his workbench. The tools lay scattered about on its surface. He stared at it, resolving for once to put everything in its place. Estelle had been saving jelly bottles for different-size nails and screws. He dumped a box of screws onto the surface of the bench and began sorting them into piles. After only fifteen minutes he grew tired of the sorting. Remembering a broken chair in Noah's room, he went up to the second floor. The chair was in the corner of the room. There was still a stack of magazines on it, *Sports Illustrated*—he had given Naoh a subscription for his birthday. Sidney looked around the room, swimming in the memories of the child become a young man. The room, the contents of his childhood, the mementos of high school, his hobbies, all were on exhibit. Noah had left this room. He could come back and occupy it next summer, on holidays, but it was no longer *his*, Noah's room. Noah was no longer *here*. They could leave the house now, it would be too big for them anyway. Why should Estelle have to clean an empty house when a few rooms would do?

He removed the magazines from the chair and took it down to the basement. Some furniture glue and a couple of screws would restore the chair to soundness. This simple task, easily accomplished, finally absorbed him, and the pain of his problems receded to an occasional palpitating reminder in his chest. He was staring with some satisfaction at the chair when he heard her call out "Sidney?" with concern in her voice. "Are you not well?"

"I'm fine."

"So why are you home in the middle of the day?"

He heard her coming down the narrow wooden steps with caution—once she had fallen on them and now she treated them with respect. The forty-watt bulb over the workbench cast a weak circle of light about him, much like the spotlight on a stage. Around him in the semidarkness, like mute witnesses, was the detritus of their life in this house, yellowed cartons with forgotten contents, objects without definition under old sheets.

Preceded by the scent of carnations, she stepped into the circle of light, glad to see him, a smile on her face. She was dressed in a peach-colored linen suit, which was a trifle tight—she had gained a few pounds again. With the dread of speaking to her now of the reality that he had kept from her and of her reaction to the shock of losing the house, he became light-headed. He thought that he might even faint, but he reached back, gripped the bench with his hand, and the dizziness passed.

"Are you sick?"

"No." He grinned a nervous, self-conscious grin. "I had a slow day, nothing happening, so I—I just came home."

She just looked at him. Then she said, "Sidney, something's wrong. I know you too well. Come upstairs and tell me about it. I've told you, you don't have to keep things from me."

"I don't want to go upstairs just now. There's the old rocking chair under that sheet. Let's just sit down here for a few minutes. It's cool." He went over to the chair, removed the sheet, scattering dust in the air, and stood admiring it. "I remember how you used to sit and rock Noah in that chair. Especially the time when he had scarlet fever. He was just four then, a tender age for such a sickness."

"Three."

"What?"

"He was three, Sidney. You've forgotten."

"Sit down, Estelle."

"Sidney, I just had this suit cleaned, and besides, it's damp down here."

"Sit down, Estelle," he repeated gently, a faraway nostalgic look in his eyes. "Remember when we first looked at this house, Estelle? Was it fifteen years ago? It was the year your father passed away."

"Sidney. You're not sick, are you?" she said, alarm in her voice. "Have you kept that from me too? You know, you're scaring me and it's even worse down in this cellar. There's some iced tea, nice and cold, in the refrigerator. Come on, let's have some with lemon and sugar. You can take sugar, can't you? It's not diabetes or something like that? Your Uncle Meyer died from it."

"It's nothing like that. It's worse," he said, the words catching in his throat. "It's worse," he repeated softly.

"Worse? Worse? What is it, cancer? You haven't got cancer?"

"Estelle. It's worse than that."

"What could be worse than cancer? You're not trying to tell me that you've got syphilis? Not at your age."

"Estelle. It's nothing like that. I'm not sick, not yet at least. But it's a disaster, a *choorba*."

"You're not sick," she said with incredulity. "Thank God. So time-out. Let me catch my breath. We'll go upstairs and sit in the kitchen and you'll get it out. When you've had some iced tea. It's Wissotsky, your favorite." Up they went, she first and he after, to catch her in case she stumbled, and both of them emerged blinking into the diffuse afternoon light of the hall. "Sidney, you forgot to turn out the light."

"Who cares anymore."

"It will burn all night. You'll forget it. The last time it burned for a week."

"Who cares anymore. We won't be here to change it when it burns out."

"Sidney, you sound as if you've lost a war or your head."

"I've lost the business, that's what I've lost. I've lo—lost our house," he said, almost shouting.

Her eyes widened. "What are you saying? I didn't hear it. What, in a poker game? Let them try to take it. Gambling debts are no good. You can't collect them. I read it in *Cosmopolitan*." Obviously stunned, she staggered into the kitchen and mechanically filled the teapot with water, then plopped down into a chair, pale and in shock.

"You see? That's why I wanted you to sit down. I knew you'd take it hard."

"Don't worry about it. How much did you lose?"

"I didn't lose last night. I won twenty-five dollars."

"What are you talking about?"

"Estelle. For once I'll get *you* some tea." And in fits and starts he told her of the long series of business difficulties culminating in the tax lien and the foreclosure notice. As he explained it, to his surprise she grew calmer rather than more agitated, so much so that he grew self-conscious and the story, like his car, finally sputtered to a stop.

He had expected tears. Instead she asked, "How much is the tax lien?"

"Twenty-five hundred."

She nodded. "And the loan? How much will it take?"

"Maybe fifteen thousand to renew the loan."

"Is that all?"

"Is that all?" he exclaimed. "I'm destroyed and you say 'Is that all?' It might as well be a million dollars."

"Why didn't you tell me about this before?" she said tenderly.

"Why? Why, I didn't want to worry you. You have enough on your mind. Besides, earning a living is my responsibility."

"What really do I have on my mind—what to make for dinner, how many raffle tickets to sell, whether Noah wears his galoshes? Sidney, there has always been plenty of room in my mind to share your business worries. After twenty years you should know that."

"But I . . ."

"But you wanted me to stay in *my* department, kitchenware, notions and groceries, while you took the bank, the business and the broker."

"You never showed any interest in it."

"You never gave me a chance. Did you think I was dumb? Haven't I managed our house well for twenty years?"

"I always saw that you had enough money for that at least, even in the lean years. And I never let you know about the problems."

"Sidney, I *knew*. I knew when you mortgaged the house."

"You knew?"

"Yes. An appraiser came from the bank when you were taking out the loan."

"Why didn't you tell me?"

"Why didn't you tell *me*?" she shouted in exasperation.

"What difference does it make now? I've lost the house."

"No, you haven't."

"Yes, I have."

"You haven't, Sidney. Sit here a minute. I'll be right back."

Sidney said nothing. The argument had taken all of his remaining energy. He was wrung out, weak, he couldn't think. He lacked even the curiosity to wonder where she had gone. He was aroused from his stupor by the slap of something on the table surface. His eyes focused on a passbook.

"What is it?" he asked.

"What does it look like, my Green Stamps premium book? Open it."

Hands shaking, he opened the passbook and saw pages of small entries, ten dollars, twenty-five dollars, eighty dollars, withdrawals, more deposits. He put it down. "So you've saved a few hundred out of the household account. Very good, but it won't save us."

"Read the last chapter."

He picked it up again, turned to the last page, and incredulously, he said, "Twenty-eight thousand four hundred and seventy-six dollars."

"Without the current posting of interest."

"Where did this come from?"

"Just call me the Wall Street whiz kid of Bolton," she said.

Sidney collapsed back against his chair. "This is all too much for me."

"Are you all right?" she asked with concern, hovering over him.

"Yes, yes. Sit down and tell me where this came from."

"It started with my grandmother. She, you remember, came from a world of pogroms, poverty, before life insurance, where they lived from day to—"

"I know, I got the same stories from my grandparents."

"Well, she told me that no matter how little there was, every woman should put away something every week, if only a few pennies, against a time when there was nothing at all coming in. And I listened to her. So every week, whatever you gave me for the house, I put something away, first in a sugar bowl, then later in that savings account."

"But how did you get to so much?"

"A few years ago I heard this commercial on the radio about some stockbroker. I forgot it. I heard it again. I dismissed it, but finally I got up the courage and went down to the office. And I met this nice young man, fresh out of Harvard. And he had all this information that I didn't really understand, but it sounded good. So he gave me something to read, and pretty soon I got so that I could understand him and participate in the trading."

"Trading?"

"Yes, I took the whole thing, all but one hundred dollars, which I left in the account, and I began trading daily, buying and selling here and there, even sometimes on the margin a little."

"On the margin?"

"Yes. I made a little and lost a little and so it went, but the pot was always growing. Until not long ago. He said to me, 'It's time to get out.' He had put together all of these economic indicators. We talked and I agreed and so I got out, just before the recession. And here's the pot."

"Don't tell me those were your Tuesday meetings?"

"That's right."

"And you'll let me have this, all of this?"

"Let you have it? It's *our* money, Sidney. Not for squandering, but for something like this. After all, you can't be blamed for the recession. You and I, we're not even a cog on the wheel, we're dust in the grease."

"But our retirement. That's what you wanted it for, I suppose?"

"Better to think about our house now. We're still young enough. We'll worry about our retirement later." She looked up at him.

There were tears in his eyes, and he said with a thick voice, "Estelle?"

"What?"

"Do you want to play a little rummy?"

13.

A Photograph

"Patience, Mendel," said Rosenzweig, pulling the fold of his cheek. "Bureaucracy moves at the speed of a cow's digestive tract."

"I'm not impatient, Rosenzweig, it's you that's impatient. After all, I didn't call me to my office for a discussion of the progress or lack of it, you did."

"Well, I know how clients get. I'm just trying to put you at ease."

"Don't trouble yourself. I have lived most of my life without the money, I don't need it, and if it doesn't come, I assure you I won't miss it."

"That's the right attitude, don't count your chickens—"

"I never count chickens, Rosenzweig. In fact I'm not much for counting. Arithmetic never interested me . . ."

He nodded a gentle look of concern, or maybe it was

condescension, maybe he was saying to himself, sure, sure, I've heard that before. And for all I know he was a little right, but just a little, for it seemed that I was getting used to the idea of having a little extra cash, not just for the sake of my generosity but for a few luxuries as well, like, for example, a good, I mean a really good, bottle of cognac or, I have to confess it, a Harris Tweed sports jacket that I had seen in the window of The Country Gentleman, a new place on Main Street where Frank's Barber Shop used to be.

"Just sign this additional form, Mendel, and you can be on about your business."

"What's this one?"

"It's the last one, I think. They even sent an English explanation with it."

"Very thoughtful of them. So what is it, a loyalty oath?"

"Just an affidavit of kinship. It's even filled out. Just sign it."

I picked it up and studied it. All the printing was in Hebrew and I couldn't make it out.

"They filled it out themselves from the information we furnished on the other application. It should be the final step before they make the determination."

I accepted the proffered gold Cross pen and signed my name.

"Done," said Rosenzweig, his hand outstretched to receive both the pen and the document. "Now, as I said, be patient."

We shook hands and I left his office wondering what it was that irritated me about him. I turned left out of the marble lobby of the Bolton Bank Building and walked a block out of my way to have another look at that sports jacket, telling myself that it was not extravagant to desire it when my only sports jacket was worn at the cuffs and one button was clinging desperately by a single thread. I looked at my watch; it was after three. Chances are Estelle will be home, I thought. In my jacket pocket was another letter from my cousin. I had been showing these letters to only three people, Nudelman, Reuven Levinson, Mark's son, and, of course, Estelle Cantor. Admittedly, it was hard for me to share them with anyone, even my friends. It was like revealing a hidden side of myself, even though it wasn't me but my cousin who had become a middle-aged man and whose life was coming into focus in fragments. This letter came with a photograph, a photograph of the family, his wife and his two children, and there was a little more of what he had done in those years. I wasn't sure that I wanted to show it to anyone as yet except for Mark, who had lived in Israel, but he was away.

Estelle I could show it to. I walked the two blocks back to where Tevye was parked, only to find an expired meter and already a ticket. Don't they have anything better to do with their time than to ticket cars like Tevye? Why, by the look of him Tevye might have been simply broken down there, unable to move a foot. I got into the car, vowing to walk downtown the next time, and drove to the Cantors'. The door was ajar; she was home. Who knows, I thought, maybe she's even baked a little something? She usually does on Fridays.

"Don't say it, Mendel, let me guess," she said as she opened the door. "It's the money. They're sending it."

"No, why do you think that?"

"There's something about your expression, I don't know, maybe I was just imagining it."

"You're half-right, Estelle, I got something in the mail, but it wasn't the money."

"Another letter from your cousin?"

"Yes."

"And he tells you more about his life, I suppose. Come, let's have some coffee. I baked a *bundt* cake. You can have a piece."

"No. Save it for tonight."

"Mendel, you know that Noah will cut a section out of it when he comes home from Pitt tonight. And if he doesn't, Sidney will when he comes home from the office, so don't stand on formalities. You know me, if I didn't want you to have it, I wouldn't offer it."

"I surrender to the power of your reason, wherever it leads me, obesity, diabetes, whatever," I said, slouching down at the dinette table. "And a little half-and-half for my coffee, please."

She brought me the cake and coffee, poured some for herself and sat down across from me, smiling and expectant. We drank and ate in silence, I looking up at her once or twice. Then I pulled the letter out of my pocket, turned the picture over, the white side up, and began to translate:

"My dear cousin Mendel."

"By now you should be well into the process of claiming the reparations money. Please let me know if there is any difficulty at all. After all, I do have a little influence; it is one of the prerequisites of government service.

"God, it's been hot here, and so dry. You wouldn't believe it, but I picked up a plum out of the fruit bowl, and before I could get it to my mouth, it turned into a prune, that dry. It's called the *chamseen*, a wind from the bowels of Arabia, or some similar place, and it drives people mad, at least madder than they usually are, which is quite mad enough. Some it gives sinus headaches, while others have an irresistible desire to take the nearest bus to the beach and immerse themselves up to the nostrils in salt water. It is, I'm told, the only antidote to the *chamseen*. So much for the weather.

"You asked if we have children. Yes. You asked for a photo. Your wish is granted. You should be able to recognize me. I am, to be sure, several years older than when we last met, but the silver hair unruly and receding gives me the look of the Old Man, I am told—that's B.G., or Ben Gurion to you. That's the only resemblance, I can assure you. Batya, my wife, you should have no trouble identifying either. As you can see, the years have treated her well. It must be all the oranges she's consumed in her life—she was literally raised in a *pardes*, an orchard. You've not lived until you've smelled an orange grove in bloom in the springtime. I hope soon you will have that experience. It is positively narcotic. We have two adult children, as you can see. Noam, the oldest, is a chemical engineer. He was wounded very seriously in the Yom Kippur War. He fought a second battle with death and won, and yet a third, which enabled him, after too many operations to count, to return to a more or less normal life. He even plays wheelchair basketball; there's a whole league of disabled sportsmen here. What about me? you are asking. Yes, I know you. Well, no visible injury. I took a shell fragment in the knee, in fifty-six in the Sinai, but not a scratch in the War of Independence, and I was safely behind the lines in sixty-seven—I was by then a reserve colonel. So much for that. Ayelet, our youngest, is a nurse, actually a surgical nurse. She is married, and although you can't tell by this picture, she is expecting a child, her first. So, although I can't believe it, I'm finally going to be a grandpa. Her husband words in the defense ministry. Don't think us a tribe of Spartans, Mendel, we don't immerse ourselves in ice water every day, just an occasional cold shower maybe, and there's still freshly baked *challah* on the table once a week.

"Now it's your turn. Send me a picture, unretouched, and not one that's ten years old, either. I want to be able to count the wrinkles around your eyes. Everyone, I am told, lives a stressful life in the United States, what with all the traffic and the climbing after careers. You see, I know something about your adoptive country. We get all the first-run movies, you see. Batya and I go at least once a week. I hope to see you soon, to hug you, to feel your bony body. (You haven't gotten fat on me, have you?) Remember the bear hugs Uncle Itzick used to give us? Remember the time he broke Cousin Zalman's rib? He even had to pay for the doctor. What a price to pay for affection. Yours, Ephie.

"By the way, isn't your birthday coming up soon? Buy yourself a book for me—a paperback, of course."

"May I see the picture?" Estelle asked me when I had folded the letter. I passed it across the table to her. She looked at it with a sober expression and passed it back without comment.

I had a few errands to run after my visit with Estelle, and put both the letter and the picture behind me for a few hours. Back in my apartment, emptying out the pockets of my jacket, it came back to me, confronted me, disquieted me. I sat down at my desk, picked it up by a corner and brought it into focus, trying to discern something of the persona of my cousin from the small blurry face. As I looked at him, another picture superimposed itself, a picture of Ephie and me with my father and mother, the only picture, in fact, that remained of them. As I thought of it, I was impelled to bring it out, place it side by side with this one and compare the man with the boy. I rummaged in my desk for the wallet where I keep my passport (I always keep a current passport, even though I never travel), my naturalization papers and a few other documents, but it wasn't there. Looking through it, I felt momentary panic until I remembered that I had put it in its own special place, a place where I thought the picture would feel quite at home and safe.

I went to the shelf next to my bed where I kept my most precious and loved books, and found the leather-bound volume of the writings of Elimelech of Lizensk, published in Lvov in 1788. I had seen the book at the bookstore, and old Shabtai Yarok, the proprietor, had given it to me with a contemptous look at the volume and a hint of warmth in his opaque eyes. I had just told him of my father's interest in the author. Shabtai had no interest in the book—it wasn't old enough for him. He couldn't even remember how it had come to be there. Even so, the gift was singular, a mark of his respect for me, for I had never known him to give any of his books to anyone.

And so that book became my family's home. It was nearly all that was left of their culture and now, as far as I knew, all that was left of old Shabtai's precious collection as well. They belonged together, the book and the picture, just as both of them belonged with me. The book fell open to the place where the picture lodged, and I saw my mother's gentleness, my father's humor and the devil in Ephie's eyes. For a moment I thought that I should put the new photograph in with them, but I decided against it. It somehow needed a different place, and I abruptly closed the book and returned it to the shelf, thinking, for some reason, not of my family, not even of Ephie or of his family, but of the bookstore.

14.
The Bookstore

Even before the bookstore burned, people had forgotten it. Rabbi Bing's survey, which I recently turned up in a miscellaneous file, proved the point. One time he asked his congregants to identify the most unique aspect of the Jewish community in their entire recollection. Why he did this no one knew; he didn't consult with the board—at least the minutes don't reflect that he did. The responses were, at most, curious. They included the following by no means complete list: the child born to the Feitelsons when Mrs. Feitelson was fifty-seven years old, her first; the year 1937, in which no sons were born; the falsetto of the visiting cantor in 1943; Mrs. Zimmer's recipe for *matzo* balls; the *Succoth* carnival of 1967, in which all the children came costumed as soldiers, even the girls; and others not worthy of mention. But not one person listed the Jewish bookstore.

Admittedly, after the establishment of the synagogue library the bookstore fell into disuse. The rabbi ordered his books from New York. He wanted the latest knowledge and there were no new books in the bookstore, only old ones, very old ones, books made illegible by time, books legible but incomprehensible, books comprehensible but as to meaning unfathomable, at least to the superficial eye.

Another thing about the bookstore was its location on a narrow side street in the oldest part of town next to a beer bar. No one ever went down there anymore, although at one time several Jewish families had lived on the very block, according to Sarah Millstein. Finally, if you didn't know exactly where the bookstore was, you couldn't find it at all, for even its exterior was obscure; a free-standing wooden building with two opaque and empty store windows and no sign, no identification to let the casual browser, the one whose periodical diversion of an afternoon was to wander in and out of stores, know that inside was a bookstore. To look into the window was to see nothing but murky twilight fading to darkness even on a bright day, for except for the storefront there were no other windows and there was no overhead light apparent. Only at night a remote yellow light revealed to the curious several rows of floor-to-ceiling shelves crowded with books and other objects impossible to identify.

Just as the Jewish community never saw the inside of the store, they seldom saw Shabtai Yarok, the proprietor, because he seldom if ever left the premises. Behind the store was a sloping shed, where he slept, and a garden enclosed by an eight-foot fence. Children who were fond of peeking through the cracks in the fence reported seeing a large and verdant vegetable garden, well-tended by a wrinkled, bent old man the color of shoe leather. One imaginative youngster described Shabtai as a mummy come to life.

Indeed, Shabtai never left the precincts of the store, for he had everything he needed: food, which he raised himself, including his precious herbs, and, of course, his books and artifacts. There were a few things that he didn't have and these were brought by his only visitors, Avram and Miriam Gan, for Shabtai was not completely cut off from the world. The Gan family saw him regularly, but they never talked about their visits to anyone. It was almost as if they had taken some vow of secrecy, so no one in the community knew or cared about their ongoing connection with the store. The only other visitor was an unobtrusive stranger, a rumpled man wearing loose, out-of-fashion clothes, his uncombed hair and beard streaked with gray. Those who took the time to notice him would have assumed him to be a bookish, scholarly type, the sort of man who on a bright sunny day would coop himself up in an airless, windowless archive and pore over obscure manuscripts, and that was precisely what he did when he came to Bolton, for the bookstore was not the place to find anything.

It was like a wilderness—the placement of the manuscripts had no apparent order, arranged neither by title, author nor subject matter. It may be that Shabtai knew the order; it may be that the key to the order of the volumes would unlock some profound secret of the essence of life, although Shabtai, by his demeanor, gave no hint of it as he rummaged among the stacks and piles, walking from here to there, picking things up, then putting them down after a moment's reflection, muttering to himself. If there was any universal truth in the order of the place, it was that chaos and disorder were the only rules of life, but that conclusion was too obvious. No, there had to be either something more profound or simply nothing at all.

What specifically were these books, these objects, these treasures that scholarly old men came seeking? There was not one but two manuscripts of Vital's *Sha'ar ha Gilgulim*, not late copies but the original editions, although one was badly foxed and some pages were barely legible, especially in the poor light of the bookstore. Somewhere—even Shabtai couldn't locate it—was an untitled handwritten manuscript attributed to Joseph Ibn Tabul. Jonah's *Wings of a Dove* lay in a corner, where the binding had been partially gnawed away by a discriminating mouse.

An enumeration of the titles covering every period of Jewish thought from biblical times up to the eighteenth century would be impossible. But, surprisingly, no volume was later than the seventeenth century, as if whoever had assembled the library had lost contact with Jewish letters after that time. Why? Who can say.

Besides the books there were other objects: *t'fillin*, prayers in ebony boxes carved with mystic signs and Hebrew letters; geometric charts on parchment, the ink faded but still legible; bits of yellowed paper on which were scrawled formulae in Hebrew letters. Were they incantations, code? Who could say, for those who wrote them were forgotten. Of all the objects there was one which even Shabtai carefully guarded. It sat on a shelf over his narrow bed, just a dark piece of old wood on a *Seder* plate under a cheese bell, not much to look at, but Shabtai knew it to be a fragment of the cedar pillars, the strong legs of Solomon's temple.

Who was Shabtai Yarok? When had he come to Bolton? Who had assembled the manuscripts? All a mystery, no one could say, but it was said that the bookstore antedated the town itself. A Mormon anthropologist supposedly did some research into the folklore of the Monoganessen Indians and concluded that they were descended from the ten lost tribes of Israel. Legend had it that their elders had communicated with other out-of-the-way Jewish communities as far away as Kurdistan, Ethiopia and Yemen. Emissaries had even traveled, at least according to the anthropologist's theory, to the Holy Land to attend meetings of learned Jewish sages of various persuasions, there to debate esoteric theological issues. On their return the sages brought back manuscripts for the ever-growing Monoganessen library, housed in the warmest and driest house in the village.

Now, how these sages got to the Holy Land before Columbus and others regularly navigated the Atlantic, the anthropologist never explained. Perhaps they hitched rides with the Norsemen or the Irish or, preposterous as it may seem, maybe they had their own boats; after all, if the Jews had gotten across in the first place, they must have known how to get back again.

In any event, with the coming of the white man, the Monoganessen sages, for some inexplicable reason, lost contact with their Jewish brethren, which might explain why the library had no volumes published later than the seventeenth century. It also explained why Shabtai, who claimed to be the last Monoganessen Indian in the county, had nothing to do with his Jewish brethren, for it seemed to him that their practices, their way of life, their customs, had only superficial Jewish content. Admittedly, they celebrated all the holidays, but in a most frivolous way. "Ignoramuses," he would claim, twisting his lipless wrinkled maw into a grimace of disgust, "with hollow knowledge. What have they read? What mysteries do they know? Nothing, nothing, a few pale hymns, some mumbled incantations of Hebrew, mostly by the rabbi, and that European music!" All of this he would say to Avram and Miriam

Gan, continually shaking his wizened head, the shiny, opaque black eyes peering out from under the ledge of his brow, eyes that would smoke with indignation.

Now, the Gans were not, as might be expected, part Monoganessen. Nor were they outcasts from the community who had sought the company of Shabtai as an antidote to their solitude. No. They had their own bizarre secrets, kept from the community, which regarded them as regular, ordinary congregants. For they were secret Canaanites, outwardly Jews whose ancestors had been converted to Jewish beliefs two hundred years after Joshua had conquered their land, but who had in secret passed down from father to son and mother to daughter the peculiar diversions from Jewish custom which marked their Canaanitic heritage. This heritage unfortunately had over three thousand years peeled off layer by layer, like an onion, until all that was left were a few singular vestiges and the important recognition that they were different from the others, they were of Canaanitic extraction, a heritage never to be abandoned. Cut off as they were from other Canaanites, their only observances, other than the once-a-month full-moon Sabbath consecrated to the matriarchal Trinity, were odd customs celebrated at Passover and *Tisha B'av*. They ate only leavened bread during Passover, while the Jews ate only unleavened bread, the bread of affliction. The reason for this difference was that while the Jews were slaves in Egypt, the Canaanites were farmers in Canaan, and their affliction was not the wicked Pharaoh but rather the wild Jewish hosts. And while the Jews were baking their bread on their heads during the flight from Egypt, the Canaanites were celebrating the coming of spring in their homes, baking leavened bread in their stout clay ovens. While Passover was a happy holiday for the regular Jews, for the Canaanites it was sad because it recalled the loss of their land. Then later in the spring, on *Tisha B'av*, when the Jews mourned the destruction of the Second Temple by the Romans, the Canaanites, in total secrecy, baked cinnamon-and-raisin *kuchen* and got drunk, for as far as they were concerned, it served the Jews right. For all outward appearances the Gans were ordinary people, and no one in the Jewish community knew of these goings-on.

If it hadn't been for nosy Mrs. Wasserman, the Gans would have gone on living their secret life and no one would have been the better or the worse for it. If the Gans hadn't moved into a bigger house, which happened to be right next to Mrs. Wasserman, probably the bookstore would still be there. Such is the nature of causation, a chain of ifs stretching back to the beginning of time, back to Adam or whoever.

The Gans, unmindful of the risk, moved into their Victorian house with its ornate gables and tall windows. Why didn't they think about the omniscient Mrs. Wasserman, with her insatiable curiosity and a tongue as ripping as a barracuda's jaw, when they held their Passover ceremony in their dining room in full view of her windows? Didn't they realize that the whole community would soon know that they ate whole-wheat bread on the first night of Passover? Fortunately for the Gans, most people don't take Mrs. Wasserman seriously—simply too much effluent pours from her mouth. But when she likened their *Tisha B'av* celebration to a three-day Polish wedding, it was only a matter of time before even the Gans' close friends began questioning them about their habits.

Believing that the disclosure would both clear the air and have a certain educational value, they confessed, to their friends at least, their Canaanitic heritage. But they were mistaken. The Gans could be either Canaanites or

Jews, but not both. When word got around, the community was soon faced with an effort to expel them from the synagogue. This in fact occurred after consultation with a learned rabbi from the Cincinnati Seminary who confirmed that such profane deviation from ceremony constituted at most an unrecognized offshoot of Judaism, such as that practiced by the Falashas of Ethiopia. But even they ate *matzo* on Passover and mourned the destruction of the Temple.

Casually, the Gans, in their innocent self-immolation, mentioned the bookstore by way of defense, alluding to the many obscure but valid customs embraced by Judaism. Inquiring eyes then began to turn toward the bookstore, and before long a stream of curious and inquisitive people discovered, or rediscovered, its dingy façade. While most did no more than eye it from a distance like jackals on the edge of a campfire, a few, more bold than enlightened, dared to enter and even rummage about under the watchful and suspicious eye of old Shabtai. Reporting back to the rabbi, they claimed that there was nothing familiar about it; no imitation copper *menorahs* from Israel, no paperbacks, no prayer books; in short, none of the usual objects associated with a Hebrew bookstore.

The distinguished scholar from Cincinnati was called in. After a consultation with Rabbi Bing he went directly to the bookstore. Finding the door unlocked, he entered and, without so much as a civil word to Shabtai, began a random examination of the shelves, taking notes with a dull tooth-marked pencil in a pocket spiral notebook. Shabtai observed the scholar at work from the door of the back room. Startled, the rabbi looked up to confront the wizened glower of Shabtai, his decimated eyebrows smoking with contempt. Shabtai said only, "Look but don't take anything, and nothing's for sale." He turned and went into his garden, where he spent the rest of the afternoon hoeing weeds, indifferent to his visitor. The rabbi stayed only long enough to discover three or four manuscripts long branded as heretical and proscribed, except to certain scholars, and which were kept under lock and key in any decent religious library, plus a few that, he had to admit, to himself at least, he had never even heard of.

It was enough. He went right to the home of Rabbi Bing and advised him that the Jewish community had a cancer in its midst and only the Almighty knew what other heretical practices had been inspired by this collection. For all the rabbi could tell, many other members of the community had their own secret practices. Rabbi Bing was admonished to take affirmative action or the whole congregation might lose its charter. With that threat dramatically and decisively delivered, the rabbi quickly departed in his rented car for the Pittsburgh airport, as the Sabbath was approaching and he didn't want to be stranded away from home, especially not in a place like Bolton.

Before the rabbi could take affirmative action other than to report the conclusions to a subdued board, the bookstore burned to the ground. No one knew how it happened, though some thought that it had been a spark from the mill —it happened on a windy night, and the old wooden shingle roof was no better than kindling. It was two in the morning when the fire was discovered. The beer bar was closed and there were no witnesses other than the fire department. By the time they arrived it was too late to do anything but keep the fire from spreading. Fires are always different and this one was no exception. It burned with a blue flame, like natural gas, and the wind around the flames seemed to moan and sigh as though the words liberated from the pages were audibly ascending from the flames.

Early the next morning, before any souvenir hunters were awake, the fire marshal was there to make his inspection. Because of the wind and the dry wooden construction, it was not surprising to him that the fire had burned to white ash, leaving no sign of what had been, except for the incongruity of the garden vegetables, roasted by the heat.

The fire marshal was poking about in the ash with a stick which he carried for the purpose when he came on something very unusual, perhaps the most unusual object he had ever encountered in the remains of a fire—a piece of wood about the size of a fist, buried in the ashes but totally uncharred. It was as if someone had buried it as a practical joke. He decided it would make an interesting subject of conversation, and he took it home with him and put it on his mantelpiece. Ultimately he had it embedded in a cube of plexiglass.

So much for the bookstore, but the whereabouts of Shabtai is anybody's guess. Since no human remains were found in the ashes, it was concluded that he was not dead but had departed for places unknown. A check of the county birth records for the past one hundred years demonstrated that he had not been born, at least not in the county, at least not so that he was officially noted. A further check by the assistant to the coroner indicated no social security number in his name and no record of payment of income taxes. It was as if Shabtai Yarok had occupied another plane of reality, for there was hardly a point of contact between him and the society in which he dwelt.

After a week or so, the assistant to the coroner lost interest in the case. Actually, it was preempted by a multiple death caused by a head-on automobile collision. So the last remains of Shabtai Yarok, consisting of a manila legal-size file, an Acco clip and three sheets of paper, eventually found their eternal resting place: the miscellaneous drawer of the coroner's filing cabinet, an unmarked bureaucratic grave.

As might be expected, the family Gan sold the Victorian and went west to Los Angeles, where nearly everything is tolerated, even the Canaanitic religion. In fact, several years later a traveler returning from California reported hearing of a thriving Canaanitic community in Anaheim, of all places, but the report was never confirmed.

Within a year after the fire, the lot on which the bookstore had stood sprouted a verdant mantle of weeds and herbs; plants which a botanist would have identified as foreign to Monoganessen County, even Pennsylvania; plants which were known to have been cultivated in the Holy Land and which were referred to in ancient tracts on medicine as well as in the Bible. But a DC-9 bulldozer made a salad of the whole crop one day, and within four miraculous weeks Bolton had its first McDonald's, complete with golden arch that could be seen all the way to Main Street, a distance of two blocks.

It seemed that the memory of the bookstore was completely purged from the collective consciousness of the Jewish community. That is, until the frumpy stranger showed up again and was aghast to find that the bookstore had been transformed into a fast-food operation. He arrived at the rabbi's study the color of refined flour and muttering to himself.

"Rabbi Bing," he said in a brittle tone, "I'm a little poor with directions, but I was sure that the bookstore was on Pine Street?"

"The bookstore?" answered the rabbi, a trifle put out that this stranger had entered his study without even knocking or introducing himself. "I'm sorry, but I don't believe I know you."

"Ruben Katz," the man replied.

The rabbi's transformation was instantaneous, as though someone had invoked the secret name of God. "*The* Ruben Katz?"

There was no reply, only a self-conscious flush. Katz was, at the time, one of three outstanding Jewish scholars in the world.

"I hope I've just forgotten the directions to the bookstore, Rabbi. Perhaps you can help me."

The rabbi felt himself shrinking in mortification until under Katz's inquiring eye he felt himself barely two feet tall. He straightened up in his desk chair to maximize his height, and said, a tremor in his voice, "Didn't you know? The bookstore burned down last year."

Katz seemed to totter at the news. "How much of the collection was saved?" he asked, his eyes wide and empty.

"Why, nothing. It burned to the ground in the middle of the night in a high wind. Nothing could be saved."

Katz's eyes accused, judged and condemned the rabbi in one moment. The rabbi, writhing under the lash of his gaze, said, "We have a modest library in the synagogue."

"A *modest* library? The bookstore housed one of the finest collections of mystical Judaica in the world. Some of the volumes"—Katz's voice broke and tears filled his eyes —"were the *only* manuscripts known to be in existence." Katz reached inside his jacket and tore the pocket off his shirt in the traditional sign of mourning, and his body stooped in grief, he left the rabbi's study without even a goodbye. Rabbi Bing sat for a long time in the twilight of his study, his eyes nailed to the shirt pocket resting on the maroon carpet in front of his desk like a grave marker.

15.
The Kite

Two blocks away from Tante Chana's house was a large green park, mostly an open grassy field with a few benches. She often sat there on a particular bench facing west, dozing, absorbing the sun's warmth, quiet as a stone. I sometimes sat with her there. I liked to listen to her. She was very wise and witty and one of the few people I knew who had found that rare middle ground between small talk and pomposity. I don't know quite how, but if she said "Egg," you saw not the shell but the yolk. She was eighty-seven and still measured a straight five-nine, though it was her eyes rather than her height that stood out. The eyes were dominant, sunken but still large, round and luminous, a sharp lens for her warmth, humor and compassion. And they fit well in a face which had strong, delicate Semitic features: high cheekbones, a knife-thin hawklike nose, a strong chin, a long forehead and crown, surrounded by a wispy silver corona of fine hair.

I wasn't there on that particular day when the kite took her away, but I'm getting ahead of myself. What I'm about to tell you, she told me and only me because she didn't think that anyone else would believe her.

On a blustery day in October she had taken herself to the park, not for sun but simply to get some fresh air. The sun was playing hide-and-seek behind cotton clouds, and a dry gusty wind was making the branches of the nearby trees dance. Wrapped in her long gray coat, she had been in her usual place only a few minutes when she saw her favorite great-grandson, Avram, walking toward her, a large kite almost as tall as he was held unsteadily in both hands. The wind was making the kite so restless that it seemed to her that it would take off with Avram. She stood and walked to meet him. Being careful not to harm the kite, she bent down and gave him a wet kiss on his cheek, saying, "Avram, what are you doing with that kite on such a windy day? Won't the wind break it up?"

Avram shook his head contemptuously. "It's big strong kite, Nana, and it has a long tail to keep it up. See?" he replied, showing her a ribbon rolled up in a tight ball.

She examined the kite as it rattled and twisted in his hands. Shaped like a shield, it was made of thin flexible wood over which was stretched white nylon emblazoned with a blue Star of David. She nodded her head approvingly. "A Jewish kite. Maybe God will protect it."

"I've got strong nylon cord, Nana, it won't get away. But you can help me get it up." Avram looked up at her hopefully.

She looked a little bewildered and said, "I've never done this before, Avram. Not even for your grandfather when he was a boy."

"It's easy, Nana," he pleaded. "I can do it alone, but it will be better if you help."

"I don't know, Avram. But tell me what I must do."

He smiled triumphantly and explained, "Just hold on to the spool and let the line out while I run down the field with the kite. When it's up in the air, I'll take it and you can watch. Okay?"

She took the thick spool of cord and Avram ran ahead, letting the ribbon dangle behind him. The kite bucked and twisted, leaped over his head, was caught by a gust and in a matter of seconds was aloft, climbing quickly on an air current, its long tail fluttering behind. Chana felt a ripple of excitement as she paid out the line, feeling the ever-stronger pull of the kite until suddenly the spool caught and the line stopped paying out just as the kite, driven by a hard gust, pulled up sharply. It was getting away from her but she had to hold on, she thought, or she would lose it. It tugged sharply again. She looked down and was shocked to see that she was off the ground, dangling from the kite's cord by the spool, and before she could decide what to do, she was already at the height of three stories and climbing fast. Below she could see the small figure of Avram running after her. She looked back and saw that he was saying something, but the wind took the words away. She was now high above the Monoganessen Valley and still rising. She could see the whole town of Bolton nestled in its dish, the muddy river twisting through it.

She should have been terrified, but for some reason she was calm; she should have been chilled by the high wind, but she found that she was warm; she should have dropped off from sheer exhaustion, but it was as if some force was lifting her bodily, so that she had no need to hold on to the spool. But after a moment's reflection, she decided on the conservative course and clung tightly to it with both hands.

In fact, she was even beginning to enjoy the experience. After all, it wasn't real, it was only a dream, or could it be death? Well, if this is death, at least the start of death, it can't be bad, she thought, but then she began to think of her family. No chance to say goodbye; that one last look at someone, the look that would have to suffice forever. She became sad. Then at the thought that maybe she would see others whom she hadn't seen in years, she became glad again. A noise startled her and she saw, not far away, a passing jet plane. She read "TWA" on the tail and concluded that she was now as high as jet planes fly. Under her the clouds seemed like lamb's wool. She could no longer see the earth, just the clouds, with an occasional view of land through a hole, and still she kept climbing, faster and faster, although she wasn't aware of the speed.

Now she could see the curvature of the earth, like the pictures the astronauts took that she'd seen on television. Imagine me, the oldest astronaut and a woman, too, she mused. But dead. Not an astronaut, just a dead old lady. She looked around for some other people, but could see nothing but the earth, now a large globe, shrinking away from her. Am I the only person in western Pennsylvania to die? she wondered. Maybe they're invisible and I can't see them and they can't see me. She spun around and saw in front of her the moon, growing ever larger, a cold desert landscape of ridges, mountains and craters. Can this be heaven? she asked herself with disappointment, but the kite was already veering away and moving past the moon into space, lonely dark space. Is this death, just flying along through the empty heavens, lonely, going nowhere? I hope not, she thought, and at that moment, ahead of her she saw an object which looked like a stone coming right at her, but as it grew closer she saw to her relief that it wasn't a stone. It looked more like a doll's house—no, a real house—just floating there in front of her in the dark, but luminescent.

The house and the kite converged, and she found herself standing on the worn stone stoop of a simple country cottage of unpainted wood, the kind that she had known as a child in Russia. In fact, to her amazement she thought she recognized the house of her parents. Hallucination or whatever, this is more like it, she said to herself. Chana was standing on the stoop, still clutching the spool in her right hand, unsure what to do, afraid that if she did anything she would shatter the image and wake up, when she heard a voice from within say with some impatience, "What are you waiting for? Don't just stand there, come in. Tie the kite to the doorknob, please."

She entered and saw fondly the possessions of her parents: the brass *menorah* that had filled the house with light on the Sabbath, the samovar that had brought warmth to the stomach on cold days, the brass lamp with the green glass shade hanging over the pine table, and all the other familiar objects which had surrounded her in her childhood. So taken was she by these remembrances that she completely forgot about the voice which had invited her in, that is, until two women stepped out of the shadows and regarded her with warmth and expectation. Overjoyed, she recognized her sisters, not as they were when they had died but as they were in their early twenties. As she approached them one raised her hand and she stopped. Sobered, she said aloud, "So this is death?"

And a voice responded, "No."

"So I am dreaming?"

"No."

"Why can't I approach you, my sisters? This has to be a dream."

"No. You see, we are not your sisters."

"Then who are you?"

"We are the Jewish matriarchs, the wives of Abraham and Isaac," said the tallest, who resembled her sister Pesha. "Although we don't like to be thought of as wives but as the mothers of our people," said Rebekah, who looked like her sister Leah.

"You mean my sisters looked like the matriarchs?"

"No," said Sarah. "It's just that we don't have any solid form, so when we are close to you, your thoughts give us a shape taken from your experience. Otherwise we couldn't be seen at all." Chana looked at them, somewhat mystified, and Sarah explained, "We look different to everybody."

"It must be hard on you to be constantly changing shape," said Chana sympathetically.

"Not at all. We remain the same. It's only the perception of us that changes. It's all the same to us."

"And this house?" Chana questioned.

"The same thing. Your experience conjured it up."

"Very nice."

"Now that you understand who we are," said Sarah in a matter-of-fact tone, "you are probably wondering *why* you are here."

"Yes."

"Sit down, Chana. Take your father's chair, the one with the arms." Chana eased herself down gingerly, expecting to fall through the apparition, but to her surprise the chair held her. "We have a proposal to make to you. Don't think of it as a proposal; rather it's an inevitable choice, but one that few can make."

"I'm listening."

"You know that death will come to you soon. You've lived a long and good life, but one day it will end. We can't tell you when, maybe five years, maybe ten years, maybe next year, but it will come."

"What can I do? I'll try to accept it when it comes," Chana said.

"We know you will accept it with courage and strength —it's the way you've lived your life. We know that. We know how you lived your life."

Chana's face flushed. "Me? Why would you be interested in me? I'm just an ordinary housewife. No college degrees, not even such a good cook. So if you looked at my life, you must have seen a million others before you got down to me."

Rebekah nodded. "We have."

"So you must have seen the dust on the mantel and the cobwebs in the corner," Chana said with a little smile.

"We were more interested in your generosity, your open heart, your honesty and your courage."

"I think you've found the wrong Chana," she said with a wry smile.

"No. It's you," said Sarah.

Suddenly Sarah's expression changed, like the sun bursting from behind a cloud. Chana saw not the face of her sister, but her mother's face, the accepting smile, the love-filled eyes. She grew weak and her heart became like butter melting in a pan.

"Time is short. We must come to the proposal. We give you your choice of death, eternal sleep or joining us. But before you choose, let me explain what we do. The choice is not so easy."

Rebekah added, "If you join us it will be a lot like

death. That is, you will lose your identity and become like we are. You will have the awareness of a stone."

Chana grew cold. "It sounds a lot like death after all."

"No. Not like death," said Sarah. "We have a specific important task. Let me explain. Do you know anything about photosynthesis?"

"That settles it. You've got the wrong Chana. I have about a fourth-grade education."

Rebekah continued patiently: "To put it simply, the leaves of the trees clean the air. We are like the leaves, only we change evil into good and send it back to earth."

"You think I'd be capable of that? My good would be all used up in a few days," said Chana.

"You underestimate yourself, Chana," said Sarah. "You could do it forever; not for the whole world, understand. There are many of us doing this. People, like you, who have been specially chosen."

"Just women?" she asked.

"No. All sorts of people, women and men, although I must confess there are a lot of mothers. But there are others, a lot of rabbis and priests and nuns."

"Priests and nuns?"

"Yes, of course. You see, each religion is responsible for its own. There are plenty of socialists and even anarchists too," explained the tallest.

"Since you're interested," continued Sarah, "I should tell you that there are even a few politicians and quite a few lawyers and judges. But I'm taking too much time. Can you make a choice, Chana, between death and this?"

"Who wouldn't choose this?" she replied.

"Lots of people turn us down. You see, this is painful part of the time," said Rebekah.

"Painful?"

"Yes. That's all we can feel. Pain and the absence of pain. It's the evil. If there's too much of it, it's like poison and it hurts."

"How badly does it hurt?"

Sarah said, "Have you ever had a migraine headache or a toothache? That bad."

Rebekah quickly added, "But it always stops on *Shabbas*, no matter how bad it is."

"Is there any time off?" she asked.

"Have you ever had time off, Chana?" asked the tallest.

"Well . . ."

"So why should you expect it now?" Sarah looked impatient and said, "Chana, I hate to rush you to a difficult decision, but there's no more time. What do you say?"

"Is there aspirin?"

"For what?"

"For the pain."

"*Shabba*s is the only aspirin," said Sarah. The women looked at her expectantly, the taller a little impatient, the shorter with a kindly smile. Chana looked at them and nodded her head.

"Good," said Sarah, knitting her brow. "Now remember, you will return to earth but say nothing about this. They wouldn't believe you if you did."

In the next instant she heard voices, and opening her eyes, she saw the concerned faces of her family gathered around her bed, looking instantly grateful that she had regained consciousness. She reached up to her head, felt a bandage and began to feel a throbbing ache in her head.

"Mama," her son exclaimed. "Thank God. How do you feel?"

"You tripped trying to keep Avram's kite from blowing away and you hit your head on a rock. You've been unconscious and delirious for nearly two hours."

"Avram. Where's Avram?" she said, and looking tearful and guilty, he pushed forward to her bedside. She reached out her hand and cupped it around his head. "Are you all right, Avram?"

"Are you all right, Nana? I'm sorry I made you fall down."

"Don't be sorry, Avram. All I got from it is a bad headache, but it will go away on *Shabbas*."

"On *Shabbas*," said her son incredulously. "Why *Shabbas?*"

Chana put her hand to her mouth. "I didn't mean it. Just an old lady's nonsense." She turned to Avram and asked, "And the kite, what about the kite?"

The boy shook his head. "God took the kite, Nana. It kept on going up, up into the clouds until I couldn't see it, and it didn't come down."

"I see." For a moment her eyes focused on something distant above her family, then she looked down at him and said, "Don't worry, Avram, I'll get you another one just like it."

The kite was never seen again in Bolton and no trace of it was ever found, but the same day the pilot of TWA Flight 427 en route from Pittsburgh to Chicago entered in his flight log the sighting of an unidentified flying object at 32,000 feet 134 miles northwest of Pittsburgh. It appeared to be white and had a long tail. There was a paragraph in the newspaper about it. But hardly anyone noticed it and those who did thought that it was another of those crazy UFO sightings.

16.

Approval

It finally came, the letter in English advising me that having proven my claim, I now had on deposit in my name IL 820,000, or translated into dollars, $75,000 at the current rate of exchange, a lot of money, even more than I had hoped for. Rosenzweig was more excited than I. For me, the news created not the thrill of winning, not the satisfaction of achieving, but a quietude, more an emptiness which people must feel when, after thirty years, they leave their office for the last time and slide into retirement. Certainly I felt here and there a little pleasant anticipation at the thought of some of the things that I might do with the money. But between these gentle waves of feeling there was nothing.

I asked Rosenzweig not to tell anyone about it, at least not until he had arranged for the transfer of the funds

from the Bank Leumi in Jerusalem to the First National
Bank of Bolton.

Unfortunately, I had to go down to the bank to sign
an authorization. The bank president himself handled it,
treating me with a deference which to me was undeserv-
ing—after all, I hadn't earned the money. Afterward I
walked around town for a time. Passing by the window of
The Country Gentleman, I saw that they had changed the
display and the Harris Tweed jacket was no longer there.
I paused for a moment with the thought that I might go
inside and see if it was still in stock in my size, but I
shrugged it off without much regret.

Then over the next few weeks, before we received the
reply to the transfer request, I began to get used to having
the money. I even did a little planning, and after hesitating
for a whole week, I walked into The Country Gentleman
and caught the disdainful eye of a salesman. It must have
been clear from my seedy appearance that I had no poten-
tial of becoming a steady patron. I tried on the jacket and
bought it and wore it out of the store, feeling as I did so
like I was wearing not simply a new coat but a new image;
the image of a man of some small means, small enough not
to be reckoned with but enough to be considered independent by Bolton standards, at least.

The jacket must have been transfiguring, for I thought
that people were noticing me as I walked by them. It even
seemed as though I saw a few smiles of admiration, obviously the imagination of a fool. No doubt about it, I
was getting used to having the money. In my fantasy I
could already see the seventy-five thousand dollars written
in a passbook. I even calculated the interest, over six thousand dollars a year, more money than I could possibly
dispose of. Think of the effort of deciding what to do with
it, which charities, which books, even a few rare books

purchased on my annual trip to New York and eventually left to the synagogue library. Five thousand I decided to give away immediately, half to the UJA and half to the synagogue. The rest would remain safely in insured accounts with the interest available for special needs and charity. That was the final plan and I was feeling comfortable with it, just as my new jacket no longer made me self-conscious. It was finally time to leak the news to my friends, although they must have suspected as much when I turned up wearing the jacket.

It wasn't my friends but Reverend Hubbard of the Pentecostal Church who was the first to comment on the jacket. I had followed his car into the parking lot that day and pulled into the space beside him.

"It's a nice day for the work of the Lord, isn't it, Mr. Traig?"

He always said things like that and he always called me by my family name, although I always replied, as I did then, "You can call me Mendel, Reverend Hubbard." Perhaps it was because he didn't like people to call him by his first name, Catledge, and I can't blame him.

"Now, that's a handsome sports jacket. I suspect that you didn't get that at Monkey Ward," he said.

"No, I didn't."

I was about to turn away, but he continued to look at me, his lips poised as though he wanted to say something more. "I don't suppose you heard that our Mrs. Paul has just returned from the Holy Land?"

"No, I hadn't heard that," I replied.

"Yes, she was on a tour of the holy places—Nazareth, Jerusalem, the river Jordan, and the Sea of Galilee. She even brought back a bottle of water from the Jordan. We intend to pour it into our baptismal fount."

"Better have it tested first."

He looked at me as though he wasn't sure how I meant that, and said, "She took some nice slides, too. Some of us saw them last night. I'm sure she'd be glad to show them to some people in your congregation as well."

"That would be nice. I'll have the program chairman call her."

His tone grew confidential as he said, "While she was there, a busload of Swedish tourists almost got blown up. They were eating lunch when a bomb went off in their bus." He shook his head. "Just a tragedy that there's no peace *there*, of all places. But we can have faith, can't we? After all, if our two congregations could work things out between us, there's hope for the Holy Land as well."

"We can hope, we can always hope, Reverend."

"It was good to talk to you about it, Mr. Traig. I don't suppose you've ever been there yourself, have you?"

"Not yet," I said, wondering if this would be the year.

"Be sure to call her, now," he said in parting as we separated and walked in opposite directions. The words echoed in my head: "Not yet, not yet." I turned to see him at the door of his church and thought back on the time when more than a parking lot separated us.

17.
Every Stream Has Two Banks

Friday at four-thirty in the afternoon wasn't a very polite time for Sennsenbrenner, the process server, to deliver notice of a lawsuit to Rabbi Bing, but his only concern was finding the rabbi in his study. Someone probably had told him that the rabbi would be at the synagogue preparing for the services, since Friday was the commencement of the Jewish Sabbath. He brushed past me in the hall, having hesitated at the library, noted the men's room, paused before the meeting room that was also a classroom, and finally came to a stop and drew himself up to his full five feet six inches before the walnut door marked RABBI'S STUDY. A nondescript man, I've been told by Hiram Guthrey, the county clerk, Sennsenbrenner's greatest pleasure is to watch the reaction on people's faces when they've been served with process. And the reaction was almost always the same—curiosity, perplexity, concern. The rabbi was no different, except that he did find the courtesy to say "Thank you," though he didn't really mean it. He is by nature a polite man who thanks everybody and God for everything. Satisfied with the reaction—rabbis, it seems, are just like everybody else—Sennsenbrenner turned and left the building without even a glance at the dedication plaque or the display of children's drawings of the *Purim* carnival.

The rabbi turned from the door, studying the formalisms of an alien discipline. "First Pentecostal Church *v.* Congregation Beth Sholem," the papers were titled. Seated at his desk, the rabbi studied the documents with the same attention that he gave to scripture, thinking that he would have to change his sermon somewhat to incorporate this new and, to him, surprising development.

What was it all about, this dispute? Its origins are obscured in the history of the county, sleeping but not dead, waiting to be revived by a curious lawyer. The year was 1878. A President named Grant was in office and great Wall Street financiers had failed, dragging tens of thousands of businesses and banks with them, including the First National Bank of Bolton. The closure of the bank combined with the drop in farm prices forced Jonah Mushrush to sell half of his 240-acre farm on Florence Road to J. Drexel Hatcher at a distress price. At least Hatcher *thought* he was buying 120 acres and never knew during his long life that he hadn't. Now, in those days, like in Poland, land was often described by landmarks. So the land sold to Hatcher was, as might be expected, described simply as all the land bounded by Strawberry Creek, Cowlick Creek and French Road.

The bank never reopened, but by 1898 the Panic of 1878 was just a dim recollection. That was the year of the great flood, brought on by torrential rains which caused the Monoganessen River to turn much of Bolton into a swirling, muddy lake. The county was never the same after the waters receded, taking with them the Center Street bridge and several historic beech trees. One of those trees had sheltered Brigadier General Hiram Bolton himself before his historic meeting with Chief Mihamappis of the Monoganessen tribe, a meeting that concluded with the cessation of all rights to the valley by the tribe in return for 24 bars of soap, 128 blankets, 17 kitchen knives and a bronze plaque. The chief, it seemed, wanted to be remembered. The plaque, too, was washed away by the flood and the town council never appropriated the funds to replace it, but none of the chief's progeny were around to protest, having moved west.

Another less dramatic effect of the flood was that Strawberry Creek changed its course, moving east by a full sixty feet. What this meant was that taking the creek as the boundary, fully sixty feet of land was amputated from Hatcher's farm unless, as Hatcher believed, the old creek bed remained the boundary. Surprisingly, both families continued to own and occupy their land through another generation of Hatchers and Mushrushes. From time to time, the location of the boundary became a temporary issue between them, to be put aside with the advent of harvest or the thaw. Both families, it seems, had in common the tendency to put off the difficult in favor of more pedestrian, attainable goals.

Nothing important happened until 1926, when the Army Corps of Engineers, largely through the efforts of an ambitious representative, undertook a flood-control project in the Monoganessen Valley which included turning Strawberry Creek into a subterranean conduit. At that time there was no one to protest the destruction of the habitat of the yellow spotted newt; in fact, only a few of the local children and a biologist from Pitt even knew of its existence. As for the Hatchers and the Mushrushes, the creek was just a nuisance that turned the surrounding fields into an impassable bog every third year, and they were glad to get rid of it.

Four years later, another Wall Street panic and another bank closure, this time the Second National Bank of Bolton, forced the Mushrushes off of their land. They sold it to Isaac Zimmerman and moved west to start a new life, presumably in the same place as the Monoganessen Indian tribe, or so it might have been, for no one ever heard anything further from them, either.

A year later the Hatchers succumbed to a form of chicken pneumonia, or rather their chickens succumbed. They sold their land to C. Walter Speck, one of the board members of the defunct bank, and they, too, moved west to South Bend, Indiana, where Harlan Hatcher got a job as an assembler at the Studebaker plant, at least I've been told as much.

After World War II, Zimmerman and Speck formed a partnership and sold off all of their land to a developer from Pittsburgh. But each of them gave a small parcel abutting Strawberry Creek and Florence Road to their respective congregations. Zimmerman was Jewish and Speck was a Pentecostal Christian.

It wasn't long after that the new Synagogue and Educational Center were built, a modern structure of yellow brick. Within a few years the Pentecostal congregation built their own more modest house of worship, a pitched-roof wooden rectangular building with a decapitated spire and a red neon sign that flashed JESUS SAVES on and off at ten-second intervals.

The construction of the Pentecostal Church was met

with something less than ecumenical tolerance by the Jewish community. Not only did the Pentecostals park their jalopies in the synagogue parking lot with regularity on Sundays, but their frequent prayer meetings were noisy and raucous, disturbing the tranquillity of the more sedate Jewish services, especially in the summer when the windows were open. Sometimes they could even be heard speaking in some incomprehensible language. But no one could knock on the door as you would with a noisy neighborhood party and tell them to turn down the music. The noise was, the Jews concluded, part of the ceremony, although no one ever ventured into the church to find out just what they did. They didn't even think to have a peaceful discussion of the subject with the pastor, the gaunt Reverend Catledge Hubbard. Nor did the Pentecostals ever express any curiosity about the customs of the Jews, although they must have seemed equally strange. At least once a year we would blow some sort of horn, once a year we erected a hut made of straw and fruit in the parking lot, once a year we had a Halloween party in the parking lot, only it wasn't Halloween, sometimes we spoke in some incomprehensible tongue and so on.

The Jews and the Pentecostals did have something in common, and that was the misunderstanding over where the church land ended and the synagogue land began, for the Synagogue and Educational Center bridged the original course of Strawberry Creek. As with the Hatchers and Mushrushes, the boundary question was an annual ritual, like *Pesach* and Easter, the longest course of correspondence between two attorneys in the history of the county. Each year in spring the law firms representing the Pentecostals and the Jews would exchange verbose, accusatory and menacing demand letters, each demonstrating their respective claims to the disputed land. Admittedly, the Jewish letter was usually the more sanguine of the two, since the synagogue enjoyed the possession of the land in dispute. The Pentecostal letter demanded, in even years, compensation for the land in an ever-higher amount, always one-third more than the synagogue board was willing to pay to settle the matter. In odd years the Pentecostals demanded the total demolition of the educational building so that they could build a parking lot. Now it can be seen why the Pentecostals were always poaching on the synagogue's parking lot. They didn't have one of their own.

A young attorney finally brought the correspondence to a halt. The threats obviously hadn't produced the desired results. He spent long hours in the county law library in the dim and dusty stacks, reading old cases in books never before opened. He studied the handwritten entries in the real estate records and finally concluded that the claim of the Pentecostal Church to the land was ironclad. Not only did the Jews have to return the land, but the church could recover at least twenty thousand dollars in rent, including interest.

New to the congregation, the rabbi knew nothing of the history of the dispute and no one had thought it important enough to tell him about it. So he called Finkelstein, the new president of the congregation, and all he could get from him was "We were afraid it would come to this someday." Finkelstein cleared his throat and said, "Rabbi, put it out of your mind. We have a lawyer to deal with it. Besides, I'll call Nudelman. You just go back to your services."

Now, a lawsuit has been likened to a civilized form of war, and that was what it was to the congregation. And as with any controversial subject, there were divergent opinions. Lawyer Rosenzweig produced his own brief, which conclusively demonstrated to the majority of the congregation the right of the synagogue to the disputed land. There were, of course, those who doubted the synagogue's right to the land, but who believed that the claim should have been raised at least fifty years ago. There was a third element in the congregation that had concluded without a shred of evidence that since all of the land had originally belonged to Mushrush, the synagogue even had a rightful claim to the land occupied by the church. One or two members thought they should pay the church for the land, but they were ridiculed by the majority for being too soft. After all, if the lawyer felt that he could successfully defend the suit, why simply capitulate? You had to stand up for your rights or you would lose all of them, they reasoned.

If the lawsuit itself provoked anger, the recognition that the lawyer responsible for it was himself Jewish spawned rage. How could a Jew, even a newcomer to the town, even one who never came to temple for services, even one who never gave to Jewish charities, even one who had no close Jewish friends, even one of those anti–Vietnam war peaceniks such as this Jonathan Fineberg, how could a Jew sue the synagogue to take its land away? But Jew he was; after all, his name was Fineberg and his mother's name was Sadie, and who had ever heard of someone named Sadie Fineberg who wasn't Jewish? So the ungrateful son of Sadie Fineberg was trying to destroy the House of Israel.

"He is Jewish," confirmed Henry Rosenzweig at an emergency meeting of the board, his face twisted in contempt. "He looks Jewish and is the most stubborn person I've ever encountered. There's no give-and-take to him at all."

"That's bad," said Nudelman. The meeting had been called to decide on a reaction to the intensified penetration of the parking lot by the Pentecostals. It seemed like there were old cars parked there day and night, cars corroded with rust, with bald tires. On Sundays the lot was so full that the synagogue members couldn't use it at all, and on top of that they often were met by the hostile stares of the Pentecostals whom they encountered on the parking lot. Aside from vigorously defending the suit, the congregation decided to go on the offensive, and the following morning a sign was erected at the entrance to the parking lot which warned, MEMBERS ONLY, TRESPASSERS WILL BE PROSECUTED.

The next morning when the rabbi arrived at the synagogue, he found a dozen round holes in the sign. Someone had apparently used it for target practice. "Hooligans," he muttered to himself. The next morning he found that the sign had been uprooted from the ground and tossed into the middle of the parking lot. The rabbi shook his head and muttered, "Vandals." Finkelstein had the stanchion embedded in a block of concrete and restored, but the following day the rabbi saw that the sign had been painted over in black paint. So the sign had to be repainted and the synagogue subscribed to a security patrol.

There was no more vandalism and the congregation basked in newly won security, at least until Sunday, when the parking lot again filled with cars.

The police refused to do anything about it, as the parking lot was private property, but Rosenzweig, sleepy though he was from a late night of poker, took down all the license-plate numbers and the next day he filed complaints with the county prosecutor, charging several of the car owners with trespass.

The day of the trial the courtroom was filled with partisans from both congregations, each believing, at least hoping, that justice would prevail. Fineberg's defense was brilliant. Since half of the parking lot was in the disputed zone, there could be no trespass unless the synagogue could prove that it had good title to the land. Of course that very question was in the courts now and was expected to remain there for a very long time. So the charges were dismissed. The Pentecostal spectators left the courtroom singing "Onward Christian Soldiers," while a few of the Jews left muttering that Judge Crawford was rumored to be anti-Semitic.

Rosenzweig was so angry when he heard the decision that he had to restrain himself from punching this upstart in the nose. He observed Fineberg looking satisfied as he chatted with the defendants. Restraining his impulse (Rosenzweig was uncomfortable with open hostility), he summoned a tight smile, more a grimace than a smile, and said to Fineberg, "I can't understand how you could take this case."

Fineberg looked at him quizzically, as though he didn't understand the premise of the question, and said, "What do you mean? It's a justiciable controversy, isn't it?"

"Well, we don't think so."

"Well, apparently the court thinks so," Fineberg replied, his voice rising an octave.

"But to take on the synagogue!"

"Oh, they shouldn't take it personally," said Fineberg. "I have nothing against the synagogue. But everyone has a right to representation."

Rosenzweig's tight smile disintegrated. He nodded imperceptibly and said, "So it's just another lawsuit. I guess we have nothing to talk about."

After the unsuccessful trespass prosecution, the Pentecostals went on parking in the synagogue parking lot, although on the advice of counsel they confined their use to the disputed portion. Across the line the Jews put all their hopes in the lawsuit, for Rosenzweig, his energies compounded by the ignominious defeat, assured the congregation that his demurrer to the Pentecostal petition would succeed, and although no one on the board knew what a demurrer was, they had confidence in Rosenzweig's judgment and ability. In the meantime the synagogue continued to suffer occasional acts of vandalism: an outside lamp shot out, "Jews beware" scrawled in black paint on a wall and a young tree uprooted, but despite the efforts of the night security service and the police, the perpetrators were never identified.

At last the day of the argument on the demurrer arrived. Partisans filled the courtroom and for the second time the Pentecostals and Jews sat side by side, though except for a few polite acknowledgments there was no conversation. Their lawyers would do the talking. The arguments were eloquent and lengthy. Judge Brock, his head shaking to the inner rhythm of his Parkinson's disease, was solicitous and patient. Without comment, he left the bench and the spectators left the courtroom in small groups, talking in subdued tones. An impasse, for Judge Brock was often agonizingly slow in coming to a decision. He had been known to take three years if he didn't make an immediate decision, and he hadn't.

With the court's indecision, the acts of vandalism increased, and disenchanted with the police, the board took further security measures, a twenty-four-hour voluntary guard armed with a pistol. At first the community responded with enthusiasm. But as the nights wore on and husbands felt the weariness of disrupted sleep or the economic loss from missed days at the office or the store, most of the initial volunteers dropped out with excuses such as health problems or wives that were afraid to be left alone.

Ultimately the job fell to a nucleus of World War II and Korean War veterans. Several of them, despite the inconvenience, were drawn on by the desire to meet the vandals just once and teach them a lesson, but for whatever reason, cowardice, caution or simply chance, weeks passed without further acts.

Just when even the guards were losing interest, their adversaries changed tactics, sending the rabbi a written threat to bomb the sanctuary itself. Outraged, the board notified the Department of Justice and a tight-lipped FBI agent began a sluggish investigation, questioning many of the Pentecostal congregants without success. After two days he left, concluding that the threat was the work of a crackpot. But that same night a small explosive charge went off in the synagogue's men's room, rattling the windows and knocking several of the pictures of past presidents off the wall. Although the damage was slight, no more than three hundred dollars to restore the plumbing, the effect on the congregation was what I would have expected. I had seen it happen before. Some families were afraid to send their children to religious school or social activities. Attendance at the services was reduced, although the guards and their families attended with regularity; they would not be intimidated. Even some who never had began attending. Strangers, itinerant salesmen stuck in Bolton on *Shabbas*, were given a careful once-over at the door, the only door which people were permitted to use. One salesman was frisked. Advised of the war with the church next door, he went off shaking his head, not even staying for the service.

Rabbi Bing endured the inconvenience. After all, the land dispute wasn't of his making, the congregation had to deal with it. He wasn't afraid of bombs or vandals, or to be more exact, he refused to be intimidated by them.

Hadn't the Jewish people always practiced their religion in adversity—pogroms, desecrations, expulsions, the burning of holy books, the burning of holy men, the burning of whole communities? This was the condition of Jewish life: finding solace in the writings of sages who had given up their lives chanting the *Shma*, wrapped in a burning Torah scroll. He saw attendance decline, he presided at meetings in which the community progressively isolated itself, likening its experience to the Warsaw ghetto. It wasn't until one Saturday morning when there weren't even enough worshipers for a *minyan* that the rabbi began to question. Then, after the bomb blast, when the board voted to remove the Torah scrolls from the ark in the sanctuary and leave them in the basement for safe-keeping, the rabbi decided quietly that he had had enough. The removal of the scrolls was only one part of it. It was unseemly to have weapons in the sanctuary, as had been suggested. Even worse, there were whispered rumors that some of the guards were planning to retaliate against the Pentecostal Church itself. "An eye for an eye," they were saying. At least until now the community had accepted the explanation that the vandalism should not be blamed on the church, but the bomb had stilled the reasonable voices.

As he sat in the perpetual twilight of his study, the rabbi came to a decision and spread the word to the key members of the board. That Friday night the attendance at the service was greater than normal, for the rabbi let it be known that he would give his views on the dispute with the church. There wasn't even a cough as, the service concluded, Rabbi Bing spread his notes, nudged his rimless spectacles up his short nose and began to speak, slowly ejecting each word as if he hated to give it up.

"I have avoided involvement in the dispute with the Pentecostal Church because, as you know, I didn't feel that it was important to the spiritual well-being of the community. I now see that I was wrong, for the problem with all of its ramifications has grown from a minor nuisance to eclipse all of our activities as a community. Education, worship, social activities, all have shrunk as the community poured more and more of its energy into the preservation of this building and this patch of land on the earth that it occupies.

"I needn't go into the antagonism, the hatred that this problem has created among us. Nor do I have to discuss the way in which we isolated ourselves from the rest of the community as we began to see ourselves as the eternal victims of hatred and persecution. I must confess that I, too, drew the same conclusions from the events of the past months. But this week I began to wonder if at least part of the problem stemmed from our unwillingness to bend, to see that perhaps there was some right in the position of our neighbors. We have been so self-righteous, so stiff-necked, so convinced of the rectitude of our position, that we thought that we had a monopoly on justice. Now, the law might be in our favor, I frankly don't know, but I do know that the law might as readily vindicate their position as ours. Whether or not it does is unimportant, for a higher standard of justice, which commands respect for our neighbors, tells us that we should open our hearts and minds to their viewpoint and settle this problem once and for all, based upon a spirit of compromise and generosity."

A few days later, I happened to be in the rabbi's study. My curiosity got the better of me and I asked him about the congregation's reaction to his sermon, assuring him that I for one found it to be reasonable. The rabbi's blue eyes, already reduced by thick lenses, receded even further into his head as he said soberly, "A few people called." It was as if the words had passed over their heads and floated out the door. As I was about to leave, the phone rang. It turned out to be the chief of police calling to tell the rabbi that they had found the probable vandal, a dishwasher at the Coffee Cup with a history of mental illness. Following up a tip from a waitress who happened to be a member of the Pentecostal Church, they had searched his room and found materials for making bombs, a rifle and anti-Semitic literature. The chief assured him that the man had nothing to do with the church. As the rabbi repeated this to me, the tension visibly left him. He looked over my head for a moment, rubbing his hands together, and said, "Mendel, what would you think if I called the Reverend Hubbard?"

"I would think well of you," I answered and without a pause, Rabbi Bing picked up the phone and called Reverend Hubbard of the Pentecostal Church.

They met the next day in the coffee shop of the Roosevelt Hotel. After the introductions, the discussions of weather and such, the rabbi came to the point. Feeling awkward, he asked bluntly, "Is there room for compromise, Reverend?"

The reverend's pale-gray eyes looked over Rabbi Bing's head. "I've had nothing to do with it, Rabbi. It's a matter for my board. I just save souls, I don't get involved in politics."

"The greatest moral issues are sometimes invested in politics."

"Be that as it may, I just save souls, personal salvation." Reverend Hubbard gazed into the rabbi's eyes. His face wore an innocent, childlike expression.

Rabbi Bing's thin lips twisted into an ironic hint of a smile. "Let me ask a different question then: What does your board want?"

"You should ask their attorney that question, Rabbi."

"Can you speculate on it, Reverend?"

"If I were to hazard a guess, I suppose it would be the right to use half of that parking lot, and maybe the right to use a couple of the classrooms, provided it didn't conflict with your religious school." Reverend Hubbard's eyes narrowed, his long head inclined slightly toward the rabbi, who nodded and said quickly, "Mmm, mmm, mmm."

The rabbi and the reverend finished their coffee and agreed to meet again, not to discuss the suit but to get acquainted. That same day, Rabbi Bing went to work on his board, seeking support for a compromise proposal. With the certainty that the vandal had, in fact, been caught with the assistance of one of the members of the church, much of the hostility subsided. Still, it was no easy task for the rabbi to muster the majority needed to approve a compromise based upon the reverend's assumptions. The meeting was turbulent. The rhetoric was as thick as the cigarette smoke. Finally at 1:45 A.M., red-eyed and weary, the board approved a compromise allocating a portion of the parking lot to the church and the use of one classroom on Sunday mornings and Wednesday evenings.

A few days later, the Pentecostal Church board of elders approved it as well. While Reverend Hubbard refused to take a position, the rabbi found a willing advocate in Vivian Hautrey, the waitress at the Coffee Cup.

Rosenzweig drew up the necessary documents, and one month later they were signed by the appropriate officers at a ceremony on the parking lot. Coffee was provided by the church and cookies by the synagogue.

A year passed, two, three. The guards formed a bowling team called the Zealots, which won the championship of the Interfaith League. Fineberg's son came of age and he enrolled him in the religious school at the synagogue. The church built a basketball court, which the synagogue youth used on Tuesdays and Thursdays. And each year the church and the synagogue gathered, one with the other, on the parking lot to eat cookies, drink coffee and socialize.

More years will pass and the long feud, except for the annual ceremony, will be almost forgotten. The common use of the classroom and parking lot, the basketball facilities, will be accepted not just as a compromise. In time it will become the way things had been and the way things are supposed to be.

Yes, things are forgotten, I thought as I walked down the corridor toward my apartment, glancing at the row of uniformly framed pictures of the presidents of the congregation and the rabbis who had served it. There was Nudelman, looking anything but comfortable. And there was Rabbi Newman, his photo showing the shy sweetness that at least the children and his few disciples knew. He, too, was all but forgotten. No one ever mentioned his sudden departure and the shock to the whole town that led up to it. The good and the bad are forgotten; the conflicts and even the miracles.

18.
Wonder Working

The news that the Rabbi Newman had cured somebody of cancer came in as I happened to be seated in Estelle Cantor's kitchen, drinking a second cup of coffee with my second piece of raisin *kuchen*. As might be expected, it was her good friend Heda Finkelstein who telephoned. After repeating it to me, hand held over the mouthpiece, with a look of ironic skepticism, Estelle said, "And who told you that?"

As always, Estelle's combination of doubt and encouragement tantalized Heda Finkelstein, and she unleashed a flood of verbiage lasting for at least ten minutes. All the while Estelle, receiver deftly cradled between shoulder and ear, attached to her friend by the extension cord, was performing meaningless tasks, adding an occasional "Mmm hmm" by way of encouragement and raising her eyebrows and shaking her head at me.

The gist of the story is as follows: On Tuesdays and Thursdays the Ecumenical Council of Churchmen of Monoganessen County rotated the sick calls at Mercy Hospital. One day the Baptist minister visited the Catholic and the Jewish patients, the next day it was the Methodist who looked after the Baptists and so on. This wasn't a happy arrangement for every sick person, some of whom were, due to their discomfort, more than a little cranky and demanding. But for others it was a refreshing change of pace from the tiresome reassurances of their own minister. Only one time was this system ever threatened, and that was when an Episcopalian was converted to Catholicism in his last days by Father Shanahan; but it wasn't just sick people who found Father Shanahan irresistible. The Episcopalian minister was, of course, indignant and embarrassed, but the rest of the council glossed over it with the judgment that there wasn't much difference between the Episcopalians and the Catholics, and who knows, things might even out in the long run. Ever since that time the Episcopalian minister has been doing his best to bring someone, anyone, into his fold, even an atheist would do, but all to no avail. The rotation plan weathered that crisis, but Rabbi Newman's miracle was not as easy.

Rabbi Newman was its only casualty, but his loss was Rabbi Bing's gain. As for the miracle, it speaks for itself, as all miracles do, in different tongues. At least that's what Rabbi Newman said.

Rabbi Newman was, as might be expected, the last man to take any responsibility for Mr. Finney's cure. He did admit reluctantly that he had visited Mr. Finney. He had, in fact, attempted to comfort him, if it is possible to comfort a man who knows he's suffering from incurable cancer of the stomach. The rabbi agreed that he at one point reached out and stroked Mr. Finney's shoulder, even applying a cold washcloth to his forehead, but he refrained from anything theological out of deference to Father Shanahan. After all, will the dog's medicine cure the cat, or vice versa for that matter? In truth, Rabbi Newman's conversation with Mr. Finney was benign and commonplace, limited to the usual questions: Could he do anything for him, was he comfortable, would he like the TV turned on? At least that's what Rabbi Newman said.

If Mr. Finney hadn't begun to rally the next day and if, within thirty days, not only was the cancer in remission but the tumors were actually diminishing, the uneventful visit would have passed without notice. The unexplained reversal of the cancer would have simply been noted by the doctors as something that happens now and then. Except for Mr. Finney himself. He would have none of that explanation. He told everyone from Father Shanahan to all the Finney family and his friends of the miraculous effect of the rabbi's laying on of hands, for Mr. Finney claimed that immediately when the rabbi touched his shoulder, he began to feel a hot tingling sensation not unlike a mustard plaster, which soon radiated to his abdomen and remained there for many hours. Pain had been Mr. Finney's constant companion and he took the burning as another torment, that is, until he felt the usual pain recede and not return.

Now, Mr. Finney hadn't been to church for many years and he took no stock in miracles, least of all Jewish miracles, so it took him some time to trace the end of his pain back to the burning and finally to Rabbi Newman's touch. Even then he dismissed it as coincidence, but the more he considered it, and he had ample time to do so in bed, the more convinced he became that Rabbi Newman's touch had cured him. During all of this speculation neither he nor his family thought to mention it to Rabbi Newman, and Father Shanahan certainly wasn't going to. In the first place he didn't believe it, and in the second place he was sure the rabbi would think him eccentric for mentioning it except as a joke, and in the third place God seemed to have given up working miracles, possibly because he was a little awed by man's technological achievements and figured they weren't needed anymore. At least that's what Father Shanahan reasoned.

Miracles were not something that Rabbi Newman had given much thought to, either. He was a practical man whose horizons were as limited as the view from Bolton, closed in as it was on all sides by hills. Rabbi Newman had even given up thinking about achievements or accomplishments, for himself at least. He had reached the summit of his career, and it was no more than 734 feet above sea level. Bolton was, had been and would be his highest achievement, a humble pulpit for a humble, unprepossessing man. In the last year, as he watched the lines in his fleshy face deepen, witnessed his hair hysterically abandon his head (did they know something he didn't know?), felt himself puff after ascending a flight of stairs (he was overweight), saw the skin on his hands become whiter and more transparent and the blue veins stand up higher—as he saw the traces of morbidity, he knew that he had already preached his best sermon.

Seated in the comfortable leather chair in his study, he would sometimes find himself lapsing into a state of suspended activity in the middle of the page of a book, and he seemed to confront an unknowing void. At such times he would secretly take stock of his worth, first appraising

his deficiencies, his speech defect that he had never overcome (he had trouble with "r," so that "roar" often came
out "war"), his slow delivery (he could see the faces growing vacant as he spoke), his unimposing form (five foot
four inches and shaped like a steel drum).

Rabbi Newman never thought at those times about the
reason for his lifetime position in Bolton: the fact that the
children loved him, that they were attracted instantly to
his easy, warm simplicity and directness, that he wove religious teachings into little stories and parables that de-
lighted even the smallest children. Some even thought of
him as one of them, although a bigger, wrinkled form.
But he took that side of himself for granted.

It's no wonder that when Mr. Finney's cure finally made
the feature page of the Bolton *Daily Observer*, the rabbi
was both embarrassed and incredulous. His first thought
was to call Father Shanahan and disclaim any responsibility for it; he wanted no part of another conflict like the
one over the conversion. To his total surprise Father Shanahan was magnanimous, even congratulatory in a way
that let the rabbi know that of course he didn't believe
a word of it and neither did the rabbi.

But then a second and a third and a fourth story appeared, circulated by other former patients, all confirming
not so dramatic a recovery as Mr. Finney's but nevertheless in agreement that the turning point in their illnesses
seemed to be the day the rabbi had come to visit and had
patted their shoulders. Remarkably, they all confirmed the
instant burning sensation, which had radiated, remained and
subsided with the symptoms of their disease, as if whatever
had traveled into them through the rabbi's fingers had
taken the disease with it when it finally left their body.
With the second article in three days, this one on the front

page, the story was picked up by the wire services. The "wonder-working rabbi" from Bolton, they called him, and poor Rabbi Newman was deluged with phone calls from all over the country, from sick people who would pay him anything just to be in his presence. So many calls came in on the day after the national story broke that I had to switch both the synagogue and his home phone to unlisted numbers. He couldn't get any sleep. Because of the time zones, when it was two o'clock in the morning in Bolton, it was only eleven at night in California, and naturally most of the calls came from there.

If Rabbi Newman had achieved instant national fame, his own congregation felt otherwise. I happened to be at his house helping him balance his checkbook when the delegation from the board turned up. At first he wouldn't even go to the door. He finally responded to the insistent knock with a querulous "Who is it?" At first the rabbi was relieved to see them, but again he shrank into himself as he saw the distance and suspicion.

When they were all seated comfortably in the living room and were offered tea, Nudelman, a gentle expression on his face, said, "Rabbi, you never told us you had this power before."

His color deepening, the rabbi raised his arms in a gesture of protest and said, "But I don't! It's all a misunderstanding, a mere coincidence."

Nudelman nodded. "We thought so, Rabbi. Obviously your congregation, at least the board of directors, doesn't believe in such things as miracle cures. We've all heard the tales of the faith healers, throw away your crutches and all that, but as Jews we're just not so naïve."

"Of course," the rabbi responded, repeatedly nodding his head.

"Understandably, we were shocked to learn that our rabbi had apparently become a faith healer without even discussing it with the board."

"I assure you I haven't, Mr. Nudelman. I knew nothing about it until the newspaper report."

"It's an embarrassment to the community, Rabbi. We're already the butt of jokes in Pittsburgh," added Feinberg.

"I regret that," he answered, too quickly, his cheeks flushing. "It won't happen again."

No more was said of miracles. They drank their tea, talked about the *Purim* carnival and got up to leave. As they were parting, the rabbi, by way of reassurance, patted Nudelman on the shoulder. Nudelman started, then jumped back in surprise or fear.

"What's wrong?" the rabbi asked in alarm.

"Nothing, nothing, just my bursitis," said Nudelman, his voice high-pitched, retreating wide-eyed. Nudelman had, for the past several months, been suffering from what the doctors had ultimately diagnosed as chronic bursitis of the elbow. Even those awful cortisone shots had failed to relieve it. He drove Mrs. Howard home, hardly listening to her rail about the irresponsibility of the press. All of his faculties were concentrated in the burning sensation in his arm.

A few hours later, as he was watching *The Tonight Show*, he realized that both the burning and the pain of the bursitis were gone. He was so excited that he knocked over Sarah's favorite vase getting to the phone to call the rabbi to tell him that the others were right, he *did* have a power. Silence at the other end of the line as the rabbi absorbed this latest testimonial, not from some naïve Catholic steelworker, but from hard-headed, practical, skeptical Nudelman, a man who wasn't given to fantasy or even rash speculation, a man whom he trusted.

The rabbi said only, "Nudelman, are you sure it's not the cortisone?"

"Rabbi, I gave up on the cortisone several weeks ago."

"Maybe it's a delayed reaction."

"No, Rabbi. It's you. You know me; I'm not gullible. Now the question is, What are we going to do about it?"

"Sam, I don't know."

The rabbi didn't have to know what to do; the events took their natural course, as they always do, and after living for a few days as a recluse, seeing no one but Nudelman and me, he was forced by the *Shabbas* service again into the public eye. He found himself facing the same congregation as before, only it wasn't the same. As he looked down from the pulpit, he saw a full synagogue, not the usual lackluster turnout; it looked like *Rosh Hashanah*. It was so full that I had to bring a folding chair from a schoolroom and sit in the back. The rabbi's eyes traveled across the faces of the congregation. Some of them seemed wide-eyed, while others bore the shadow of skepticism.

The service over, the rabbi timorously embarked on his sermon with his usual lame delivery. Twelve minutes later he concluded. There wasn't a single nodding head. People had actually listened to him. After the service many people even complimented him, seeing much more in his remarks than was actually there. The rabbi looked pleased, more so than I'd ever seen him except when he was teaching the children.

The next day he resumed his rounds at the hospital, not simply visiting the one or two Jewish patients but seeing everyone, and to his astonishment the next few weeks saw each of them recover. Some, to be sure, would have recovered in any event. Others were goners until the rabbi showed up. A few, admittedly, didn't make it, but through no fault of the rabbi. One fell out of bed and suffered a fatal head injury. Another choked on a piece of chicken which became lodged in her trachea.

For a few days the hospital occupancy level declined to the point that they were afraid of bankruptcy. A hospital, after all, is like a hotel: the beds have to be filled to meet the expenses. The doctors were thinking seriously about charging the rabbi with practicing medicine without a license. He was threatening to put them all out of business. Then the convoys of sick began arriving in wheelchairs, in ambulances, on crutches; people bent over, emaciated people, people yellow with jaundice, people red with hypertension. They filled the hospital, and the doctors were reaching the point of exhaustion trying to treat them. It was like a town afflicted with an epidemic or a military hospital after a battle. And Rabbi Newman saw them all, reassuring them, touching them, asking nothing from them, still in awe of this power that he was sure was not his.

As might be expected, not everyone in the congregation was of one mind on the subject of the rabbi's powers, for the rabbi, as he devoted more and more of his energy and time to healing, gave less and less to the congregation. There were those who went around clucking their tongues and repeating, "What good is a golden wine goblet if there is no wine?" This comment, likely as not, would be met with a shrug, followed by "The rabbi doesn't mix into my business and I don't mix into his." A few of the rabbi's followers would look down their noses and say, "God's cup is filled with life, not Manischewitz." None of these conversations went much further than that, for in Bolton it is said that a person's opinions are as precious to him as his savings passbook.

The only question which provoked true speculation among the congregants was the nature of the rabbi's powers. Of the many theories, the one espoused by Meyer the pharmacist was the most popular. It held that the purity of the rabbi's soul neutralized the energy of disease in much the same way that Bromo Seltzer neutralized the acid in a stomach.

Whatever the reason, the rabbi was giving of his life to those he cured. He was becoming visibly weaker each day. His stocky physique was shrinking. His skin was drawing back against the bone, was becoming pale and, in certain light, almost transparent. And as his body wasted, his eyes grew larger and shined with a feverish intensity.

The rabbi was oblivious to all that, working longer hours each day, totally absorbed in what he was doing. At least he was until the panel of New York rabbis flew into town and perched behind him like four stoop-shouldered crows. They followed the rabbi on his rounds, saying nothing, their sharp eyes taking in every gesture as though they had expected some sleight of hand. One of them, a tall, distinguished man with a neatly trimmed graying beard like Lenin's, took copious notes and questioned Rabbi Newman with transparent condescension. Of course, the rabbi could provide no answers. He had no explanations other than that some power had been bestowed on him.

The rabbis went away without even a goodbye and released to the Jewish press a denunciation of Rabbi Newman as a mendicant, a mystic and a charlatan. Even worse, they recommended that his privileges as a Conservative rabbi be revoked. They had seen no evidence that there was other than an empirical explanation for all of the cures, and their physician consultants confirmed their opinion.

When the rabbi's followers heard the news, they quickly gathered at his home. I must confess that I was among them. Everyone but the rabbi was in a state of agitation. It was as if they, rather than the rabbi, had been discredited. Siegelman, the leader of the group, suggested an objective demonstration.

The rabbi listened with a weariness that could have been mistaken for calm. With a lull in the discussion, he raised his palm and said, "God doesn't need anyone to make a demonstration."

"You're wrong, Rabbi," said Siegelman. "You have a duty to get the message to the people."

"Which message, what message, Allen?"

"Simply the message that God has actively intervened in your life, endowing you with a rare power to cure the sick. And that as he has acted, he remains a positive force for limitless good."

"And what if it's not good?"

"What else could it be?"

"We have no way of knowing," said the rabbi softly, almost to himself.

The lines deepened on the rabbi's forehead; he brought his hand across his eyebrows and sighed. "What do you propose?"

"Just a publicized, witnessed demonstration."

The rabbi's eyes grew distant, his head cocked to one side, his gaze fell to Siegelman's feet and remained there. Then he looked up with surprise, as if he had not expected to see the people around him, and he said, "If that's what's to be . . ."

Siegelman rose, touched the rabbi's shoulder and left the room, the others following silently.

Siegelman arranged the demonstration, as they called it, for five cancer patients certified as terminal. The reactions and hoped-for recovery were to be scientifically monitored by disinterested volunteer cancer specialists. Rabbi Newman had no part in the planning. Each day he went through the hospital seeing more and more people, passing from one to the other, finding the strength to focus a little of himself on each of them. He gave no thought to it, but it appeared as if he was engaged in single-handed combat, not simply with disease but with death itself.

The day of the demonstration approached, yet nothing was said to the rabbi until the morning of the meeting. At a few minutes to ten Siegelman came to him and led him like a blind man into a circular surgical amphitheater filled with distinguished doctors, clergymen of every denomination and representatives of all the wire services and television networks. The glare of the surgical lamps made him blink, but he discerned the dim shapes of the witnesses.

His eyes adjusted to the light and he saw five stainless-steel gurneys in a row, on which lay five people under white sheets. From their wasted shapes and their eyes, he could see that they were all very close to death, that they had suffered much and that they understood how slight was their hold on life. Three of them were old, at least in their seventies, and time, not sickness, had slowly worn away life like water dripping on limestone. A fourth was middle-aged, with eyes that hope had left. The last was young, too young to meet death. The rabbi's eyes touched hers, eyes which begged for help, but not with desperation. Rather they were opaque, bottomless, serene, even indifferent.

The room was so still that the rabbi's heels scraping the rubber tile seemed loud. For the first time since the gift had come to him, he found himself thinking that he could do nothing—nothing for those whom age had brought to the point of death. Nothing for those who had given up all hope. He turned to the young woman and saw again the serenity which transcended death.

His head bent upward and he stared into the lucid whiteness of the overhead surgical lamp. The coruscating light drowned his senses, his ears began to roar, he lost awareness of his surroundings and he saw, forming out of the searing white, a shapeless pulsating black mass. Despite the heat of the surgical lamps, a chill passed through his body and he closed his eyes and turned away. A murmur rippled through the crowd as the rabbi hesitated, his eyes closed. Like a stirring of wind, the whisper reached him, and without so much as a glance back at the patients, he left the amphitheater, only to find his way blocked by a distraught Siegelman.

"What are you doing, Rabbi!" he said, his voice pleading and anguished.

"Let me pass, Siegelman," the rabbi said gently. "I have nothing to give those poor people. They are even beyond comfort. Why make a spectacle of their death?" His voice was calm and his eyes steady but showing hurt.

"They'll think you're a fake," Siegelman cried out, his eyes filling.

The rabbi said nothing. He only looked Siegelman in the eye, a look of sadness and fatigue. Then he said, in almost a whisper, "I have seen death."

Above them in the gallery the spectators, their voices growing, were standing in their places and moving toward the exits. Siegelman gave the rabbi a last pleading look, the rabbi looked back, but his eyes were not there. Siegelman, his shoulders slumped, looked to the ground. He turned and let Rabbi Newman pass, then raised his head to watch him as he walked alone down the white hospital corridor.

The press relegated the story to the back pages, devoting only a few paragraphs to it. Rabbis and doctors returned to their homes, their convictions affirmed.

Within a week the consensus developed in the congregation that the rabbi should be asked to resign, his good works having brought just too much stress to the community. But there was no need to request his resignation, for the rabbi had already left town. The last time I saw him, it was only to make arrangements for a moving company to pack and forward his belongings. I heard nothing from him for at least a year. Then, at last, I got a postcard, the message crammed on the back. He was well and working in Denver; not as a healer, not even as a rabbi. He had become a social worker in a ward for terminal cancer patients, giving whatever solace he could to the dying. And the rabbi's gift? He wrote nothing about it.

19.
First Snow

I could tell from the somber tone of his voice that Rosenzweig had received bad news, so bad that he didn't even want to discuss it on the telephone. Rather, he asked me to come down to his office. "Somber" is too strong; it was more the tone of a hurt child, I thought as I left off my writing and drove down to his office, expecting to be told that it was all a mistake, that there was no money for me after all, that it had been given to someone else in 1957. Who knows what excuse or explanation I expected? Reality was descending like a window shade, closing off my fantasies.

Stopped at a traffic light, I looked around me. The weather was mirroring my oncoming gloom. It was early winter, the sycamore trees on Main Street were bare except for an occasional tenacious holdover dangling brown from the edge of a bough. The sky above was neither white nor gray, the chill but humid air was biting and there was a frame of frost around Tevye's windshield. It looks like the first snow will fall soon, and even as I thought it, what looked like dandruff began to touch the windshield and disappear, leaving behind a speck of moisture.

I turned my collar up as I got out of the car, and hurried half a block to the entrance of the building. The fluted brass handle of the door was cold to the touch and made me flinch, but it was warm in the lobby.

By the look of Muriel's face as she told me to go right in (for some reason he calls her his "girl," although she has to be in her middle fifties), by the look of her it was bad news. So what? I said to myself. I never wanted the money in the first place. Rosenzweig looked up from his yellow legal pad as I came in. He put down his pen and gestured to a chair, a pained expression on his face, which he was trying to dispel with a dubious smile.

"So, Rosenzweig. What's up, more papers to sign?"

"No. Not exactly."

"Let's have it, then."

"You want the good news first"—his voice ascended the scale—"or the bad news?" The words tumbled down again.

"You should know that I'm always prepared for the worst, but let's have the good news first; it will take the edge off the bad." I could feel my face getting hot as I waited for him to speak.

He picked up a letter and said, "The good news is that the transfer from the government trust for undistributed reparations has been conditionally finalized. The money is in your name in an account at the Bank Leumi, in Jerusalem. You are free to withdraw it."

"So fine. When will the bank make the transfer?"

"That's the bad news, Mendel. They can't."

"Why not?"

"Government regulations. They say you have to go there and draw it out personally."

"That's not so bad. It seems convoluted, but if I must it will give me an excuse to go visit my cousin." I was relieved, even exhilarated. Without the complication I know that I would never have planned an immediate trip to see him, although I had intended to do it eventually.

"The trouble is, Mendel, you'll have to spend it all while you're there, because they won't let you take the money out of Israel. It's some rule they have about reparations paid to the State of Israel on behalf of families that didn't survive the Holocaust, you see."

"I don't see. I did survive."

"It's a legal problem. Had you applied directly to Germany, it would have come to you anywhere. But these reparations were paid to the State of Israel on behalf of all of the European Jews. So the State of Israel is willing to partially undo the fact that they already have the money and have probably even spent it by letting you have it, but only on the condition that you spend it in Israel."

"I see."

"They don't have any obligation to give you anything at all at this point. But they want to encourage immigration."

"Immigration?"

"Yes. You can't get the money as a tourist. You must first become a permanent resident, and the money is supposed to be used for things like an apartment, a car, appliances, furniture and your support. It's up to you how it's spent, within those limits, of course."

He stopped speaking, waiting for me to react. I was prepared for some technicality which would deprive me of the use of the money, but this "immigrant" condition took me by surprise. There were crosscurrents of feelings beginning to circulate in me; on the one hand a fear born of resistance to change and its uncertainties. I believed myself to be settled here in Bolton, even though I was in so many respects an alien, an outsider. Still, I belonged, I had friends, work that satisfied me and my small apartment. I even saw myself buried in the cemetery one day, not too soon I hoped, but eventually lying in this my adopted soil beneath the daffodils and turf. I had never been a Zionist, as was Ephie. I belonged to a universal Jewish community, particularized there in the town of Zamosc, nourished by tradition, realized by ceremony, family and a common outlook. Maybe I was myopic, as Ephie always said, but it was enough for me. Of course, when all of this was taken away from me, Israel did, over the years, begin to occupy some of the space that had been vacated by the destruction of my own community, but it remained remote, untouchable, exotic, still hanging above the clouds like some eighteenth-century engraving. I probably couldn't bring myself to grasp the reality of it out of the fear that if I once made it concrete in my mind, like Zamosc, it, too, would turn to dust and blow away. Now suddenly I *had* to cope with it; I was faced with the choice to retain my engraving of a claustrophobic Wailing Wall or to replace it with a bank, automobile traffic and disorderly jostling crowds of people, most of whom just happened to be Jews.

"Mendel?" Rosenzweig looked at his desk clock. "I'm sorry, but I just squeezed you in. I've got a settlement conference at the courthouse in about five minutes. The last thing I wanted to mention is, I think your cousin told you that the right to claim the money even in Israel expires in about six months. If you don't take it, it will revert to the state for good." He stood up and looked around him. "Muriel, have you got that Fenniker file?"

"It's on your desk."

"Oh yes," he said, picking up the file and stuffing it into his attaché case. "C'mon, I'll go down in the elevator with you. Looks like snow, doesn't it?" Then, as we waited for the doors to slide open, he added, "I wonder what the weather's like in Israel at this time of the year?"

"I'll write to my cousin and ask him," I said, and we parted shaking hands. I looked at my watch and realized that Nudelman was probably already waiting for me at the synagogue. He had the afternoon off and had agreed to listen to my Zamosc speech again. I started toward Tevye, unsure whether my apprehensive state was due to my meeting with Rosenzweig or to the thought of going through the speech again.

20.

Negative Responses

Everybody is afraid of something. Some of the things we fear have validity, some are foolish; only the fear is always real. I've had a lot to be afraid of in my life, although I won't go into that. Not the least of my fears is the fear of making a fool of myself speaking in public. So you can imagine how I felt when I opened this letter from the Pittsburgh Jewish Center and found a request that I speak on my childhood in Zamosc.

It seems that they were having a picture exhibition of the Polish Jewish community, and why not complement it with a speech? After all, there's something morbid about an old still picture; it's like a skewered butterfly. So they heard about me, but for Ephie the last of my tribe, a living complement to all those pictures, but they didn't know of my fear of public speaking.

I couldn't bring myself to say yes and I didn't want to say no. So I let the letter sit on my desk, taking up its own space; not covered up by magazines or anything like that. No, it lay there looking me in the eye each time I sat down, giving me the jitters. Well, two weeks passed and I still hadn't answered the letter, thinking, although I wouldn't admit it to myself, that if I didn't respond they might forget that they had even written. I remember having just such thoughts on cold, dark winter mornings as a child. If I lay there ever so still, maybe my mother would forget me and not shake me out of bed to go to school. Well, it didn't work then and it still doesn't work, because there came a second letter to shatter my late-afternoon tranquillity, and this one by special delivery, at that.

So I got Nudelman on the phone. He had just taken an aspirin, as he had a headache, and I almost didn't even get around to the subject of the call. When I finally did, after I had told him what he already knew (my fear), he thought for a moment and said, his voice sluggish and far away, "How much time have you got before the speech?"

"About two months."

"No problem, then."

"For you it's no problem."

"You'll go in training."

"What do you mean?"

"Just what I said. You'll write the speech and give it to some of your friends until you feel comfortable. You worry too much, Mendel. We'll help you." His voice faded and I knew the headache was getting the best of him, so I didn't press the issue further this time; however, his usually good advice gave me no reassurance, not even a little bit.

Despite my fear, the special-delivery letter, combined

with Nudelman's dubious support, tipped the scale of indecision, and before I could change my mind I called Mr. Fishbein, none other than the director of the whole center, and with muttered apologies for the delay, accepted his invitation. He sounded like one of those very busy people in a hurry to hang up to get on to the next abrupt phone call. When I finished with my message, there was a pause as if he had left the phone, then a terse "Thank you," a "Do you need directions to get here?" and a "Goodbye." A busy man. The head of a big center, and that's the way it is in the city, no time for small talk. Not like here in Bolton, where there's no time for big talk. The telephone clicked down on the receiver and I vowed to start work on the speech, rework it a few times and take up Nudelman's offer. And I did.

The speech turned out to be about sixteen pages typed, double-spaced. Poor Nudelman, poor Finkelstein, poor Sidney Cantor. They sat there at the end of the day, in the front row of the sanctuary, insisting on simulated battle conditions. I stood on the *bima*, clutching the oiled walnut lectern, my knees shaking and little quivers rolling up and down my back. As bad as I felt, I wasn't too nervous to see Finkelstein fidget and grimace and Sidney slump forward into a doze, only to be nudged awake by Nudelman halfway through.

When I had finished, Nudelman patted me on the back and said, "That was a pretty good speech." That's what he said with his voice, but his expression told me another thing. It said, "God in heaven help poor Mendel out of this fix."

A friend is somebody like Nudelman. The next time I called the audience, Sidney had to work late and Finkelstein was committed to cleaning the refrigerator. But Nudelman, suffering from a winter cold, his fleshy, prominent nose looking like a red light, came back for more punishment and offered more words of encouragement.

"Come up for air," Nudelman said as I plowed through the text, my head so close to the page that my nose was almost dragging across the paper. Nudelman's coaching worked, for I had to admit that I was, in fact, feeling more confident.

I had more confidence, at least, until the day of the speech. A cold shower and a glass of milk made me feel better, until I looked outside. What I saw was nothing, nothing but white, a blizzard such as I had not seen since my childhood in Poland. It's from God, I thought with relief, he's sent this blizzard to prevent me from dying of fright on the platform.

It must have been a busy day for God, because by noon he'd gone off and almost forgotten about the blizzard, and owing to his neglect, the snow was falling only lightly. Depressed, I called the state police, and the recorded message confirmed that the weather was indeed clearing and the Pittsburgh road was icy in places but open.

I put on my parka and went out to see how Tevye was doing. "Tevye," I said, dusting off the windshield with a broom so he could see me, "how do you feel about going to Pittsburgh this afternoon on an icy road in a snowstorm?" Tevye just looked at me through the hoarfrost, and I could tell that Tevye was about as enthused as I was about the trip. I got inside the car, thinking maybe Tevye wouldn't start, but to my disappointment the engine turned right over. That was that. One thing I've learned in life is to accept something that can't be changed. As my Uncle Berl, the floorwalker, used to say, "You can't go around in the revolving door after the store closes." I went back into my warm apartment and practiced the speech a few more times, even making some notes so as not to be totally dependent on the text.

We got an early start, Tevye and I, and except for an anxious moment when a gust of wind pushed us laterally across the road into the center line, we made it all the way to Pittsburgh intact and in time for a bowl of heavy barley soup and a thick corned-beef sandwich at Jack's Delicatessen in Squirrel Hill. For my taste, it was still the best place in town to get real European Jewish cooking, even if it had been taken over by Koreans after old Mrs. Jacobson died. I must confess that I can't tell the difference in the cooking anymore, although by now maybe I've just forgotten what her cooking was really like.

The Pittsburgh Jewish Center makes our Synagogue and Educational Center look like a shoe box. It's sort of a cross in appearance between an engineering school and a hotel. The lobby was marble, with a large rosewood reception desk and clusters of uncomfortable-looking chairs apparently designed for people with short backs. There were people with regular backs all over the place. As I looked at them, it came to me how true it was that Jews are a nation of many different types: there were tall blond women who looked like Scandinavians, swarthy Mediterraneans, black people, people who looked like they had come from Central America and even a few who looked like the stereotype of what some people take for Jewish, only to find that the person is a Swiss Catholic. There they all were, the whole mosaic, in jogging clothes, their leotards, carrying gym bags; there were even a few elderly people over in the corner.

My watch said seven-forty; I had twenty minutes to find Meeting Room B. I asked a tall black man wearing blue-and-white basketball trunks. He looked puzzled for a moment, then pointed me down a long corridor to the left. Just as I turned the corner into it, I was knocked against the wall by four angular women careening down the hall on silent roller skates. I had only a glimpse of bottoms crammed into shorts, long legs in motion and hair drifting back behind them before they were gone. I looked up the hall to make sure nothing else was coming, a mini-bus maybe, and picked up the scattered folio of my speech. Meeting Room B wasn't far down the hall. I timorously peeked in; the wings of my heart flapped against my chest as I saw a crowd of at least sixty gathered in a semicircle on padded chairs. They'll be comfortable at least, I thought. No one noticed me, no one introduced himself, so I just sat down in front waiting for the moderator. A few minutes passed, long minutes, before a middle-aged man with thin hair, thick glasses and a red face went to the rostrum. I thought it best to do the same just so he would know I was there. So I summoned my courage and introduced myself to him. He looked irritated, and without even reciprocating he said, "Please sit down, sir. The program is about to start."

"But you don't understand—"

"Please sit down so I can make the introduction."

I sat down. He must know what he's doing; at least he knows I'm here. I had to send them a photograph. He must have recognized me. He watched me sit down, then turned to the group and said, "We are pleased to have with us to-night a man of considerable reputation in the community" —that doesn't sound like me—"a graduate of Georgetown" —that's not me—"Father Boniface O'Leary, S.J., who will discuss the topic of his recent book, *Guilt and the Concept of Original Sin in the Catholic Church.*"

I got up and approached him, saying, "I had a lecture scheduled here tonight."

At the same time a delicate man in black was approaching from the other side of the circle. The moderator looked from one to the other of us. It was obvious who was Father O'Leary and who was not. He said to me with restrained hostility, "The other lecture must be in another room. Unless you want to hear Father O'Leary, a very interesting speaker, I would suggest that you go and find the other room."

He looked as if he wanted to say something else, but the time was passing and I had the vision of a restless crowd sitting in some other part of the building, a moderator looking at his watch and wondering whether the snow had delayed me. Feeling the sting of a hundred eyes probing my back, I left the room and closed the door behind me, already glancing down the corridor, resigned to try every door if need be until I found the right one. Inside the first room I found an underfed fiddler, a woman tootling a little tin flute and an old man playing an accordion and singing in a dialect of Hebrew that I'd never heard before; perhaps it was Sephardic. "Pardon me, there isn't supposed to be a lecture in here, is there, a lecture about Poland?"

"Poland? No, not on your life. We're the Kilkenny Caelie Band, we've got a concert in about an hour in here and I can tell you there'll be . . ." I didn't wait for the rest. In the next room several women in tight black body stockings were walking about or lying contorted on the floor as if in pain. What sounded like the space between two shortwave radio stations was blaring over a sound system. I didn't even ask. Panic welling up inside me, I hurried on to the next room. I opened the door a crack and was relieved to see a crowd of seated people. This had to be the place, I thought, but as the door opened further, I saw that someone was already speaking. A woman saw me and got up from her seat. Holding her finger to her lips, she gestured toward an empty chair on the aisle. When I just stood there, she approached me, looking irritated. The speaker was drawing a picture of a bird on the blackboard, and her eye drifted from me to the board.

"This isn't the lecture on Zamosc?"

"No, it's a visiting professor of linguistics from Cairo University, giving a talk on Egyptian hieroglyphics. It's very interesting. Please sit down. It's only just started," she whispered.

"I'm actually trying to find the lecture on the Polish Jewish community."

"I wouldn't know."

"It was supposed to be down the hall," I said, about to lose my power of speech.

Her eyes passed over my shoulder. "I think that's a schedule on the door."

I turned to the paper and was relieved to find that the fourth entry from the bottom was my lecture, in Room 236A. She had already returned to her seat. Lapsing into a fractured speech pattern, as I sometimes do when I am nervous, I asked, "Do you know where is Room 236A?"

"Down the hall, then left into the old building."

My watch said 8:07. They'd blame the weather. Certainly no one should even be impatient as yet. Jewish programs never start on time, I said to myself as I ran down the hall, came to the end, turned left and entered another time—a narrow hall lit by dim, incandescent hanging glass globes with faded red floor tile and wood doors, the varnish black with age. The change somehow calmed me; I felt more comfortable out of the fluorescent hospital glare. My head turned from side to side as I read the numbers. At last at the very end of the hall, I saw the door with "236A" painted in white letters at eye level. I flung the door open, only to face the blind indifference of thirty wooden folding chairs. The room was empty. I pulled my head back around the door and checked the number. It was the right one. Relief, anger and despondence were chasing one another through my head. I entered the room, if only to catch my breath. The room was not bright, and at first glance I hadn't seen the old couple seated at the back in the corner. They were small, although by the look of their clothes, age had shrunken them. They were sitting in the last row, leaning together like two old walls holding each other up. The man was wearing rounded metal spectacles of an almost antique appearance, his eyes were dark brown and his thin white hair was falling over his wrinkled forehead. The woman looked like an engraving of a Slavic *babushka*, her nose receded into, rather than protruded from, a potato. Well, I thought, it isn't exactly the Jewish community of Pittsburgh, but here at least are a couple of Old World Jews who want to share their memories. I spread my text on the lectern and began to talk, feeling about the way I would feel after a little sip of port in Nudelman's living room. Don't get the wrong impression. I wasn't miraculously converted into a Demosthenes. I was a little nervous all the way through.

By the looks of them, the old couple liked what I had said, for when I finally folded my text and looked up, they both smiled and nodded approvingly. I waited, expecting them to come up and say something, but they only nodded again and left the room to me and the chairs.

I sat down, feeling both fatigue and satisfaction. Maybe, I thought, maybe the Bolton congregation might like to hear it sometime when Rabbi Bing has laryngitis.

The door opened and the red-faced man from the first room came in.

"I'm very sorry," he said with an undertaker's tone of

voice. "I thought that you were just an eccentric come to take in the lecture. The photo exhibit about Zamosc finished last week. With all the activity, I guess—"

"Don't worry about it."

"The staff had to change the rooms at the last minute, and I guess nobody in the office thought to call you."

"No harm done. Not many people were interested, anyhow."

"How many came? Twenty or thirty at least?"

"Not quite that many. In fact just two. But they made up in quality what they lacked in quantity," I said bravely, putting on a smile.

"Not the old couple I just passed in the hall?"

"Sounds like a pretty good description of the crowd," I said.

He just shook his head, apparently undecided whether to be saddened or amused.

"They come here often. He's the custodian of the Catholic Church down the street. A sweet couple."

"It seemed like they enjoyed the speech."

"You never know with them. I don't think that they speak twenty words of English."

"Oh, I know that," I said. "The speech was in Polish."

"But I think they speak Slovak."

"That was no problem. I did a simultaneous translation."

I left him looking as though he had swallowed a fly. Looking both ways down the hall so as to avoid the minibuses, bicycles and roller skaters, I walked as fast as I could down the long corridor, past the Irish band and the hieroglyphics professor, past the contortionists listening to the static and the guilty priest and into the lobby, where the three elderly folks were playing cards in the corner, then out the automatic door, across the snowbound parking lot to where I had left Tevye. The familiar door lock clicked, Tevye coughed once or twice and started, his warm instrument lights began to glow. I eased the car into first gear, thinking, How good it will be to get back to Bolton. One thing was certain, I had overcome my fear of public speaking.

I thought that that was the end of it, at least until I got another letter from Pittsburgh, this one in a quavery vertical European script. The letter follows:

Dear Mr. Traig:

We liked very much your speech about Zamosc, Poland. We never been there but are interested since we had with us during German occupation of our country, a child which became like a daughter to us, a little Jewish girl from Zamosc. Right after war she was taken to Palestine by Jewish refugee organization and live there to this day on a kibuts with her husband and children. She still write to us and we still write to her. We go to Jewish Center and find out much about Israel, her home. Now we tell her we know some about where she born. If you come again to Pittsburgh we invite you to have tea and cake. Sorry our English not too good. It is hard for old people to learn well new language.

Anton Zarich

Their English was good enough for me.

21.
A Game of Chess

By coincidence, the next week after receiving the news
that I had to literally settle in Israel in order to get the
money, I had been invited to dinner at Reuven and Dalia's.
Reuven had come back to Bolton after his father's—my
friend Mark's—death to take over the family business—his
mother wasn't fit to run it—and it was the kind of old-
fashioned department store in a steelworkers' neighborhood that produced a good income for the family but, due
to its location and somewhat antiquated appearance, would
not have brought much more than its liquidation value, at
least that's what Reuven told me. His wife, Dalia, a Polish-
looking young woman with straw-blond hair and narrow
blue eyes, wasn't very happy about leaving Israel and her
family, and for that matter Reuven had a hard time with it
himself. After all, had he wanted to remain in Bolton he

wouldn't have gone to live in Israel in the first place. It was natural for him to leave home, to make a new life for himself with his own values. It must have been hard for him to return, but they seemed happy enough living with their young son in Reuven's parents' large and comfortable home, at least three times the size of their apartment in Haifa, and enjoying the mixed blessing of Mark's wife, Hannah, who provided them with both the freedom of a built-in nanny and the interference of a mother-in-law, at least part of the time. Hannah spent half the year in the family condominium somewhere in Florida.

I must say that the news had immobilized me for the rest of that day and the next day. People asked me questions and I usually responded after a delay to allow for the penetration of the thought through the fog that had closed off my mind. When it finally began to disperse, I was left with a confusion of scenes ranging from stereotyped images of sandy beaches, flat-roofed Mediterranean houses, robed Arabs leading donkeys, casually dressed soldiers with machine guns slung over their shoulders, dense groves of lemon trees, healthy-looking youth hoeing weeds in shorts —in short a composite of all the programs, posters, slide shows and photographs that I'd ever seen about Israel. And somewhere in that confusing collage was me, wearing sandals, khaki pants, my face tanned and wrinkled, my hair steely gray, wandering from place to place, essentially not knowing what to do with myself. For even in the place of the Jews I saw myself as the outsider.

It was not that I had decided to leave Bolton, far from it. I couldn't bring myself to do that, but I couldn't see myself just turning my back on seventy-five thousand dollars, either. There I was, bumping into things, picking up a pencil and forgetting why.

In my present state of mind Reuven and Dalia were the

only two people in town who I could really talk with openly about my dilemma, they having both lived there and come here.

One thing was certain, if Dalia's cooking was a fair example I was sure to suffer gastronomically by the move. Not that there was anything bad about the food, I thought, pushing my plate away from me and wiping my mouth on the paper napkin; it's just that it lacks that indefinable component *tam*, a Yiddish word that means something like taste.

"Some tea, Mendel?" Dalia's high melodic voice brought me out of my reflection.

"Mmm? Yes, some tea please, no sugar."

"You sure are quiet tonight, Mendel," said Reuven.

I hadn't had the courage to mention it, even to him as yet. Here goes, I thought. No more shally-shillying. I swallowed and said, "How do you think that"—I pause for a deep breath—"I"—my throat constricted—"would like Israel?"

Reuven's cheeks wrinkled quizzically and he pulled on the red bristles of his mustache (he does that when he is perplexed).

"Are you thinking of taking a trip to Israel to see your cousin?" Then after a moment he added, incredulity in his voice, "You're not thinking of living there, now that you've got this money coming?" A pause, then a weak, "Are you?" Reuven's brow was raised, crushing his freckles.

"No, of course not," I blurted. "But after all, why not? It's as much my country as here."

Reuven looked distracted for a moment; he fumbled in his pocket for a pack of cigarettes, drew one out, lit it, exhaled and appraised me from behind the screen of smoke.

"Read me a story, *Abba*." Gavriel came to the dining room dressed in red fuzzy pajamas with feet.

"Dalia, has he made pee-pee?" Reuven called into the kitchen.

"*Ken*." They speak a mixture of Hebrew and English in the house for the sake of Gavriel, whom they want to be bilingual. "Excuse me, Mendel. I'll just get Gavriel to bed and be right back. Why don't you set up the chessboard in the meantime? You know where it is."

He returned after about ten minutes to find me sitting at the table, my teacup half-full in front of me.

"You don't feel like some chess tonight?" he asked, sitting down across from me.

"Reuven," Dalia called from the kitchen. "*Hoo yashen?*"

"*Mekevan she ken,*" he replied.

"Maybe later. I'm having trouble concentrating. You would take me to the tailors."

"You mean the cleaners," he said with an indulgent grin, then, jumping up, he added, "I've got something stuck in my teeth. Be right back."

And from the kitchen: "Mendel, you want a pear?"

"*Ken,*" I said, tentatively trying out the language.

"Oh, so you are speaking Hebrew now?" she said, bringing me a pear already cut into quarters.

"Listen, Dalia, let me ask you something. Do you think I would like spending some time in Israel? I mean, more than a vacation; even two or three years?"

She raised her eyebrows in a "Who knows?" expression and said, "That depends."

"On what?"

"On many things." Her undulating voice finished on a minor key still up in the air. "Why, Mendel? You want to move to Israel? All the best," she said. Reuven returned and sat down.

"You think someone like me would be content there?"

"For a while," she said. "Many people go. Many people leave. It is a hard country, you know. Not like here."

"So what are you saying, Mendel? You want to go live

with your cousin?" asked Reuven, taking out another cigarette.

"Reuven, enough cigarettes already! You want cancer?"

He looked at Dalia, sighed and put the cigarette back in the pack.

"Not exactly," I replied. "I have been told that I must live in Israel to get the money." At that a smile flickered across his face and was gone.

"You wouldn't have to stay if you didn't like it."

"But that's the question. You have known me all of your life. You also knew Israel. I'm too old for coming and going. I've had enough of that in my life. Obviously I'm not thinking seriously of it. This is my home, but . . ."

"I understand."

"So?"

He shrugged. "I really can't say. The people are different than they are here. I think that you would meet people that you liked. After all, your cousin is somebody there. He would get you settled in and you'd probably do fine. And with the money and your simple style of living, you'd get along." He paused. I looked at him, telling him I wanted to hear more. He tossed his head as though he was having a conversation with himself, then he said, "And that's it." He looked at me for a moment, then asked, "Have you ever met anyone from Israel? Do you know anyone there, besides your cousin, I mean?"

"Not really. I've met a few people at meetings but never gotten to know them. Then, of course, there are the Independence Day speakers that they send us from Pittsburgh; all young students except for the Arab Deputy Minister."

He looked at me in disbelief. "They sent you an Arab?"

"Yes. Last year, in fact. You were still in Israel."

"How about that?"

"I'll tell you the story sometime, but I'm surprised your

mother never mentioned it." We sat quietly and I fiddled with my teaspoon, then looked at him. "Are you sorry you left?"

Reuven looked up at Dalia. She turned and went into the kitchen. "Yes and no," he said. "But neither the yes nor the no would be much help to you. I will say this, Mendel. If my father were living and alone, I would say to him that—that it's easier for a younger person to move to a new country. Oh, I saw lots of people in their middle age who had come there, but it seemed more like they *had* to. There was something bad about where they had come from that made them want to move. I guess what I'm saying is that I can't be of much help to you. I can answer specific questions about the—well, the cost of living, the bus service, the climate, even neighborhoods, but more than that . . ."

"Yes. I just thought I'd mention it. Having all that money is tantalizing. And the thought of being near my cousin."

With an apprehensive glance at the kitchen door, he quickly took out a cigarette and lit it. "I'm no philosopher, not like my father, but it seems to me that we have in life a lot of choices to make. But . . . when we look back on many of them, we see that it really might not have made a lot of difference which way we turned. What I mean is I'm just not that expressive . . ."

"No, you are, Reuven, go on."

"When you have a really hard choice to make, that means that there are enough advantages and disadvantges to either choice so that A, you'll never know if what you did was the right thing to do because you'll never know what would have happened if you'd done the other instead."

"And B?"

"B? I guess there is no B. And that's the point. When you make a choice you wipe out the other possibility." He inhaled, blew the smoke out and watched it diffuse in the soft yellow light of the crystal chandelier. "Sure you don't want a game of chess? Just a quickie?"

With him there was no such thing as a "quickie," but as it was still early, I said "Sure." As he went for the chess set, I thought, He wasn't much help. I know what Mark, his father, would have said in a minute: "Don't go, stay here." But he wasn't here to say it, he was gone.

Not that it matters, but Mark, I mean Reuven, wore me down and beat me that night, and he made me tell him about the Independence Day speaker before I left, on top of it.

22.
The Independence Day Speaker

For a Jew Israel is the Jewish state, just as for a Frenchman France is the French state. Which is not to say that there aren't others who don't happen to be Jews living there. It's just that we don't think of them as being part of the *state*. Part of the place, yes, and they are welcome; but after all, as Finkelstein would say, "Do you put a Baptist, no matter how good a person he is, on the board of the synagogue?" So it came as a shock when Nudelman got the letter telling him that the UJA was sending an Arab to speak at the Israeli Independence Day celebration.

I was the first to see the letter, as I open the mail and put it in the appropriate boxes in the hall outside the library. I enjoy doing it. I'm a little nosy and find out what's happening that way. Like the postmaster of a village. I was surprised when I read the letter—but not as surprised as

Nudelman was when I hand-delivered it to him, eager for his reaction. He did not disappoint. It was as though someone had just stolen his color television set. When he recovered he smiled conspiratorially and said, "Get on the extension, I'm going to call Finkelstein."

"Did you hear the news?" Nudelman said.

"What news?" answered Finkelstein irritably. "I missed the seven o'clock news and the newspaper was so soaked by the rain that I couldn't read a word. So don't ask me about the news," he continued, clearing his throat.

"No, I mean the letter we received from the UJA. They are sending us an Arab to speak at our Israeli Independence Day celebration."

"An Arab? They've run out of Jews? Nudelman, you must be joking. I know we're a small, unimportant community, but it could at least have been one of these Israeli students at Pitt."

The Program Committee met the next night in special session at the Abrams' house. Harry and Dora Abrams frequently hosted meetings, mostly because Dora baked the best cakes in town. If you had to go to as many meetings as Nudelman, you would appreciate the reward of a superlative pastry after hours of endless repetitive discussions.

Nudelman was sitting in the cramped living room, inhaling the fragrance of buttery pastry and cinnamon and wondering how soon Dora would produce the *kuchen*, not till after nine probably. Heaven forbid, the evening might be over at eight-thirty, and then what? But he knew he could count on Henry Rosenzweig's verbosity to prolong it. If I had only a nickel for every word Henry speaks tonight, I'd make a tidy profit on the meeting, Nudelman concluded. His glance turned to Linda Joyce, who never listened to what the others were saying and repeated the same ideas in a slightly negative way. No, there would be no hazard of this meeting breaking up before the cinnamon *kuchen*. Not a chance.

No one objected to hearing an Arab speak about Israel, but this was the wrong occasion! As Harry Abrams put it, "It's like the Pittsburgh Pirates sending over one of the Chicago Cubs to speak at the Booster Club banquet."

"Not exactly," said Linda Joyce. "After all, he is an Israeli and a poet and a *doctor* and Deputy Minister of Transportation."

Henry Rosenzweig, it turned out, had laryngitis, and his usual flood of words was reduced to a muddy trickle. After a circuitous discussion they decided not to request an alternative speaker; if the UJA thought it wise to send an Arab, they must have a good reason.

"It's not for us to complicate their decision by interfering in their policies," said Henry. "Not unless we are willing to move to Israel ourselves, at least." Nudelman found this reasonable, while not exactly understanding the logic of it. He was starting to think that having an Arab speaker would be a good idea as he recalled the tedious bore they had sent last year, a chicken farmer who talked about chickens in broken English. Deputy Minister of Transportation: an important person. "If he's good enough to be Deputy Minister of Transportation," Nudelman said out loud, "he must be okay. After all, there are probably a lot of qualified Jews who could have filled the job, and an Arab would have to be a cut better to get the job, wouldn't he?"

"Not necessarily," Linda Joyce interrupted; she was always interrupting, and she fixed her unblinking sparrow stare on him. "He could be the token Arab in the government. What does a doctor know about transportation, after all?"

Henry nodded and whispered, "I heard somewhere that

the drivers are crazy in Israel. The highways are like a war zone. Maybe they put an Arab in so they could blame him for the carnage."

Nudelman leaned forward in his chair as the cinnamon *kuchen,* brown, flaky and shining with butter, was brought into the room. He reached for the biggest piece, took a bite and nodded his approval to an expectant Dora. Now the meeting could conclude, so Nudelman outlined, in a few words between bites, a simple plan for the evening: dinner at the Rosenzweigs for a few couples, well chosen, including himself and the rabbi, of course, followed by the speech at the general meeting and no protest to the UJA.

Everything had been arranged—or so I thought—until several nights before the dinner, when I got a call from Rosenzweig. I could tell right away from his sweet tone that he wanted something of me. I was put on my guard quite correctly, for he soon came to the point. The speaker's plane was arriving too late to make bus connections. Would I please pick him up and bring him with me to the dinner? Now, this was news; until then I had not been invited to the dinner; but I suppose it just wasn't in him to ask me to play driver and stay up half the night taking the speaker back to the airport without some reward. Since my old Chevy doesn't care much for the open highway, the prospect of dinner with the elite of the community did not move me to accept the offer. When I said no, it seemed as though Rosenzweig had fallen off a cliff. He must have asked just about everyone in town who could drive before he got around to me.

"*Pleeeeease,* Mendel," he said, drawing out the word. "Please. The community is counting on you. I'd love to do it myself, but I've got to help with the dinner and play host with the early guests, and Nudelman's bursitis is acting up. Finkelstein would kill them both, it's got to be you, I've asked . . ."

I had to stop him; I had to agree just to stop him. So there we were, Tevye and I, Tevye and I would go and come four times, returning long after we both should be asleep. Yes, I said. I'll do it. Rosenzweig climbed back up the cliff, said, "Thanks so much Mendel," and hung up.

Tevye wouldn't start at first, but once he gets going he's perfectly reliable, and the trip from the airport was more pleasant than I had imagined. Al Zaki and I hit it off from the beginning, he being a poet and I a writer of sorts and an avid reader, so we discussed poetry the whole distance and I was hardly aware that all the while Tevye the Chevy was diligently plodding home at a leisurely fifty miles per hour.

The dinner guests looked anxious, expectant and a little tipsy when we arrived. Rosenzweig had been pouring extra-strong drinks to calm those who found dining with an Arab member of the Israeli government a tense experience. We entered to find the guests gathered in a semicircle, all eyes fixed on Al Zaki. He was a tall man, over six feet; his face was brown, the color of olive wood, and rough; thin skin was drawn tightly over sharp cheekbones; he had a strong jaw and a knife-edged aquiline nose. His hair was black with no sign of gray, although he was clearly in his forties. He was wearing a black suit and was a little stoop-shoul-dered. Nodding politely, he went around the room shaking hands and addressing a kind word to each in a soft voice and tolerable English. It was apparent by the wide eyes that several of the women found him not a little charming and attractive.

Never had a dinner party been assembled with greater care in Bolton. Al Zaki sat at the long Chippendale table laden with crystal goblets filled with ice water, Spode china, a delicate floral pattern and a waxen floral centerpiece. On one side was the hostess, Harriet, a sharp wit, well-read and well-traveled; on the other the rabbi; across the table the assistant principal of the high school and his wife, an attractive social worker. There was even Dr. Zucker, an internist who knew nothing about Israel but was Bolton's only resident Harvard graduate.

Dr. Zucker began the conversation: "Has the Zipfer technique for diagnosing cancer of the cervix been introduced yet in Israel, Dr. Al Zaki? I was reading in the medical journal—"

"Cy!" his wife, Miriam, interrupted, "the Deputy Minister didn't come here to discuss medicine." She shook her head apologetically and said, "That's all he talks about."

"I'm sure your patients appreciate your zeal, Dr. Zucker." Zucker nodded eagerly and was about to continue the conversation when Al Zaki added, "But I'm sorry to say that I have grown quite out of practice. You see, my political life in the Knesset has so completely taken over and I have no time to practice."

Disappointed, Zucker leaned over to his wife and whispered, "Is the Knesset their legislature?" She nodded, looking apprehensively at the guest to be sure he hadn't overheard and understood the level of her husband's ignorance, but Al Zaki was engaged in a conversation with Nudelman, who had asked, "Are you an observant Jew?" to which Al Zaki replied without the slightest trace of discomposure, "I was raised a Moslem, but I don't practice it."

"I had the impression that the Moslems were very observant," said Harriet.

"The same as Jews in Israel, I suspect. Most Jews have no formal observances in their life, especially the ones on the *kibbutzim*," said Rosenzweig, who had recovered from his laryngitis.

"How can they think of themselves as Jews if they don't practice their religion?" asked Sarah Nudelman.

"They see themselves as Israelis. They don't define their identity by their religious, religious—I can't think of the word . . . Rabbi, can you help me?" and Al Zaki rolled off a sentence in Hebrew that made the rabbi writhe.

"I'm sorry, Doctor, but my modern Hebrew isn't quite as fluent as yours," Rabbi Bing said, his cheeks flushing.

"Ah, but your classical Hebrew is better than mine. I've thought of the word, 'affiliation,' religious affiliation."

"Then aren't they throwing the baby out with the bath water?" asked Harriet. "Why a Jewish state if they don't want to live as Jews?"

"Come now, Harriet, we all know why we needed the Jewish state," intoned Rosenzweig, drawing his lips back. "We certainly don't need to get that information from Dr. Al Zaki."

Nudelman then asked Al Zaki for his opinion of Menachem Begin, whom he had mistakenly thought to be the leader of Al Zaki's party.

Singer, the assistant principal, looked scornfully at Nudelman and said, "Begin is the head of the Likud. Dr. Al Zaki's party is on the other side of the Knesset."

Nudelman recoiled momentarily, thinking to himself, Not only did they send an Arab but a Communist to boot?

Al Zaki looked around the table. "You seem surprised. Didn't they tell you I was a socialist, just like the *kibbutzim*?"

"I knew the *kibbutzim* were communal," said Rosenzweig, "but I didn't know they were all socialists."

"The food is excellent, Mrs. Rosenzweig," said Al Zaki.

"And how thoughtful of you to have the Middle Eastern salads."

With a lull in the conversation, Singer said, "Forgive me if I ask this question, Doctor. I wasn't going to ask you, but I must." He ran his hand through his head of unruly black hair. "What I want to ask is, Don't your fellow Arabs think you a traitor, excuse the word, for serving in the Israeli government?"

"How can you ask such a question?" interposed Rosenzweig sternly, having doubted the propriety of inviting the teacher in the first place. Al Zaki raised his hand slightly, focused a kindly eye on the teacher and said, "No, no, that's a very good question. I can answer it."

He paused, and with the agility of a basketball player, Rosenzweig intervened with, "The Israeli government has many Arabs in the Knesset and in ministerial positions. It is, after all, an integrated society and one in which Arabs have the same rights as Jews. Isn't that so, Doctor?"

Dr. Zucker started from his reverie and said, "What? Oh, I really don't know."

"Shut up, Cy," said Miriam. "He was addressing Dr. Al Zaki."

Al Zaki nodded and with a smile of circumspect politeness replied, "You have answered for me, Mr. Rosenzweig. You are well-read on the subject."

"Thank you, Doctor. I try to keep up on things, with the *Jerusalem Post* weekly overseas edition. I speak on the subject occasionally." Silence settled over the table like a bank of fog and remained until Rosenzweig said, "Well, Doctor, if we keep badgering you with difficult questions, you'll have no energy left for your speech. Besides, we haven't given you a chance to finish your dinner, we've had you talking so much."

As a rule, most of the community turned out for the

celebration of Israel's independence, although it must be said they came for different reasons: some for the Israeli dancing by the synagogue youth group, others for the reasonable facsimile of a *falafel* that the women's group served with grapefruit juice, while some came out of curiosity. What, after all, was a celebration of Israel's independence without a real live Israeli in some capacity or other?

This particular year, however, there was grapefruit juice but no *falafel*, since the woman who made them was in Israel visiting her daughter. The leading dancer had broken a bone in his foot playing basketball, and the dancing would not be up to par. So the Arab Israeli, or the Israeli Arab, was the big attraction.

It was ten past the hour and the crowd was already growing restless when the guests from the dinner party, feeling conspicuous and self-important, entered the hall from the rear and advanced down the aisle like a wedding party. And like guests at a wedding, all necks craned for a look at the speaker. Al Zaki moved calmly down the aisle with all the self-assurance of the president of the congregation. An audible murmur ran through the room as he took his seat and acknowledged the crowd with a traveling glance.

Rosenzweig went right to the podium and began his introduction. A heavy speaker, he clung to his words like a miser before dropping them like nondescript rocks on the heads of his audience. A lawyer's summation is limited only by the patience of the judge, and it was in the spirit of summation that Rosenzweig embarked on a prolonged exposition of the history of relations between Arab and Jew from the "salad days" of Andalusia to the "mosaic of Alexandria"—all of this in the guise of introducing the speaker.

At last, after about twenty minutes, Nudelman walked up to the rostrum and handed him a note. Creases furrowing his leonine face, he announced in a tense voice, "There's been a bomb threat. We must clear the hall calmly but quickly." With panic in his voice, he admonished the crowd, "Don't panic, just leave row by row," but in his haste to leave himself, he neglected to tell them which row was to leave first. The group rose as one and choked the aisles.

Al Zaki remained seated until the crowd had thinned before joining Rosenzweig outside the building. "How could you remain so calm?" Rosenzweig asked him.

"Such threats are almost always false. They are intended to break up a meeting. Someone who wants to plant a bomb in a crowd doesn't give warnings. The bomb is the warning," replied Al Zaki in a steady voice.

Rosenzweig shifted his eyes toward the crowd standing in front of the building in conversational groupings. Some were talking with animation, others were looking expectantly at the building. He turned back to Al Zaki with a look of embarrassment, a look of someone whose collar is too tight, and said, "My apologies to you, Doctor. You came all the way down here from Pittsburgh and didn't even get a chance to speak."

Al Zaki smiled reassuringly and replied, "No matter, I'm not much of a speaker. And this sort of thing happens occasionally back home."

"Still, I'm afraid my introduction got a little drawn out."

"It was very interesting, very educational."

Rosenzweig looked around expectantly as the crowd began to disperse in twos and threes. "I wonder why the police haven't arrived as yet?"

"Perhaps they have other more pressing matters."

"No, not in Bolton, Doctor. Nothing ever happens more pressing than a bomb scare. Nudelman," he called out, "why haven't the police arrived?"

Nudelman approached them, looking at his watch. "I don't know. Maybe they don't know what to do."

"Well, if the place blows up before they get here, they'll hear about it," Rosenzweig said indignantly.

Al Zaki said to Rosenzweig, "Thank you for your hospitality. I hope I can reciprocate when you are in Israel. If you come, perhaps we can arrange a meeting for you."

Nudelman nodded. "Then *you* can make the introductions."

As we left town in the reluctant Tevye, Al Zaki turned to me and said, "I'm surprised the police weren't there when we left."

"Who knows, maybe they were never informed."

He pondered my answer before asking, "Do you have any idea who might have done it?"

"Not really. But if you want my honest opinion, Dr. Al Zaki, it was a member of the audience who saw it as the only way to stop Rosenzweig."

Al Zaki laughed quietly and we resumed our discussion of poetry. Sometime later he sent me a book of his work, which had been translated into Hebrew.

23.

Refugees

It was cruel of the board to put me on the Committee on Refugees and inhumane of them to make me chairman, especially when I was thinking about becoming one, of sorts. But this they did with the charge that the community would undertake to raise enough money to sponsor *one* family. I read a little note from Finkelstein informing me, and shook my head sadly. They must have thought it an honor for me. They didn't know that it made me feel like the chicken walking around the farmyard helping the farmer decide which of my fellow birds should be taken to market. Finkelstein said to me, "Mendel, we thought about it and came to the conclusion that of all of us you were the natural choice."

I said to him, "Finkelstein, selecting one family is like condemning all of the rest of them."

He put his hand on my arm and said, affection spreading across his creased face (Finkelstein had more creases on his face than the Bolton city map has streets; it wasn't that he was old, he was made that way), he said, "Mendel, it's not the boat people, it's the Soviet Jewry. Don't feel so bad. If we don't take them, some other community will, and, after all, if they don't find a place here, there's always Israel."

"That's the whole point. Somebody will take them. Understand, I feel for them as I do for the others, but they have a place to go, while the others are drowning, dying in crowded, leaky boats, starving—"

"Mendel, Mendel, you sometimes talk as if you had made the world."

"Not me. But since I'm staying for a little while, I thought I'd like to fix the place up any way I can."

"Mendel, all we can do is what we can do. We must leave some of the good works to other people, other generations."

"Do we ever know when we've done enough, Finkelstein? Can we sit back and congratulate ourselves and say, 'Aren't we good because we're going to make a place in our town for a family of refuseniks?' "

"Mendel."

"That's four Mendels already. We both know my name."

"You're agitated. I'll call you later, and if it's too much for you, this committee, I know Nudelman and the rest of them will understand . . . I'm sure Rosenzweig would be glad—"

"Don't give it to Rosenzweig, whatever you do," I blurted out. "We'd end up with three more lawyers."

"The third member of the family will be a child."

"So he can practice in juvenile court."

"Mendel, you know nothing about the law."

"Only that it's like a taxi on a rainy day—when you most need it, it's unavailable."

Finkelstein started clearing his throat and I told him I had an appointment with the custodian (he'd been doing a sloppy job, cigarette butts in unseemly places), so Finkelstein gave me another pat on the shoulder and we parted.

I went and talked to the custodian, a retired steelworker with an occasional drinking problem. He promised that he would do better, and by that time I was resigned to writing letters and talking on the telephone to officials and representatives of the refugee relief agencies to find a suitable family for Bolton. Obviously it had to be people who could earn a living in Bolton, so we couldn't have, for example, a mining engineer—there are no mines in Bolton. Nor could we have a professor of history, for there are no universities in Bolton, either. We do have a pretty good community college, so a teacher would do, assuming he or she spoke fluent English. Then there was the matter of housing; a lot of details, but the big detail was finding the family, and that proved to be the hardest. When I announced to the committee that I couldn't find a suitable family, Nudelman shook his head in disbelief. "That can't be. That simply can't be."

"I didn't say there weren't families. I said suitable families. There is one family with six children, from Georgia."

"Georgia?" said Finkelstein. "Stalin came from there."

"Yes, but I'm sure they're not related."

"Mendel," said Finkelstein.

"The head of the family is a shoemaker. The only shoemaker in town, Mr. Baltucci, is eighty-three years old and has arthritis."

"He's had a pair of my shoes for two weeks now," said Dr. Zucker.

"Bolton could use a shoemaker. Nobody wants to do

that kind of work anymore," I said. "I went down to talk to Mr. Baltucci. He told me he's been trying to get an apprentice for two years."

"Six children is a lot for a small community like ours," said Linda Joyce.

"I thought you'd feel that way. And one of them has an orthopedic problem, according to the report."

"Really?" said Dr. Zucker, his interest waxing. "Was there a diagnosis in the report?"

"No, there was no diagnosis."

"Too bad," he said. Obviously disappointed, he dropped his head and began riffling through the pages of a medical journal that he had brought with him.

"Seven more Jews in town would be good for the community," I said. "Children to fill up the Sabbath School, more *Bar Mitzvas*. Who knows, some of them might even stay here, get married, raise children here."

Linda Joyce nodded and said, "Mendel has a point. The rate of attrition among the youth is almost a hundred percent." That was the first time I had ever heard her agree with something said in a meeting.

"If they all grew up and stayed, it would change the character of the community. They would be a community within a community," said Finkelstein.

Nudelman shook his head. "Give them twenty years and they'd all be good Boltonians. The big question is whether we can support them. Although a shoemaker ought to be able to support his family . . . given the need."

"You never know. Maybe in Russia they don't fix shoes the same way they do here," said Finkelstein, clearing his throat. "We might have to send him to shoemakers school."

By the time the committee got around to taking the process a step further, the shoemaker had decided to move to Omaha, Nebraska, where apparently there was an even greater demand for his trade. And to make matters worse none of the newcomers, it seemed, wanted to be the only foreigners in the community. It would be better, the representative of the agency told me on the phone, if there were at least a few other families in the community with whom they could share the difficulties of adjusting to our society. I told him that there were still quite a few older people who were fluent in Russian, although, I had to admit, the Jewish community had little or no contact with them, as they were the parents of steelworkers and of the Russian Orthodox faith. "We'll keep you on the list," the official said. I reported all of this to the committee and they had a mixed reaction to it.

"It's like trying to adopt a Jewish baby," said Nudelman. "Thank God there's more demand than supply."

"It's too bad. It would have been nice to have found a shoemaker," said Rosenzweig, looking at his shoes. "Call them again, Mendel, and ask if there are any secretaries. Mine just got married and moved to Beaver Falls. Tell them I'm willing to convert my office to Cyrillic script even, ha ha."

"Who would know the difference?" said Nudelman to all of the non-lawyers.

"What about a Vietnamese refugee?" I asked.

Nudelman smiled understandingly. "Mendel, it's just like you to say that. And you're right, of course, that no one wants them and there are so many. But don't you think the community would prefer a Soviet Jewish family?"

"The situation reminds me of the way it was for us," I said. "It would be a *mitzva*." I stopped and looked around the room, measuring the reaction. The way I had put it, I knew no one could oppose me, at least not to my face. There was silence as they all digested it, and I could see by their expressions that they understood.

"Of course, if we did that we wouldn't have them in the Jewish community," said Rosenzweig.

"What if—what if some of them were Jewish? After all, there used to be Chinese Jews," I said. "I read about their community in a book in our synagogue library . . . and there are Indian Jews," I added, building my case.

"Have you ever heard the story about the Jewish traveling salesman who went to Friday night services at the Chinese synagogue?"

"Later, Saul," said Nudelman to Finkelstein.

"It might be easier to find a shoemaker than a Vietnamese Jewish family," said Rosenzweig, wearing his most skeptical courtroom face.

Nudelman looked at me, his expression shifting from doubt to whimsy. "There's no harm in trying. After all, we couldn't do any worse than we have in finding a Soviet Jewish family." The vote was unanimous in favor of trying to find a Vietnamese Jewish family. Rosenzweig, who must have had a hole in his shoe, suggested that we should also ask for a shoemaker. I wasn't sure whether he meant a Jewish shoemaker or just a shoemaker, and no one at the meeting asked.

The necessary inquiries were made, without much hope, and were probably punched into some computer somewhere. I was sure that the computer would come up tilt. But I was startled a few weeks later to find that in fact a family had been located that one, was willing to come to Bolton; two, had only one child, a girl six years old; three, had one shoemaker, the man, twenty-eight years old; *and* four, was Jewish. I simply couldn't believe it. What did it matter if they spoke only a few words of English and some French? We would teach them.

That night the committee met right after dinner at Linda Joyce's house. I wasn't happy about that and neither was

Nudelman. All she ever served was instant coffee and Oreo cookies; her children would eat no other, she claimed.

What was the first question that was asked? It was Finkelstein, I think, who said, "They're not orthodox, are they? They wouldn't be very happy here if they were."

"I really don't know," I replied. And I had no time to find out because they arrived in an army truck no more than forty-eight hours after I phoned in the committee's willingness to sponsor them. I even had to sign for them—it was like receiving freight—but there they were, three small, thin, pleasant-looking young people with black hair, narrow eyes and small features, high cheekbones, not very Jewish-looking, but the sight of them brought with it such a wave of memories that I could just barely control my emotions. The man was smiling, nodding, glad to be here, his eyes said. The woman seemed shy and apprehensive, and as for the little girl, she was hanging on to her mother's skirt with one hand and clutching a stuffed doll with the other. I bent down to her level and smiled, and she overcame her shyness and smiled back. It's difficult for me to put into words my feelings at that moment. It was more than empathy, it bordered on the feeling that she was an extension of me and I of her. She was Mendel, alone, torn from his life, his family, and I was she, my arms around my mother, not knowing at the time that soon, in a matter of days, she would be taken away in a truck by cold men in uniform, and that I would never ever see her again.

I asked them if they spoke English. He nodded and said, "Little, little." Touching the man on the shoulder, I brought them inside to my apartment and served them some fried eggs, tea and some of Sarah Nudelman's cookies. I tested out their English, and although the man smiled and nodded, it was apparent that I wasn't getting through.

In anticipation of this problem, we had scoured the town

for someone who might speak Vietnamese. Fortunately there was someone, a new assistant librarian at the town library who was Chinese but who had been raised in Hanoi. While they ate I called the library, and he agreed to come right over. Then I called the committee, and Nudelman and Linda Joyce agreed to come over too.

It was after I had made the last call that I noticed the crucifix, barely a half an inch long, hanging on a silver chain around the woman's neck. Maybe they have mixed marriages in Vietnam too, I thought. After all, how many eligible Jewish girls could there be? Maybe none at all. The letter had said "Jewish," there was no mistaking that. Perhaps they wore it to avoid persecution. What if they weren't Jewish at all? What would the committee do now that they were here, signed, sealed and delivered? After all, it wasn't like a defective washing machine; there was no warranty. You can't just send people back because they don't meet specifications.

As I sat there smiling at them and thinking these thoughts, Nudelman, Joyce and the librarian all arrived within a few minutes of one another. I gave everyone some tea, brought in a few folding chairs and Mr. Chin the librarian began to find out something about Thrang Van Doc and his family. It turned out that he was in fact a shoemaker from a small town in the highlands, which is why he spoke no English and only a little French. At least that question was answered right. Then came the question of religion. I looked around at the committee and saw that I was not the only one to notice the cross.

"Are you Jewish?" Nudelman asked through Mr. Chin.

"Oh yes," came the reply. "Very certainly Jewish." Everyone relaxed.

"And your wife, is she Jewish too?" An anxious moment while the question passed into Vietnamese.

"Oh yes."

"Then why is she wearing a cross?"

"All Christians wear crosses."

"Then she's a Christian?"

"Oh yes."

"But you are not?"

"Me too."

Nudelman looked around at our troubled, perplexed faces. "At least they're half Jewish," he said with a wry smile. "What's going on?" He looked at me.

"Maybe it's an old Jewish community that didn't get the message that Christ wasn't the Messiah," I said. "After all, the Yemenite Jews had never heard of the Talmud."

"Or maybe he knows something that we don't know," said Nudelman. "You ask a question, Mendel."

So I did. "What do you call your religion?"

"Messianic Jew," he said through the translator. Then it came out. Some missionaries had visited the town where he lived, missionaries from an obscure sect based upon early Christian teachings. They were essentially Christians who celebrated both religions, believing that Christ was Messiah and Jewish. His family and some others were converted from Catholicism. He was both Jew and Christian. Yes, his family practices all Jewish holidays. To convince us (he saw the skepticism on our faces), he reached into the bundle which enclosed all of their belongings and produced a brightly colored silk shawl.

"What's that? Not a *tallis*," said Nudelman.

The man nodded. He recognized the word.

With that thought, everything stopped as if time was suddenly frozen. Nobody moved. Mr. Chin was waiting for the next question, the shoemaker stood watching us, the permanent smile on his face, the child looked at her doll, Nudelman seemed away on some thought. Then he looked up and a warm light was playing in his eyes as he went to the man, grasped his hand in both of his and said, "Welcome, you are welcome." The man turned expectantly to Mr. Chin and joy lit his face as he heard the translation. His wife looked up with the shyest smile and touched her fingers to her eyes. She turned her back to us for a moment before she took the child gently by the shoulder and said something to her in their language, something which made the girl look at us gratefully and say in English, "Thank you so much."

So the town of Bolton got its cobbler and Rosenzweig got his sole repaired and the congregation got a new family; but not quite, for we have to share them with the Pentecostal Church next door.

24.
Flight One

That same week it looked as though providence had arranged a trade: me for the refugees. My cousin sent another letter, a thick one with an airplane ticket on El Al, Flight 1, New York–Tel Aviv, departing on May 15 at 4:35 P.M. in about four months.

The letter read,

My dear cousin:

My friend at the reparations office called to tell me the news. I'm sure it must have surprised you. I know it must be hard for you even to think about moving here, let alone deciding to do it. I suspect, if I know you, that you will just think about it and think about it until it is too late because the money has gone back to the state and then you will simply put it behind you with a philosophical "It was meant to be." You know that I am not the same, which is why I left the ghetto to join the partisans in the forest and you stayed behind. I know that I can't make the decisions for you, but I can make it easier for you to decide. The ticket is intended to do that. Don't worry about the expense, you can pay me back or not, depending on how well you like it.

I have also taken the liberty of putting option money down on a nice studio apartment in an older stone building in a very nice district. It's walking distance from us, a quiet street with Jerusalem pines and even a view of the surrounding hills from one side. It's a corner apartment, so the circulation is good when it gets hot. A friend in the foreign office has been assigned indefinitely to the French embassy, and the place is too small for him in any event. It's a bargain at $27,000 at the going rate of exchange. Take a deep breath. I've even gotten a commitment of a job at an institute that does scientific translations. I know that you would like that sort of work, but if you didn't it would get you started at something and I'm sure we could find something else. The best thing about it is that you don't have to make an irrevocable commitment to Israel or Jerusalem. You can come as an immigrant, get set up, take an *ulpan*—that's a six-month course in Hebrew. If you stretch it to a year, you'll be reading the newspaper and talking politics even. If after two, even three years, you don't like us, the Israelis, the taxes (they are appallingly high), you don't like me or my family, you don't like the weather (too hot *and* too cold), whatever, you sell the apartment and return to Pennsylvania (you still haven't told me how far it is from Chicago).

Now, don't go resenting what I've done. If you don't like it, you have only to return the ticket. The apartment I will have no trouble getting rid of for more than the option price. I've done this only because our lives are passing and I want to see you again while I can. Don't misunderstand me, I'm not ready to turn in my own ticket. It's only that I fear that we both have more years behind us than ahead of us and you never know.

Honestly, Mendel, now that you know that I am alive, how can you not come and spend even two years with me? Can you live your life without having once experienced Israel, and I don't mean from the narrow window of a tour bus. From what I understand of your life from your letters, you have nothing substantial to keep you from packing up and coming here for two years, even for good if you like it. You are not married, you have no children, no property that isn't portable, no work that can't be duplicated more or less. If you are worried about friends, I will guarantee you at least five people who you will enjoy meeting and being with; people of some depth and experience who have much to give. I don't want to scare you, but there are even eligible widows, lovely, intelligent people who you would enjoy being with, and who knows? it is never too late for such things. Mendel. Please think this over seriously before you make a decision, whatever it is. I can hardly wait to see your wrinkled *pisk*.

My first reaction to the letter was anxiety. Resentment followed. Then I read it again and experienced a surprising exhilaration. So I said to myself, Just what do you have to lose? That sentiment lasted for about five minutes before, like a teeter-totter, my mind was asking me how I could possibly leave Bolton. It's amazing, I was already taking for granted what I had been yearning for, a connection to my family.

This went on and on and on. It was worse than a toothache. My cousin had shrewdly concluded that by creating alternative conditions of security for me in Jerusalem, he would draw me toward him.

I decided to proceed one step at a time: to ask the board if they would consider giving me a two-year leave of absence without pay. When I asked Nudelman if he would bring it up with the board, he passed right over it as if he hadn't heard what I said.

"Listen, Mendel, have you hired the orchestra yet for the

Purim dance? Somebody gave me the name of this wonderful new band from Pittsburgh. Oh, and listen, before I forget I've got an interesting story for you, for your collection. I'll tell you about it the next time we get together. In fact, why don't you come over for dinner tomorrow night? You haven't been over for a few weeks. We miss you."

"Nudelman, I asked you if you could discuss with the board a leave of absence to go to Israel."

"To visit your cousin? No problem. I'll raise it at the meeting tomorrow night. Why only two weeks, though? It's silly to spend all that money for such a short time. Why not go for a whole month?"

"I didn't say two weeks, I said two years."

"Two years!"

"I might like to see what it's like there," I said.

"That's what they all say when they invest in a condominium in Florida, Mendel."

"It's not the same. I'm not retiring. I haven't taken off more than a week a year for twenty years. Consider it an accumulated vacation without pay or something like that."

"If you must go, so just go for a few months; after all, it's a small country, how much is there to see?"

"Nudelman, I haven't decided yet. I just want to know how the board would feel about it. My bags aren't packed. I don't even have a big suitcase, just the one I take to New York to the book show every year."

That seemed to reassure him, for he said more calmly, "I can't argue with that. Besides, I would be tempted to do the same thing, I suppose. What's the situation with the money? When is the transfer coming?"

"That's the whole problem." And I told him about the latest letter.

"So why didn't you tell me that in the first place?" he said. "There's a meeting of the board tonight, as you know. Do you want to raise it then?"

"Tell you what, Nudelman. I won't come tonight. You raise it and you can all talk about it freely without me listening in."

"That's not necessary."

"It will be better, believe me."

"As you wish."

"What time should I come to dinner?"

"Why ask? The usual time, whenever you feel."

Estelle Cantor is the other person who should know about this right now, I thought. I had an excuse to go out, I needed a new heavy-duty extension cord, so why not combine a trip to the hardware store with a visit?

I got to the Cantors' house just as Sidney was hurrying out the door. "Well, Mendel," he said, "come for your coffee klatsch, I see. You'll be disappointed, though. Estelle isn't baking this week. Dr. Zucker has me on a diet. Has the money come yet?"

"There are some complications with the money."

"Isn't there always complications with money?" he said, closing the door behind him, leaving me standing in the hall alone.

"Estelle?" I called. "It's me."

"What a pleasant surprise," she said, coming to the door of the kitchen at the far end of the hall. "I was just thinking about you, wondering why you hadn't called."

"Just too many things going on. I'll tell you about it all in a minute."

"Put your coat over there on the kitchen stool. It's getting colder," she said, looking out the window at the bare branches of the apple tree in the backyard. "Sorry I haven't baked. Dr. Zucker—"

"Yes, Sidney mentioned it on the way out. He must think I come here only to *shnor* the cake or something. He always mentions the cake when I see him."

"Sidney has trouble making small talk with people. You know that. He's all business and poker." She poured some coffee for us both and sat down, giving me a searching look. "So what's with the money? If you're looking for somebody to help you invest it, I've got just the person for you."

"I wish that were the only problem." With that introduction I pulled out the letter from my cousin and brought her up to date. She said nothing, but I thought I saw a note of regret in her eyes. "End of bulletin from Jerusalem," I said and picked up my cup.

"So what do you think you'll do?" she said quietly, looking down at the table.

"What should I do? What would you do? My mind is like a merry-go-round."

"No one can stand in anyone else's shoes, Mendel. I have a different life and it's hard for me to even imagine how you feel. But I suppose if I had no family here and just a few friends, I would . . . go. Yes, I'd give it a try," she said.

"My cousin makes it sound as if I could transplant myself and feel, well, at home—I hate to use that phrase—almost from the beginning, at least after I got comfortable with the language."

"Yes, it's strange, though, almost as if he'd planned it that way. As if he knew from the beginning that you would have to go there to live to get the money."

"Dumb of me not to think of that. But it's reasonable. He knows me. He knows that he would have to bring me along gradually. Probably if he had said it from the beginning I wouldn't even have bothered to apply. Yes, he's capable of that," I said, thinking of some of his childhood escapades. "He is capable of that."

"There's nothing bad about it, even if it is the case," she said. "I'd call it just intelligent planning. In his place I might have done the same." A spark flashed in her eyes.

"Yes, you probably would have. You and Ephie have that in common, you're both acters. Me, I'm a reacter. You take the bull by the seat. I let it chase me around the block and I slip into a narrow doorway."

"Don't knock yourself, Mendel. You're really a very organized person. You'd be missed, you know that, don't you?"

"Nothing I do that a few volunteers couldn't do. If you want to know the truth, my job's a sinecure."

"Come on now. Don't knock yourself. You know how hard it is to get people to volunteer for anything. Everybody's busy with family, making a living, whatever."

"You're making it harder for me, Estelle. You, Nudelman, Ephie, you all are."

"You should be pleased. Next thing you know, the board will want to raise your salary or something radical like that."

"Never." But she was right, for the next day when I went to Nudelman's house for dinner, he told me that they had in fact done just that and established a two-week vacation with pay on top of it. But the leave of absence was tabled.

"The board just wants some time to get used to it," Nudelman explained, and he was right. At the next board meeting they agreed to a two-year leave of absence and to hire a temporary replacement, which just shows how indispensable I really am. I had only to tell them my decision and they would begin looking. Hamlet, I said to myself as I got the news, for the first time in my life I really understand your character.

Nudelman took my hand in his after he told me. "We

hope you'll be back with us, Mendel. But if you don't you'd better keep a rollaway bed. Everyone on the board will come for a visit."

"Don't rush me into a decision, Nudelman. I haven't decided yet," I remonstrated. And I wasn't fooling him, I hadn't. There was no time for further discussion just then, as he had an appointment and I had to go down to Grover's to renew the floral contract for Ellen Yanow's grave. Sam, it seems, had let it lapse.

25.

Sam Yanow's Reflection

No one ever had such a funeral. Sam Yanow's wife, Ellen, was buried in flowers, at least it seemed so. There were so many that I had to rent a pickup truck to cart them away after they also died.

Her death had come without warning, like a summer electrical storm. Sam had no time to prepare himself for it, if it is possible to prepare for death. A cerebral vascular accident, they called it. The best way to die, he ultimately concluded, as abrupt a transition from life to death as an electrocution, and without the pain and awareness. She had gone to sleep one night, and gone to sleep, and gone to sleep, as if the record had stuck. He awoke to find her lying cold beside him, and he, too, almost died in that moment, that moment which had taken him by surprise like those snipers in the war. In that first searing awareness his own heart reached out to her and stopped too. Stopped and grew cold and could have remained so if some life-seeking force within him hadn't given it a squeeze and started it moving again.

For months after the funeral he must have come to her grave at least once a day with fresh flowers. I would see him there, just sitting on the ground, shoulders and head bent. I wanted to say something to him, but it looked like he most wanted to be alone with whatever part of her he still carried with him.

After six months Sam stopped coming as often, and like an old flower he, too, began to fade. Only his fading was more a gradual withdrawal, like the coming of night in the early summer, a fading away of the landscape into memory. What happened came as a surprise to all who knew him.

Withdrawal was not in Sam's character. He was even more than a participant.

He liked to have control of things when he could, and a lot of his energy had gone into getting what he wanted. Not that he was avaricious or a manipulator of men, and he was certainly not an opportunist. It was only that what he thought worthy he tried with his whole being to achieve. At sixty-five he had become a moderately successful builder of tract houses, small subdivisions, not more than twenty at a time, in Monoganessen County and in the surrounding counties as well. He had invested in commercial real estate and the stock market, had a comfortable home, unpretentious but reflecting an easy taste for good things. His children, a son and a daughter, were educated and independent. The daughter had attended Bryn Mawr College, married a stockbroker and lived in Philadelphia. His son also lived in Philadelphia, having entered a large law firm by way of Columbia. Like Sam, they were steady, success-oriented people, drawing strength and stability from a good family foundation. For Ellen, his wife, had been a loving, nurturing mother, and Sam, too, had made the children a high priority in his life, having always given more of himself than he had given material things.

Now with Ellen gone there was nothing more for him to do. He had built the business and sold it, his investments required little or no attention, and besides, he had grown bored with just sitting watching stock market transactions projected on the wall of the stockbroker's office. He was equally tired of pinochle, television, the movies, gold, the continuous round of dinners with friends; they weren't the same without Ellen, they just aroused painful memories. He had tried painting; he had no patience or talent. There was travel, but how many places could you go? Crossword puzzles had interested him for a time. In time even that grew tedious.

Sam was not the kind to sit around and feel sorry for himself, but the longer he sat around in his comfortable paneled den measuring time by the ticking of the antique regulator pendulum clock and the mountain of gray ash from his favorite Havana cigars, the longer he sat there letting *The Wall Street Journal, Business Week* and *Time* pile up beside his leather armchair, the more he began to feel that it was not himself but the world that he felt sorry for. After all, he reasoned, I'm still fairly healthy; of course, my hair is thinning, my eyes don't focus just like they used to, but bifocals take care of that. I tire more easily, I don't have the strength that I used to have, but the doctor says my heart is strong and my mind and memory are good. But the world, the world is different.

Sam had taken to sleeping later in the morning and reading late into the night, an antidote to the sleeplessness that had afflicted him after Ellen died. He would build a fire in the stone fireplace after Yetta, the maid, had cleaned up the kitchen and gone home, leaving him all alone in the house. Then he would go around and turn out all of the lights except the one that hung in the hall, and sometimes he would first prowl through the house like a voyeur, stopping in one room or the other to look at pictures, mementos, pieces of furniture, often lapsing into a trance-like state as shadows traversed his memory like moths. Eventually he would close himself in behind the paneled door of the study, turn on the brass reading lamp with the green glass shade and read magazines, *The Wall Street Journal*, history books—he belonged to several book clubs—often until three in the morning.

And it seemed to him that the more he read, the more depressed he got. Everything seemed to be hopeless, falling apart: the bankruptcy of the city of New York, international terrorists, oil spills polluting the ocean, the depletion of our natural resources, hunger in Bangladesh, drought in the Sahel, a devastating earthquake in China, killing nearly a million people, the destruction of the ozone layer, the specter of mass plutonium poisoning, air pollution, inflation, a privileged bureaucracy responsible to no one, corporations more powerful than countries, the precarious state of world finance, the corruption of government and burgeoning crime, violence, drug addiction, unemployment, the breakdown of family life—there was no end to the list. Compared with the world's problems, his loneliness, his not knowing what to do with his time, his lack of purpose except to live out his life, were nothing, the self-indulgence of a spoiled man.

There had been a time, he reflected, when he had believed in something. He had believed for a time that Roosevelt would restore the fractured well-being of the country, but he hadn't; it took Hitler and Tojo to do that. He had believed that the United Nations might help bring about world peace, but it hadn't. Dominated by the bullies, it had instead become a propaganda platform for the have-nots. He had believed that it was important for the United States to support the free world against the Communists, but that hadn't worked and we were the worse for it. He had believed that we, though not perfect, at least had some moral integrity, but Watergate, the CIA and ITT had shattered that illusion. He had believed that government could solve or help solve social problems, but more and more was spent and nothing changed. He had thought that money spent on education was well spent, but the children graduating from high school were increasingly illiterate and those who got through college had no jobs. He had believed that hatred and racism could be eradicated, but the white robes and the swastika were still around and on the streets again.

So Sam gradually turned his back. He canceled his subscriptions first to the local newspaper, later even to *The Wall Street Journal*. Next he rerouted all of his magazine and book club subscriptions to the county library, and then one night after a particularly depressing news program, he threw a glass ashtray through the screen of the color television set. A few days later he tossed the radio into the garbage can. Sam stopped smoking; why pollute the lungs? The air was bad enough. He stopped shaving; why bother? He stopped visiting with his friends; he had nothing more to say to them that after forty years hadn't been said many times over. And as for cards, a silly waste of time, just as well to dance yourself into a frenzy around a campfire to amuse yourself. At least it would tire you out and you'd get a good night's sleep, he reasoned. He stopped taking walks, gave up the gardener, stopped even going to the barbershop. His hair grew longer, his beard sprouted, the grass, too, grew long and went to seed, weeds choked the flower beds, the neat shrubs that Ellen had been so proud of grew undisciplined and rank, but Sam didn't notice and didn't care. He remained nearly all of the time in his study, the heavy drapes drawn night and day, seeing only the housekeeper, who brought him meals, and occasionally talking listlessly to his lawyer, who he had entrusted with the management of his investments. He even refused to see his son or daughter, although they called frequently and even came down to Bolton a few times, only to be told that he was out of town on business.

If he hadn't been so stable in his lifetime, if he wasn't so well-heeled, his friends might have concluded that he had had a schizophrenic break and even encouraged his children to have him committed to a mental institution, but his behavior seemed to them so incongruous, so out of character that they attributed it entirely to the death of Ellen, concluding that he would get over it in time. Besides, he still answered the telephone. He had to—his lawyer called him several times a week—and while he sounded vague and distant, he was still communicative and hadn't lost his sense of humor. Sam was never much for long telephone conversations anyway, and they took his silences for granted. Everyone was concerned, but believing his state to be temporary, they left him alone, and not even Yetta the housekeeper knew what he was doing behind the heavy paneled door; maybe writing his biography.

Sam wasn't writing, he wasn't reading; he was for the most part sitting, although he did do some exercises three or four times a day—stretching, touching his toes, even a few push-ups. Otherwise he just sat with his eyes either closed or fixed on a landscape that hung over the mantel, an almost abstract view of a still sea on a gray day, almost monochromatic.

If Sam had been familiar with the many forms of meditation that had become popular of late, his activity could even have been classed as meditation, but he knew nothing of it except that he was in a sense inventing it for himself. Sam thought of it as washing his mind. He put aside nearly everything that had occupied him and found that he needed very little. Of course, this didn't mean that he had altogether given up interest in his investments; only that they had been given a less, a much less, important place in his life. Yet the more he sat trying to think of nothing at all, the harder it was. Thoughts and images kept slipping under the closed door and stalking across his consciousness. That is, until he discovered the picture over the mantel. He had never really liked the picture, finding it too flat, too colorless. Once he had nearly donated it to a synagogue rummage sale. Now he found its simplicity soothing, and the more he looked at it, the more he saw in it, finite gradations of tone, texture and hue. While he looked at it the crack in the door was sealed and fewer and fewer images intruded.

The door was sealed at least until early one morning when, as he was dozing in his chair, he heard a stirring in the room. He opened his eyes to see before him, seated on the ottoman, an old orthodox Jew, barely two feet tall, wearing a faded gabardine caftan which reached his ankles and a black wide-brimmed hat.

Recoiling slightly, his brow deeply furrowed, he simply stared down at the incubus or succubus, he wasn't sure which was which. Sam composed himself and studied the man's features, thinking that he resembled his paternal great-grandfather, at least the old family picture of him. There were the distinguishing features of his family: the pointed chin, the thin, crooked nose and the short forehead. He knew the features, for they were his as well. He closed his eyes, concluding that the form in front of him was hallucinatory. Hearing nothing after a time, he again opened his eyes but found that the little man was still seated before him.

"You can close your eyes, but I'm not going away," the man said in a reedy voice that matched his size.

"You're not," Sam repeated, his tone guarded. "What—what do you want here? What—maybe that's the first question—what, who are you?"

"Last question first or first question last?"

"You choose."

"I'm your caseworker."

"What kind of case? You mean welfare or something like that?"

"Not just so. I should tell you I'm your great-great-grandfather, Reb Shmuel Berl Yanofsky. And my present address is, well, up there," he said, pointing to the ceiling.

"I'm sorry to disappoint you, but I don't believe in such things. So I'm afraid whatever you do or say, I'll only think that I've gone off the deep end."

"All the same, you'll listen to what I have to say."

"I won't get up and leave the room, if that's what you mean."

"That's a start. I was saying that I am your caseworker."

"And what does that mean exactly? A kind of guardian angel?"

"Something like that. But we've had a change of job description. Modernity." The little man raised his eyebrows and shrugged his shoulders apologetically.

"Even up there."

The little man shrugged again.

"What do you do? You've never come down to visit me before. Why now?"

"Sam, my son. Don't think that because I haven't appeared as I am now that I haven't been paying attention to you."

"What do you mean?"

"I don't want to brag," said Reb Yanofsky, cocking his head back, "but now and then ideas have sprung into your head. Do you think that they were yours alone? We put those ideas there to help you along. And you're lucky, you've got a caseworker like me with business sense. Some people are not so lucky, as you well know." Reb Yanofsky nodded his head and stroked his beard.

"You mean I don't get any of the credit?" said Sam with a wry smile.

"Well, some, of course. But the big decisions were mine."

"Like what?" Sam was convinced that he was experiencing some sort of hallucination, but he had to admit to himself that he was enjoying the company, dream though it was.

"Like marrying Ellen."

Sam started to shake his head, but the old man shook his thin finger at him and chided, "Don't you remember? You wanted to, you almost married Selma Vapnik from Union City, you *shlemiel*. A narrow escape that was."

Sam didn't respond, except that his expression hardened in its usual way when he realized that his adversary, usually in a business deal, was getting the best of him. At the sight of him, Reb Yanofsky turned gleeful, his eyebrows went up and he said, pressing his advantage, "Let me give you another example. Remember your first big real estate investment, in 1955? The building on Third Avenue in Pittsburgh?" Sam nodded. "You were going to buy that apartment house instead, and look how the building turned out. You quadrupled your money in two years, didn't you?"

"Who knows what I would have done with the apartment house?" Sam muttered.

"I know," the old man piped, a quiver of feeling in his voice. "It would have driven you *meshugge*."

"So you're the brains behind it all?" Sam said, an ironic smile creasing his lips. "And now that it's over, you're here to welcome me to wherever you've come from, I suppose."

"Not very likely, Sam. Not in your condition. And it's *not over*. That's why I'm here, Sam. You may think it's over. I'm sorry to disappoint you, Sam, but we've got other plans for you."

"Who's *we*, Grandpa?"

"Sam. You know perfectly well who *we* is."

"Look, Grandpa—is it all right if I call you that?"

"What else would you call me?"

"Grandpa, I don't have to tell you that *plans* are just what I don't want; I've had a life of plans. Now I'm happy just to sit here, at least for the time being. And I can tell you that I'm feeling better, now that I've closed *that* door," he said, pointing at the door to the study, "on what's beyond it."

"All right, Sam," the old man said soothingly, "all right, I know what's in your mind. You don't have to tell me. You look out at the world and you see death and misery and stupidity and corruption and suffering. But don't forget, Sam, there is also joy and love and trust and honesty and even nobility. All of those are also there, Sam, and it's not that you've been a stranger to them, Sam. You've tasted them all. Haven't you? Haven't you?" he said, shaking his finger.

Sam's chin was cradled in his hand and he was looking thoughtful. "I've put that all behind me."

"You can't, not while you're alive, you can't. Look, Sam, let me show you something." And as he said it, Sam found himself standing in a child's room. He recognized it as his son's room as it was thirty years ago. And there beside him was Ellen, looking much younger, thin, with no gray hair at all, and in her arms she held his son, a small bundle no bigger than a loaf of bread, it seemed. Suddenly the baby looked up at him, the round eyes widened and his whole face smiled; the baby had recognized him for the first time. The warmth touched his heart and spread through his body. The love of a parent coursed through him for the first time, moving him toward the baby. He took him from his wife and held him gently, feeling the warm softness of his son's skin against his. Alive. Life was warming the baby, life that he and Ellen had given, and for the first time his son had experienced happiness and affinity and cognition, the best of what it was to be alive and a person.

Abruptly the nursery vanished and he saw Reb Yanofsky before him. Tears filled his eyes and streamed down his cheeks. His chest heaved convulsively and he wept without restraint, loudly, inconsolably, for the first time since Ellen's death. All of the dammed-up sorrow came pouring out of him like a spring charged by winter's thaw. Reb Yanofsky flew to the back of his chair, wrapped his arms around Sam, and his tears stopped. He couldn't feel the old man's touch, but he knew himself to be in the embrace of a field of energy; it was a pool of emotion, love, the same that he had felt for his son, for his wife, for his daughter, for others he had known, and now he was immersed in it.

"Sam. What you have felt in your time, what you now feel is reason enough for you to go on living." Before Sam had a chance to reply, the little man lifted into the air and ascended through the beamed ceiling, leaving behind a dispersing trail of milky dust. And before he had a chance to reflect, Sam fell into a deep, untroubled sleep.

The next morning Sam awoke feeling fresh and relaxed. He opened the drapes and looked out. The sun, its strength growing, was drying the dew on the grass. He blinked at the light, stretched and went up to the bathroom for a shave. He ate a big breakfast at the Coffee Cup, got a haircut and bought a scythe at Miller Brothers' hardware store.

That same morning Mildred Bickle, his neighbor, was surprised to see him in his undershirt cutting the high grass.

"Good morning, Sam," she said. "We haven't seen much of you lately."

"I've been sort of doing my memoirs, Mildred. But I think I've finished with them."

"Nice to have you back, Sam."

Sam Yanow smiled and went back to his scythe.

26.
The Beginning of the End of the Beginning

It's spring, the sun is filling everything it can touch with tonic, the young grass is bright, the soil gives when you walk on it, from the recent rain. The air is scented with leaf mold and hyacinth. Some of the trees look like they've got a green web around them from the leaves that are just beginning to show. Clusters of daffodils are everywhere, seven varieties, all of them looking up at the sun.

But for all this beauty, it's not a happy day. There's a funeral going on right at this very minute, not ten yards from where I'm standing. Sidney Cantor died a few days ago, suddenly, of a heart attack, right at the table of the weekly synagogue Men's Club poker game. He must have gotten excited. They say there was twenty-four dollars on the table, and he had a full house or something like that.

People have died over more frivolous things, but not much more frivolous.

Sidney was known to be a generous man. He had had some bad times with his plumbing business, but things were going well for him. His son, Noah, the tall, thin one, is holding Estelle by the arm. A good thing he's so close; she will need him. She's pressing a white handkerchief to her eyes, trying her best to control herself, but her body shakes as they lower the coffin by the tapes into the grave. Rabbi Bing is singing *Kaddish:* "*Yisgaddal v'yiskaddash shmey rabboh* . . ." The rabbi's nasal tremolo touches the mourners, passes from grave to grave and wanders into the trees. Noah is crying too now, and he's not the only one in the crowd. So are Nudelman and Finkelstein, standing together, heads bent.

No one disliked Sidney; some people loved him. The last words of the *Kaddish* die. They're bending down now and throwing a little of the damp soil on the coffin. The crowd is leaving quietly, except for Estelle, Noah and me. They are no longer crying, just standing looking into the grave.

Noah has taken her arm, they turn and walk slowly down the gravel path. Estelle turns and walks back to stand there beside the grave. She's saying something, but I can't hear it; a wife's last words to her husband. She looks down into the grave for a long moment, looks with her soul into death and turns back to life. Noah takes her by the arm again. He says something to her and they walk together among the cut stone and young grass toward the gate. Now he bends to pick a daffodil near the path and is giving it to her. I, too, have been weeping, for at every funeral I bury those I could not bury.

They've gone through the wrought-iron gate. There's no one here but the dead and me. I must lock the gate and get back to town. I usually walk around the place before I leave just to make sure everything is in order, that the gardener has done what he's supposed to do, that there's been no vandalism and so forth. But I must confess that's not the only reason. I like to visit some of these people; not just my old friend, Mark, but some who were dead before I came, others who I knew.

People don't come to the cemetery like they used to when I was a boy. Families used to come regularly for a visit, to say a few prayers, even talk a little or just to be close. Even though I'm just an acquaintance, my visit must be better than nothing. Take this gentleman, Chaim Schwartz. He died when he was eighty-seven and I swear I saw him dance the *kazatsky* at a wedding the same month that he died. He was filled with life. He had a good sense of humor, was equally conversant in international politics and Talmudic commentary and could switch from one to the other with agility. He and his first wife, Sarah, raised seven children; one still lives here. As he lies here, he must still have all the hair in his head and the teeth in his mouth, he was that healthy. There are none like him, I can tell you that.

Here's a fresh stone, the one with the roses carved on it. Tante Chana died last year. She was ninety-two. It was after a *Shabbas* meal which she had cooked for her family. They had just finished their tea and *mandelbrot*. She was seated at the head of the table, for some reason wearing her best violet silk dress. She looked around, smiling at each of them, as if she wanted to fix them firmly in her mind. Most of the family was busy talking and only a few noticed. She slumped forward as though she had dozed off, but there was no waking her. Her family said that her face was beautiful, serene and smiling. There is no more like her.

Don't misunderstand. Not that there aren't good people,

learned people around, but it seems that the learning is specialized now, a good doctor, a good engineer. You don't see many people with the understanding that Chaim and Chana had. Take humor, for example. There isn't that spontaneous wit. All I hear are the same old ethnic jokes. Conversation isn't pungent like it used to be. People work hard, they're tired, they don't want to be bothered or annoyed, they don't want to offend people and so on.

Now here's another, Jennie Burstein. She was seventy-eight, still playing the gypsy violin. If she knew one Yiddish song, she knew a hundred. Did anyone think to write them down? I doubt it. She also baked *challah* every Friday of her life, two braided loaves, enough for the weekend.

Her husband, Lev, is buried next to her. He had actually written an unpublished Talmudic commentary. He wasn't a rabbi, only a student. An orthodox man but not severe. He had a shoe store on Main Street. There isn't a single orthodox Jew left in Bolton. And the people hardly came to the services except, of course, during the High Holy Days. There are so many other things to do, it seems.

I've just padlocked the gate. And as I walk back to town —it's a narrow road through pasture land, only two miles— I will think about tonight. I'm having dinner with Reuven, Dalia and Gavriel. After dinner we'll play a little chess, and I will say over and over again to Reuven, who is very methodical, "It's your move, Reuven. It's your move."

27.
After Dawn

Dear Ephie

It is very late, or rather very early. Outside my window the light of morning is touching the early apple blossoms on the tree that I planted just last year. It is still, except for the sound of my pen on the paper and the squeak of my chair, which, as always, needs oiling, one of those tasks that I never seem to remember.

I have just made myself some strong coffee. I have been up most of the night and there is another day to get through and this letter to write. It's unlike me to do it immediately. My usual inclination would be to let it mulch.

I have been with a friend most of the night. No, nothing like that; just sitting up with her, talking, drinking tea. We didn't talk much, although she did take to reminiscing a little as memories came to the surface at random. The death of someone you've been married to for twenty-one years is something like a mental earthquake. It brings a lot to the surface: regrets, anger, affection, events long forgotten, yet cherished. My friend lost her husband a few days ago, quite suddenly, one of those heart attacks that are so massive that you don't recover, although the doctors at our local hospital did their best for him. There were warning signs, of course, but who doesn't have them at our age? There was no preparing for it, you see.

My friend Estelle, perhaps I've written about her, Estelle is a strong woman, well organized, self-sufficient. She has a son who is in college. She's been a good *baleboosteh*. She called last night, this morning really, about one-thirty. She woke me up and came right to the point. "Mendel," she said. She didn't have to say more than that. It was the bruised tone of her voice, something that I had never heard in it before. "I'm afraid," she went on, "here, in the house, all alone. Noah has been here since the funeral, but he had to go back to Pittsburgh this afternoon." Then, a little calmer, she said, "I'm sorry to wake you, but, well, I just *had* to talk to someone, to tell them . . ." She took a breath and I heard her blow her nose.

"I'll get dressed and come right over. You put the tea on. I won't be ten minutes. In the meantime turn on some music, anything, one of those all-night stations. You'll have some sounds in the house at least."

"No, Mendel, you don't have to come over. Go back to sleep. I just needed the reassurance of another voice. Not *just* a voice; a friend. I feel better now, I—"

"Are you sure, Estelle?"

"Yes. I'm sure. No, not really. Please do come."

And I did. We talked, rather she talked. I suppose Sidney was still around the house, and she was talking to him rather than to me. She finally grew weary enough to sleep

—besides, the dawn dispels those night fears. They do for me at least. I'll go back there later this morning and let her make me some coffee. I'll see if she wants me to do anything. She'll be fine. She's one of those people who . . . well, enough of Estelle Cantor.

What I have to say in this letter, Ephie, is painful and hard, and I will probably regret it as soon as I say it. I do in fact already, but I can't come, not for the two years at least. Oh, I promise you, I will come for a visit, and this year. And I promise you that I will stay for at least two weeks, maybe three. I'll get one of those charters, and it won't be the only trip either. I'll let you show me everything. I'll try to make the trip coincide with your vacation so that we can go places together and I can see it with your eyes. Also, I hope to be there after your daughter, Ayelet, has her child. Meeting and getting to know your family and seeing the start of a new generation of our family will be most important for me. I want to speculate in person about who the baby looks like and whose character he or she is already showing signs of acquiring. Yes, that for me will be a great joy.

I will come to see you, but I am not prepared to leave my home. Yes, it is my home. I know myself, just as you know me. I know that, with your help, I would adjust to my life there. I know it would be a good life, and I know that when the time came to leave I would remain, with regrets at what I had left behind me, but remain I would. I even know that this would be good, but it would be bad as well.

You see, my outlook has been changing since the abandonment of my Zamosc book and the start of my collection of stories about Bolton. It's more than that, though. You recall that I wrote to you about the refugee family from Vietnam. I saw them get off the army truck, and I had the image of another army truck taking away Father and Mother. That double image, like a twice-taken photograph, answered a question that I've been quietly but persistently asking myself for thirty years: What kind of a God is it that takes parents, good people, away from children, even grown children? Oh, I accept disease, even accidents. I mean in the back of an army truck. The answer is, no kind of God. God had no hand in it. I know, Ephie, you're an atheist; the question is irrelevant for you, but not for me. I finally understand that God is probably looking for another place to start over, to try again. Whatever comes our way as human beings, indifference, compassion, injustice, better or worse, it is always man's choice. Our choice to redeem or condemn, to help or to hinder one another. And that's how it is: one truck goes off and years later another returns.

At first it was hard to get used to the sight of Oriental Jews. They don't look at all like we do, but I learned something from that too. Looking at them, it came to me that we are all of us Jews, all devoted to life, all intent on survival, all random victims of others. When I saw that, and when I accepted the reality of my own dislocation, I began to see myself no longer an outsider but as a part of a community, as much a part as anybody, and not just a part of Bolton, either. So now you see, a little at least, why I must—no, choose—to stay here. A rationalization, you say? Perhaps. Well then, I confess to a fondness for hamburgers just the way they make them at the Coffee Cup, buried in grilled onions, the American cheese melting over the side. And I even like the winters; it gives me something to complain about.

Now, as for the money, I never had it. As I sit here, I know that I won't even miss it, although I must confess that I was already growing accustomed to having it and the cares that come with it. In the end I'm exactly one sports jacket ahead. So, if possible, I leave the disposition of the money to you. If it is possible without my living in Israel to distribute it in Israel, I would like you to find one or two schools for disadvantaged children and transfer the money to them. I have an acquaintance, an Arab Israeli, Al Zaki, the only Israeli that I know in the Knesset and a poet as well—I'm sure you know of him. If at all possible, I would like some of the money to go to a children's school or home of his choice as well. I will sign anything to make this happen. If it does not, I hope that the government will at least promise to attach the money to the budget of one of its social welfare departments. Please try to do this for me. It is very important that you try at least.

It's growing late. I'll close this letter, as I've got to unlock the doors of the school in a few minutes. I know you're sad. I too am sad. I will sit here nights and imagine what life would have been like there with you in Jerusalem. I will visit you. But I want you too to visit me here in Bolton. I will show you the quiet, unassuming beauty of the countryside, and most important, you will meet some of the people that I've written about. I know there's nothing special about any of them, but they are all of them special.

Love to you and to ours,
Cousin Mendel

About the Author

SHELDON GREENE grew up in Cleveland
Heights, Ohio, and is a graduate of
Case Western Reserve and its law
school. He practices law in San
Francisco and lives in Berkeley with
his wife and young daughter.